The Clerk's Tale

The Clock's Tale

The Clerk's Tale

M. J. TROW

LUME BOOKS

LUME BOOKS

Published in 2022 by Lume Books

Copyright © M. J. Trow 2022

ISBN 978-1-83901-511-3

Typeset using Atomik ePublisher from Easypress Technologies

www.lumebooks.co.uk

Chapter 1

He sat bolt upright in bed. There had been a thudding in his dream, a loud and determined thud that reverberated from hell. But that was then, when he'd been asleep. Now, he was awake and the thud was still there. He blinked, clutching the bed covers under his chin. The vague light of dawn peeped through the shutter slats, but he had no idea what time it was. The bells had not started yet, so it couldn't be …

'Chaucer!' a voice barked from beyond his door. 'Geoffrey Chaucer!'

Gratified at least to be reminded who he was, the man whose peace had been shattered scrambled off the bed and tottered to the door. 'Yes?' he asked a knothole in the wood.

No answer, just another terrifying thudding, rattling the bolts on his side. Chaucer grabbed the ironwork, cold in his hands at that time of the morning and the door swung open. Armed men faced him, with iron kettle-hats shading their faces and swords at their hips.

'Good morning, Master Chaucer,' the man in the centre growled. 'You will come with us.'

Chaucer blinked again, trying to find some clue as to who his uninvited guests were. They wore livery, but there was no device on their sleeves or chests, and he really didn't care for the glint in the one good eye of the man to his left.

'Where?' Chaucer asked. 'Why? At whose behest?'

Geoffrey Chaucer was a man of substance. He was Comptroller of the King's Woollens, for God's sake. Poet Laureate to the same king, by God's grace. And if that king happened to be a snivelling fifteen-year-old with more spots than royal castles, time alone would remedy that.

'You'll find out,' the centre man grunted. He glanced down. 'Er … you might care to dress yourself, Master Comptroller. This *is* Aldgate Ward and there *are* standards.'

'Yes.' Chaucer adjusted his nightshirt, although there was strictly no need. 'Give me a moment.' He scuttled back into his rooms in search of his houppelande.

'Hobson,' the man grunted– and he of the single eye marched into Chaucer's inner sanctum and stood there.

'Do you mind?' Chaucer said to him. 'A little privacy wouldn't come amiss.'

'Hobson,' the man grunted again and the soldier spun to his right, with his broad back to Chaucer.

'What *is* this all about?' The comptroller was hauling off his night-shirt and adjusting his subjaculum, as you do when your sleep has been so rudely disturbed.

'Orders,' the man said. 'No, you won't need your purse, sir.'

Sir. That was more like it. Oafs though these ruffians may be, they at least knew their better when they met him. Chaucer instinctively reached for his belt, the one with the poignard dangling from it.

'Knife!' Hobson yelled, although how he could see it with his back turned, Chaucer didn't know. The comptroller found himself flattened face down on the bed, Hobson's knee in the small of his back and his right arm wrenched behind him.

'You won't need your dagger, either,' the man said.

Hobson hauled Chaucer upright.

'Now, be a good gentleman and get dressed, will you? Sir Nicholas Brembre wants a word.'

'For God's sake, Nicholas!' Geoffrey Chaucer was not usually a man to fume, but the events of the day so far had changed all that and now, he was ready to fume for England. 'Picture the scene. I am sleeping the sleep of the just in my little room over the Aldgate when half a dozen morons armed to the teeth burst in and pin me to the bed. You and I go back a long way. If you wanted to talk to me, all you had to do was ask.'

'Yes.' Brembre was already pouring the wine. 'I'm sorry about Pettifer. He's new. A little over-zealous, perhaps.'

'Perhaps?' Chaucer shrieked. He was past caring how much like a girl he sounded.

'You know how it is.' Brembre handed over the goblet. 'Ever since that wretched peasant business, we've all been a little on edge.'

Chaucer looked at the goblet. 'And it's a little early for me,' he said, taking it and immediately putting it down. 'I am due to leave London in less than an hour. My pilgrimage, you know – the one I haven't been on for the last two years, through no fault of my own.'

'God.' It wasn't too early for Brembre and he took a swig. 'Is it that time of year already?'

Chaucer stood with his hands on his hips. 'You *know* it is, Nicholas,' he said. 'You mentioned the peasants only a moment ago. Although I'd choose not to celebrate it myself, this is something of an anniversary—in that they nearly killed me the last time I tried to get to Canterbury.'

'Lord, yes,' Brembre sighed, swigging again. 'Put like that, I suppose it is.'

'Well? Now that we've caught up, what is it that you want so early in the morning?'

Brembre looked grim. 'I've had some bad news,' he said.

'Trouble on the Rialto?' Chaucer was used to Brembre's dodgy dealings; if it was bad news, it *had* to be business-related.

'The Rialto be damned,' Brembre said. 'This is personal, Geoffrey. It involves my family.'

Family and Nicholas Brembre did not go hand in glove. His wife had left him years ago, preferring the endowments of a man from the Bourse. He had no children, at least none that he acknowledged, and his parents had long since shuffled off into God's twilight.

It was as though Brembre read his mind. 'My sister's boy, Hal.'

'What of him?'

'Well, that's just the point, Geoffrey.' Brembre topped up his goblet. 'He's dead.'

'Oh, I'm sorry.' The platitude dropped easily onto Chaucer's tongue though he knew neither Brembre's sister nor her son. 'But I don't see how ...'

'When I say "dead", it goes without saying that I also mean "in mysterious circumstances". Oxford.'

'Ah.' That seemed to say it all.

'I had a letter from the Warden of Merton a couple of days ago. The boy met his Maker.'

'College fever?' Chaucer guessed. 'Scholar's ague? Mother of God, not the Pestilence!' Both men crossed themselves.

'I did say "in mysterious circumstances", Geoffrey.'

'You did, Nicholas, you did. But, to us, many of the ways of the Lord are strange.'

'Ways of the Lord be buggered!' Brembre snapped. 'Not to put too fine a point on it, I believe that little Hal was murdered. A hammer fell on him, they say. Oh, I know builders can be careless, but …'

Chaucer stared at the men. Then he reached for the goblet after all. 'Just how little was Hal?' he asked.

'Sixteen,' Brembre said.

'Quite elderly for an Oxford scholar,' Chaucer commented.

'He'd been at Merton for two years. Reading for his Quadrivium.'

Chaucer looked blank. Brembre sensed it.

'You and I, Geoffrey, are men of the world. Not for us the cloister and the hearth. Apparently, it's arithmetic, geometry, music and astronomy.'

'Oh, yes,' Chaucer smiled. 'It's all coming back to me now. We covered it during my brief sojourn at Lincoln's Inn. Number in the abstract, number in space, number in time, number in space and time.' He caught Brembre's face. 'With me so far?'

Brembre laughed. 'That's what I love about you, Geoffrey,' he said. 'Never met a trifle you left unconsidered. Will you do it? I'd go, of course, but I've got this meeting with half the Hanse on Tuesday. Make or break for me.' It was always like that with Brembre; every business deal could make or break him. Chaucer knew he'd hang one day.

The comptroller sampled a little of the Romonye. Not bad. 'Expenses?' he asked. He knew it wasn't one of Brembre's favourite words.

'Absolutely,' the merchant nodded. 'And a little something for yourself. Take Pettifer with you.'

'Pettifer? Why?'

'St Scholastica's Day,' Brembre rumbled like the voice of doom.

'Come again?'

'You and I were boys, Geoffrey. 1355, to be exact. A couple of scholars poured wine over an innkeeper; the good citizens of Oxenford didn't like it and there were three days of carnage. You may need to watch your back.'

'If Pettifer were with me, I certainly would,' Chaucer said. 'Thank you, but I'll make my own arrangements. Do I report to you?'

'If you would,' Brembre said. 'It's tricky in the Cotswolds, Geoffrey; take care of yourself.'

'That I will, Nicholas,' the comptroller said. 'That I will.'

It was the usual chaos in the courtyard of the Tabard later that morning. Rounceys, palfreys, donkeys and nags of every colour and size stamped the straw, whinnying and snorting, ready for the off. One of them was Chaucer's grey, from whose back he jumped down and handed the reins to a lackey.

'Just in time, Master Chaucer,' his host greeted him. 'I'd nearly given you up.' He glanced across the yard to the comptroller's mount. 'No luggage?' he asked.

'No pilgrimage, Harry,' Chaucer shrugged. 'I've been called to higher things.'

'Higher than a Harry Bailly peregrination to the shrine of the Holy Blissful Martyr, Master Chaucer? Is that even possible?'

'Affairs of state, Harry,' Chaucer said in a half-whisper. Looking about him, this year's potential fellow-pilgrims seemed a rough lot; you couldn't be too careful.

'Oh, dear,' Bailly looked concerned. 'Another year, then?' He brightened up.

'Indeed,' Chaucer sighed. 'I thought it only right that I should let you know of my sudden cancellation in person.'

'Good of you,' Bailly said and the two stood looking at each other. The unspoken words, the elephant in the courtyard, was the deposit that Chaucer had already given to Harry Bailly. There was no way in hell that the proprietor of the Tabard was going to return that. And Geoffrey Chaucer was too much of a gentleman to ask for it.

'A bientôt, then,' Bailly said, 'as they say in Stratford-at-Bow,' and he went in search of his water bottle.

Chaucer reclaimed his horse. Pilgrimages were not his friend lately. Last year he had been driven back by revolting peasants laying waste to half of Kent. The year before that, he'd been called to help out an old friend. And now …

Now, Geoffrey Chaucer made a decision. The short ride from the Aldgate to the Tabard had reminded the comptroller that his old trouble threatened to return. Four days in the saddle over God knew what roads would do nothing for his condition. No, he'd go to Oxford by boat, up the Thames and into the Styx.

'What?' the boatman bellowed over the incessant clang of the Steel yard. 'Where?'

'Oxford,' Chaucer shouted back. 'It's …'

'Oh, I know where it is,' the man was sitting cross-legged on his deck, twisting twine. 'And I know *what* it is.'

'Oh?' Chaucer said. 'How do you mean?'

'Proper shit-hole is Oxford,' the boatman six boats along the quay grunted, an echo of the first man Chaucer had spoken to. The smiths' cacophony was at least a little further away now and Chaucer could hear himself think. 'You know that thing they say, about the dreaming spires an' that?'

'Yes.'

'That's rubbish, that is. Place is falling apart since the Pestilence. The arse has fallen out of the wool trade ...'

Chaucer knew all about that.

'and the place is going to rack and ruin. Carfax is a pigsty. And there's a knocking shop to the north-east of the castle the size of the great outdoors. I wouldn't be seen dead in it.' He nudged Chaucer. 'At least, that's what I tell the missus.'

'Oxford?' a third boatman frowned. 'Ooh, you've got me there. West country, isn't it? Near York somewhere.'

'Shipman,' a fourth corrected Chaucer. 'I'm not a boatman, I'm a shipman. See that?' The man pointed to his barque and the name in burnished letters on the side. 'The Madeleine. That was my ship. Out of Dartmouth. I lost her to those bastard French pirates a few years back. And I'm just biding my time until I can afford to refit her. If you want to go to Oxford, it'll cost you.'

'How much?' Chaucer asked.

The shipman looked him in the face. Then he reached across the deck and picked up a quill and ink. He scribbled a figure down on a piece of parchment and handed it to his putative passenger. The comptroller hoped that his eyebrows hadn't disappeared into his hairline with the shock of what he saw.

'Done,' he said. What the hell? Nicholas Brembre was paying.

The shipman looked at him silently, holding out his hand. Chaucer was not au fait with the habits of seafarers and so held his out, to shake on the arrangement. The shipman guffawed and held Chaucer's hand in a grip that was as rough as rope and smelled of tar.

'If you think I am going to trust a landlubber like you on the shake of a hand, Master ...'

'Chaucer.'

'Master Chaucer, then you can think again. I want your seal at the very least on that piece of parchment in your hand. And the money of course. Up front. Before you leave the dock. Because I know your kind ...'

'I would have you know, Master ...' Chaucer could be as terse as the next man.

'Zouche,' the shipman said.

'Master Zouche, that I am Comptroller of the King's Woollens, Court Poet and a confidant of the king himself.'

Zouche looked at him without speaking and then picked up two lengths of rope and began to unravel the two ends. The conversation appeared to be at an end.

Chaucer could feel himself getting testy. He could see a week of sitting on a horse's back in his future and his condition simply wasn't up to it. Even the ride to Canterbury would have been too much, he now realised. 'Did you hear me?' He all but stamped his foot.

Zouche looked up slowly, his hands still busy with the rope. 'I heard you,' he said. 'But I confess to you, Master Chaucer, I don't see quite what you are trying to say. Is it that, because you are Comptroller of the King's Woollens and some fancy poet, I should take you to Oxford for nothing? That my time is worth nothing compared to yours?'

Chaucer shook his head. 'No. Of course not.'

'Are you saying that I am to trust you to pay me when you fancy, or not at all?'

9

Chaucer did stamp his foot this time. This rogue was going too far. 'I simply assumed, Master Zouche …'

'Ar.' Zouche looked up at the sky. 'Breezy for April, ain't it? You'd think the old March winds would have died down by now.'

'What?' Chaucer could have screamed in frustration. 'What's the wind got to do with anything?'

'It's got a lot to do with the price, Master Chaucer,' Zouche told him. 'If that turns to a headwind, you can add another quarter to that price. Here, give me that parchment a minute.'

Chaucer was so surprised he handed it over without thinking. Zouche scribbled something under the price he had quoted and then signed it with a flourish. He looked up and winked.

'Surprised to see me writing, Master Chaucer?' he said. 'Owning a ship isn't just about scraping off the barnacles, you know, before they turn to geese. Oh, no. If you deal with the Hanse, you'd better know how to write *and* to read, as small a print as you can, or the bastards'll do you for every penny they can get.' He waved the parchment to dry the ink. 'Here. See if this still suits you.'

Chaucer took the page from the man's calloused hand and looked at it. It seemed the Hanse didn't have a monopoly in small print and he had to ferret in his houppelande for his spectacles, which he perched on his nose, turning the parchment to the light. The man had added certain conditions, all dependent on wind, weather, extras such as … What was this? Provision of a pot to piss in? This was really too much. But then, as he read on, he saw that there were also concessions. If they reached Oxford in less than eight days, there would be a discount. If Chaucer provided a daily allowance of wine or ale, a discount. He began to nod and reached into his breast again to fish out his seal, carried on a chain around his neck whenever he was away from his rooms above Aldgate.

'So?' The shipman cocked his eyebrow.

'Do you have wax?' Chaucer waved his seal.

The shipman chuckled. Chaucer would find out soon enough that he had everything to make the world wag; no good being a businessman without the accoutrements of business. He fished out a stub of green beeswax from the pouch at his waist and lit the end with a practised flick of his thumb on his steel. Chaucer pressed his seal onto the drips that fell on the corner of the parchment and the deal was done. He handed over two angels, which the shipman bit and added to the bulging purse.

'You have baggage?' the shipman asked.

'I will need to bring some things,' Chaucer said. 'Some clothes. Some books to amuse me on the journey. Some wine …'

'You can bring one change of clothes,' the shipman said. 'No need for books. I have a Bible if you need amusement. But the wine can come along, we can ship it in the gunwales.'

'*One* change of clothes?' Chaucer was not a man of fashion, but that seemed a little niggardly. When he got to Oxford, Heaven only knew what exalted company he would have to keep.

Zouche looked at his passenger-to-be. 'You look like a man with a man,' he said.

'A woman, actually,' Chaucer corrected him.

The shipman raised an eyebrow. 'I didn't see that coming,' he muttered. 'Whoever you have to help you in the house, get them to pack some clouts and send them by road. They'll get there before us, that I can guarantee.'

Chaucer nodded. That did sound like a sensible suggestion. All he needed to do now was to get an address from Brembre for sending the clothes on ahead, find a likely lad to push a barrowload of wine to the quay and they could be off. It hadn't been easy nor yet had it been impossibly difficult. He lamented the loss of his pilgrimage yet again, but the prospect of a gentle river voyage had its charms. And the shipman was literate at least, his craft seemed watertight and the weather was set fair. What could possibly go wrong?

Chapter 2

'Master Zouche.' Chaucer had learned to pitch his voice to be heard only over the gentle lap of water on the sides of the barge and not the cacophony of the city. The wind was still quite sprightly and the barge was nipping along smartly. He had hoped that his *mal maris* would not translate to *mal flumenis* but he already knew he would be doomed to disappointment. He sat in the prow and tried to keep his eyes off the banks as they flew past.

'Master Chaucer?' Zouche was manning the tiller and could only begin to guess at the shade of green of the comptroller's face, judging by the livid hue of the small bald spot on his crown.

'Do you have plans for stopping somewhere for the night?' Chaucer tried to keep the desperation out of his voice.

Zouche looked up at the sky, still a wall-to-wall blue, though perhaps a little paler than it had been. 'Not night yet, Master Chaucer,' he said simply.

'No, not *yet*.' Chaucer tried to keep all suggestion of the sulky child from his voice. 'I was just wondering where we would be lodging.'

'Lodging?' Zouche sounded confused. 'I had no plans for lodging,

Master Chaucer. I just tie up and sleep in the boat. There's nothing nicer than being lulled to sleep by the lap of the river.'

Chaucer clenched his hands in his lap to stop himself from screaming. He had maintained his savoir faire by a whisker since they passed Putney, Zouche calling indecipherable greetings to the ferryman who feathered his oars to allow them past. The river was narrower and faster now and there seemed to be very few signs of civilisation along the banks. He thought he had seen Mortlake Manor through the trees and since then he had been as lost as if he had been on the moon. And now – he stifled a sob – he was going to have to sleep in the bottom of a boat, wrapped no doubt in some noisome tarpaulin, having feasted on nothing at all, if his rebellious stomach had any say in the matter.

'Don't worry, Master Chaucer,' Zouche called above the flap of canvas. 'I have laid in provisions. We ought to sup on the bacon tonight. It'll be good eating when I've cut the green bits off. And I've got a heel of bread could do with using up. There are some apples not too soft with keeping. And of course, there's always your wine. We'll dine like kings and sleep like babies, I can guarantee.'

Chaucer closed his eyes and gave himself up to the rhythm of the river. In his life he had had worse experiences. He just couldn't remember, what with one thing and another, exactly when.

William Zouche liked his solitary life. Although he had had a crew on board the original *Madeleine*, he could take them or leave them. He found in his line of business it was no good getting too fond of his seamen – decisions needed to be made using criteria such as how much cargo could be saved, how much plunder could be stowed aboard his already groaning craft, not by how long he had known the skipper's mate. Working alone suited him well and he could tie up and batten down by himself as quickly as many crews of five. He had finished doing just that when a startled crowing sound from the direction of Chaucer, now huddled under his cloak in the prow, told him he must become mine host for the evening. The dark was almost complete in this tiny backwater off the mighty Thames and the only sound was the lowing of some cattle over the brow of the hill and the occasional grunt of a frog as it fell prey to a marauding otter. It was the kind of peace which William Zouche loved best of all, but he appreciated that it could be disorienting to a townsman just woken from a deep sleep.

'Over here, Master Chaucer,' he called. 'The *Madeleine* is tied up for the night. Wait where you are a minute, till you get your night eyes.'

Chaucer licked his dry lips and tried to get up but although most of him was awake, his left leg was reluctant to rouse itself for the moment, so he had little choice but to remain where he was.

Zouche poured some wine into a horn beaker and took it over to his paying guest. 'Sip, Master Chaucer,' he said. 'Just let yourself come to, slowly. You've been asleep for quite a while. The river does that to people. I've had passengers topple over the side before now, so you dropping down in the prow was a wise choice on your part. Being fished out of the Thames half awake is no fun for anyone.'

Chaucer took the beaker and tried to sip, but his thirst got the better of him and he drank greedily. He handed back the beaker and Zouche sighed.

'I hope you are not a drunkard, Master Chaucer,' he said, reprovingly. 'A drunkard is dangerous on any vessel, even my little *Madeleine* on a river.'

Chaucer never made much of a dent in his gallon of wine a day from the king and when he could, negotiated to get the equivalent in nice hard cash. He liked a drink, he would never deny that, but drunkard? That was not fair and he struggled to his feet to defend himself against the slur. His left leg still wasn't keen to comply, but it didn't let him down at least, although he was a little slanting. He tried to straighten up and the boat lurched alarmingly.

'Steady, Master Chaucer,' Zouche laughed. 'You're not on solid ground now, don't forget. You must tread light and always be ready for the deck to shift under your feet. Now, steady as she goes, come on down amidships and we'll be more stable.'

Treading like a heron in deep water, Chaucer moved the yard or two towards the rather over-grandly named amidships and saw that a rudimentary meal was in the process of preparation. Earlier, he had thought he would never want to eat again but now realised he was hungry and sat down carefully in front of a low table made from a board stretched between two beams. He suspected they had some fancy maritime name, but was not intending to ever venture on a boat again after this, so wasn't interested enough to ask.

'You'll find the fare simple,' Zouche told him, 'but I hope acceptable. River gives you an appetite as well as the need for sleep. It's a healthy life.'

Chaucer took a hunk of bread and bit into it. That it had once been moist and fresh he didn't doubt, but now it was more of a challenge to teeth used to the finer things.

Zouche leaned forward. 'Best thing with two-day bread I find,' he said kindly, 'is to have it with a chunk of cheese or a slice of bacon. That way, the fat helps it slide down neat as you please.'

Chaucer looked around. Perhaps it was the dark, though a small rushlight was burning, tied to a rowlock. 'A piece of cheese might do nicely,' he said, his voice still croaky from his sleep.

'Got no cheese until day after tomorrow, when we pass the dairy at Maidenhead. Nice cheese they make there. People come from miles.'

Chaucer forced a smile. 'A slice of bacon, then,' he said and Zouche carved a sliver from a hunk of greyish looking meat at his side. The knife he used made the hairs on the back of Chaucer's neck stand up. It was fully a foot long and the edge shone in the rushlight, sending glitters into the air from the burrs along its wicked length. Chaucer took the bacon wordlessly and set about trying to eat it and the bread.

The sound of chewing added to the night sounds and Chaucer found his appetite took over and he made shorter work of the old bread and bacon than he had made of the finest foods at less friendly boards. With an apple to finish and enough wine to mellow but not intoxicate, he leaned back at the end of the meal and toppled inelegantly off his bench.

Zouche laughed, the laugh of a man with nothing to worry about and a good night's sleep ahead of him. 'One thing to remember, Master Chaucer,' he said, helping his guest back onto his seat. 'No chair backs on the river.'

Chaucer settled his houppelande more comfortably about his shoulders and tried to regain some dignity. 'You seem happy in your life, Master Zouche,' he said.

'I was sad to lose my *Madeleine*,' Zouche said simply. 'The ship and she who she was named for.' He looked down for a second and then brightened again. 'Women, eh?'

'Indeed,' Chaucer said, in what he hoped was an understanding tone.

'Are you married, Master Chaucer?' the shipman asked.

'Oh, yes, indeed, yes. My wife lives elsewhere. Lady in waiting to the Duchess of Lancaster.'

Zouche's eyes widened. 'You move in exalted circles, Master Chaucer,' he said. 'Even more than I thought. So I must ask – why are you travelling in my humble craft? And why do you want to go to Oxford, of all benighted places? Surely you have people who could go for you? When I still had my ship, I had men of business to do things for me, and I had never been within spitting distance of the king, or John of Gaunt.'

Chaucer thought for a moment about how much he could trust this man. He seemed a simple soul on the surface, but he had met such men before who had turned out to be lower than the serpent and twice as slippery. They were alone, tied up to a riverbank under a canopy of willow, with only voles and cows for company. But there was something about the soft night air and the friendly tones of this shipman which made the comptroller more than usually honest.

'I confess, Master Zouche, that I don't often think of my circles as exalted. I see the king a couple of times a year and often across a crowded room. His woollens, which I comptrol, do have something of a life of their own. The merchants tell me what they are doing, I believe half of it and react accordingly. I am almost certain that they are robbing the king blind, but he can afford it. My role of court poet brings me more pleasure …'

Zouche interrupted. 'I was going to ask about that,' he said. 'I like a bit of poetry, though you might not think of me as a poetry sort of man. William Langland, now I do like him. I know a ferryman who took him across the river once.' He beamed in the glow of reflected proximity. 'Would I know anything of yours, perhaps?'

'I don't know,' Chaucer said, modestly. '*The Book of the Duchess*?'

Zouche thought for a moment and shook his head. 'No,' he said, finally. 'I'm sure it's very good, though. I like something with a story, myself.'

'I'm working on something at the moment,' Chaucer said, 'when I'm home. I'm thinking of calling it *The Parliament of Fowls*, or something like that.'

Zouche screwed up his face and wagged his head. 'Doesn't trip off the tongue, does it?' he said. 'Can I hear a line or two?'

Chaucer cleared his throat and struck an attitude, as he did when performing for the king and his cronies. 'For this was on Seynt Valentynes day, Whan every foul cometh ther to chese his make, Of every kinde, that men thynke may; And that so huge a noyse gan they make, That erthe and see, and tree, and every lake So ful was, that unnethe was ther space…'

The shipman looked polite but unimpressed. 'It's still a work in progress, I expect,' he said, kindly. 'I'm sure it will be very good, though, when it's finished.'

Chaucer dropped his pose and looked into his goblet, which was empty. If he had found one thing in his life, it was that everyone was a critic and not a very informed one at that. 'Indeed, Master Zouche,' he said, flatly. 'It is a work which is very much in progress.'

'I interrupted you,' Zouche said, apologetically. 'You were telling me about your wife.'

'I was?' Chaucer was startled. He rarely talked about Pippa. He kept her life with the second duchess as something of a closed book.

'She is a lady in waiting, you said.'

'Yes,' Chaucer said. 'That's right.' He yawned and stretched extravagantly. 'Is it bedtime yet? It seems very dark and even the cows seem to have gone to sleep.'

The shipman smiled to himself. He could tell a change of subject when one got up and punched him on the nose.

'I have made you a bed here in the stern,' the shipman said. 'It's

19

wider here and you can sleep straight, as you would at home. I curl up in the prow myself. It's what I'm used to.' He pointed to a pile of what looked like discarded clothing and rubbish at the far end of the boat. 'It's not raining or even cold, so I haven't put out the oiled linen I use for wet weather. You can arrange the bedding to your liking. And for your information ...' he leaned to one side and looked up through the sheltering willows 'it is near to ten o'clock, by the set of the moon. She'll be going down soon and it will be black as pitch. We might as well go to bed, though it's good to have someone to yarn with.' As he spoke, he was packing the food away in a sturdy rat-proof box. He moved the plank of wood which had been their table to one side and stepping neatly past Chaucer, turned to the river, unlaced his breeches and urinated lavishly into the water.

Chaucer, while a touch taken aback, was in another way relieved, almost as much as the shipman clearly was. He had been wondering how to broach the subject of such arrangements and he could not have wished for a clearer answer. Zouche looked over his shoulder and answered another unspoken question. 'If you need to answer any other call of nature, Master Chaucer,' he said, 'you will find two short ropes tied to the side, just behind you.'

Chaucer looked and sure enough, two short lengths of hemp lay hanging just along from the rowlock. Each had a hefty knot tied at the hanging end. 'Umm ...' As a poet he had quite an active imagination, but this had him stumped.

'Hang your arse over the side, hang on to the ropes and do what you need to do,' Zouche explained. 'Don't let go and don't worry about where it's going. Downstream is the answer and it's not yours to worry about once it hits the water.'

Chaucer muttered his thanks and went to his bed in the stern. He pummelled the hanks of unwashed wool, heavy with lanolin and sheep shit, into place and spread a blanket over it. He lay down and wriggled himself into position. It was, to his surprise, really rather comfortable. He turned on his back and looked up at the stars as they twinkled through the willow leaves. Catkins shed their golden pollen through the starlight and the boat rocked gently, making his eyelids flutter lower and lower.

'Oh, and Master Chaucer,' the shipman's voice came from the prow, 'if the third call of nature overcomes you, try to keep it quiet. It upsets the cows otherwise and there was a nasty incident last Michaelmas.'

The shipman didn't go into further detail and any nascent desire which may have been forming in Chaucer's head left and didn't return.

Breakfast was the same as supper and the midday repast the same as breakfast. And so the days meandered by, with Chaucer learning some simple rivercraft and finding he could bend more easily and sleep more soundly. Zouche was right, it was a healthy life on the river, but even so, the comptroller was not sorry when, on the morning of the seventh day, the shipman announced that they would soon be at their destination and Chaucer hurried to the prow, looking out anxiously for the first signs of the town of Oxenford.

The river widened before it reached the bridge and the barge groaned as the shipman steered to the right. Ahead, Chaucer could see the grey walls of the Dominican abbey and the great wheel of the Blackfriars mill grinding in the shadows.

'This is Grandpont, Master Chaucer,' Zouche said, 'close as I can get. Any further and I'll hit the weir at Trill Mill and then God help all of us.'

'I'm sure he will, Master Zouche,' the comptroller said. 'Here will be fine.'

'Oh-oh.' Zouche pulled hard on the tiller. 'I was afraid of this.'

A boat was cutting through the water to the *Madeleine*'s right, along the stream called Shire Lakes from the Cherwell beyond.

'What's this?' Chaucer asked.

'Welcoming committee,' the shipman told him. 'Tell me, Master Chaucer, is that poignard of yours just for show or do you know how to use it?'

Chaucer wore his dagger like he wore his belt, liripipe and houppelande – it went with the territory. 'I've had my moments,' he said, neglecting to tell his river-companion that all that was rather a long time ago, in the days when the comptroller could still see his knees when standing up.

'All right,' Zouche murmured, 'but in the first instance, leave it to me.'

The shipman lifted a huge club from a hiding-place under the deck planking. Solid oak a cloth yard long, it was studded with iron. 'My little persuader,' he winked at Chaucer.

'Ho, the *Madeleine*!' someone called from the boat, slewing towards the bank in line with Zouche's craft.

'Ho yourself,' the shipman called back. 'Who are you?'

'The Safety Commission of Oxenford,' the voice came back. 'State your business.'

'Safety Commission?' Chaucer muttered to Zouche.

'You won't find 'em in no statute books, Master Chaucer. Nor the rules and regulations of the University – particularly there. They're self-appointed nobodies anxious to make sure no one treads on their precious rights. Publicans and wool merchants – oh, saving your presence, of course.' He raised his voice. 'You know me, Marriott. I am William Zouche, of the *Madeleine* out of London, bringing a visitor.'

There was a moment of muttered discussion on the other boat. 'Who's your visitor?' they wanted to know.

'I am Geoffrey Chaucer,' the visitor said, 'Comptroller of the King's Woollens and Hides.' He held up the gilt hart that was the royal crest and it glinted in the pale spring sunshine.

More muttering. 'Are you here on the king's business, Master Chaucer?'

'Always,' Chaucer said, 'but specifically I have come to retrieve the body of a scholar, recently deceased.'

'Which college?' somebody else called from the boat.

'The House of Scholars at Merton,' he told them.

One of them spat into the water.

'Was it something I said?' Chaucer murmured to Zouche.

'I did try to warn you on the way up, Master Chaucer,' the shipman said. 'Town and gown don't mix here. It'll be all right once you're in the High – I hope. But unfortunately, these arseholes control the ways in and out.'

'Is there a problem?' Chaucer called. There were five men in the townsmen's boat, all of them built like chantries and all of them armed.

'That depends,' the answer rang back.

'On what?' Chaucer asked.

'The size of the toll.'

'And who decides that?' Chaucer asked. 'You or me?'

There were guffaws from the boat. 'What do you think?'

'The bridge there,' Chaucer called, pointing ahead. 'Who owns that?'

More guffaws. 'We do,' was the answer.

'And the street ahead?'

'Grandpont? That'll be us.'

Chaucer was pointing still further into the distance. 'And there, beyond the town gate?'

'That's Fish Street,' they told him.

'Precisely,' Chaucer said. 'And beyond that?'

'The High.'

'Short, if logic and law serve, for the King's Highway. The same holds true for Grandpont, the bridge, Fish Street and the waterway at my back. It all belongs to the king, knarre, and as the king's man, I have full right to use it – without toll.'

There was a stunned silence on the boat, then more muttering.

With a clank of oars, the boat pushed off from the bank and turned in midstream, the water rippling through the reeds. The Safety Commission was going home.

'Don't think this is over, Chaucer!' one of them shouted.

'It never occurred to me,' the comptroller said, determined, as always, to have the last word. He turned to the shipman and shook his hand. 'Master Zouche,' he said. 'Thank you for the safe journey. You'll be making your way back?'

The shipman smiled. 'Not just yet, Master Chaucer,' he said. 'I've met the Commission before. They don't take insults lying down. Unless, of course,' he patted his cudgel lovingly, 'they're lying down permanently. Think I'll stick around for a day or two. I would have said I know a comfy little inn near Merton, but in the circumstances, I think I'll sleep with *Madeleine* tonight. And you'll need a boat to get you home.'

Chaucer looked askance. 'And how much …?'

Zouche laughed and clapped the comptroller on the shoulder. 'No charge, Master Chaucer. No charge. Tell you what, you can be cook on the way home; work your passage, eh?'

Chaucer looked at the man. It wasn't often in his life he had been able to trust another human being completely, but he knew instinctively that this was one of those times. 'It would be an honour, Master Zouche,' he said. 'But can we agree – no bacon?'

'No bacon it is, Master Chaucer,' Zouche laughed. 'And don't forget, I'm here if you need me.'

It had to be said that the proctor of Merton left a lot to be desired when it came to civility. Even he, however, knew the king's crest when he saw it and led Chaucer through a labyrinth of passageways south of the High and across a neat quadrangle with new-looking stone buildings all around it. Everywhere was scaffolding and put-log holes, workmen sauntering about with planks under their arms and nails clenched in their mouths.

The proctor, in his rough grey fustian, poked his head around a door, grunted, 'Visitor, Warden,' and left.

There was a genial 'Come in,' from the tiny room and a tonsured head emerged from the academic gloom. 'Good morning,' he said. 'John Bloxham, Warden of Merton.'

'Good morning,' Chaucer smiled, trying to hear himself think above the noise. His ears had adjusted to the quiet of the river and the reversal was taking time. It had taken most of his walk through the meandering streets to regain his land legs and although he was almost back to normal, he was nevertheless glad to be in a space which didn't yaw about from time to time. 'I am here to collect the body of the late scholar Hal Golightly.'

'Ah,' the warden extended his hand. 'Would you be Sir Nicholas Brembre?'

'Not for ready money,' the comptroller shook hands. 'I am Geoffrey Chaucer.'

Bloxham blinked. 'Not *the* Geoffrey Chaucer?'

'Well,' the comptroller felt he ought to be accurate, 'I am *a* Geoffrey Chaucer. I'm not sure how many of us there are.'

'Geoffrey Chaucer, the poet?' Bloxham enthused.

'I dabble,' the comptroller told him.

'Indeed you do,' Bloxham ushered Chaucer to an inner sanctum. 'Come through here. It'll be quieter. When the trustees told me we had money for the rebuilding I must confess I had no idea how noisy it would be.' Bloxham was shouting above the hammering, sawing and profanities. Beyond the next oak door, however, all was calm. Chaucer accepted Bloxham's spare chair and the warden sat grinning at him.

'Well, well,' he said. 'Geoffrey Chaucer, here in the flesh. Here at Merton. Dick will be delighted.'

'Dick?'

'Richard Congleton, my Master of Logic. He's a *huge* fan.

'Well, I'm flattered,' Chaucer said. 'But I fear I am here on more pressing matters.'

'Yes, yes, quite.' John Bloxham was as grey as his stonework and looked as though he could give Methuselah a run for his money in terms of age. That said, his eyes were alive and kindly, twinkling below the silver tonsure. 'I understood that poor Hal was Nicholas Brembre's ward.'

'And nephew, yes,' Chaucer told him. 'But Nicholas is a man of business and he was unable to tear himself away. I am his humble substitute.'

'Come, now, Master Chaucer,' Bloxham beamed, glowing in the presence of greatness. 'There can be nothing humble where rare talent is concerned.'

Chaucer smiled. He would never be a modest man, but there was something about unrelenting hero worship that could wear thin extremely quickly. 'What happened?'

'Well,' Bloxham leaned forward. 'This is a little awkward. You probably noticed as you came in that we're having a little building done.'

'Hmm,' Chaucer nodded.

'Well, I don't know the exact details, nobody does, but poor Golightly was found with, not to put too fine a point on it, his head smashed in. Roger would know more.'

'Roger?'

'Roger Allard, my Master of Medicine. He it was, I believe, who wrote to your friend Brembre.'

'May I talk to him?'

'Of course. He's lecturing now, but I'll see that he's available this evening. You'll join us for dinner?'

'Thank you, Warden.'

'Where are you staying?'

'Er ... nowhere, as yet.'

'My dear fellow, you must lodge with us.' He caught the look on Chaucer's face. 'Oh, no,' he chuckled, 'not here in Mob Quad; it's a tip at the moment. No, we have halls for the scholars and guests at Frideswide Grange. Harriet's an excellent hostess. She'll look after you.'

'That's kind,' Chaucer said. 'May I see the boy's body?' He felt it was the least he could do.

'Of course. Of course. We placed young Golightly in Frideswide's Priory. The prior's an old friend of mine. We academics must stick together in troubled times, eh, Master Chaucer? I'll get Watkin to take you.'

'Watkin?'

'The proctor you came in with.'

Chaucer forced a smile. 'Wonderful,' he grated through gritted teeth.

Bloxham caught the man's mood at once. 'I know he is not the most genial of men; something of a token, to be honest. His old pa was a groundsman here for years and the boy was a little on the simple side. We took pity, you understand. As long as any instructions are made in plain speech, he will carry out your wishes promptly and well, if not with much small talk.'

Chaucer smiled. He could list a dozen such men, some quite high up at court.

'By the way.' Bloxham stood up to fetch the proctor in question. 'Which college did you say you went to?'

'None, I'm afraid,' the comptroller admitted.

'Oh.' Bloxham looked a little disappointed. 'Cambridge.'

'Not even that,' Chaucer said. 'I did once spend a term at Lincoln's Inn, but the law and I soon parted company, in the nicest possible way of course.'

The crypt of St Frideswide's Priory was cold as a witch's tit. Watkin the proctor had led Chaucer down cobbled lanes and around corners, with Canterbury College looming to their right and the pair squeezed through a narrow gateway into the grounds of the priory itself.

'Prior,' Watkin had grunted to a tonsured Augustinian crossing the burial ground. 'Visitor.'

'Geoffrey Chaucer,' the comptroller had said. 'Warden Bloxham told me I might view the body of the late Hal Golightly.'

'Are you family?' the prior had intoned, his hands tucked into his sleeves.

'Friend of,' Chaucer had told him. 'I have come to inter the boy or take him back to London.'

The prior led Chaucer to a flight of stone steps that ran below ground from outside the walls. He fluttered his fingers at Watkin, who grunted something and made himself scarce.

'Uncharitable though it is of me,' the prior said, 'I can't warm to that man. Talking of uncharitable,' he stopped Chaucer at the doorway, 'can I trouble you for a small donation to the spirit of St Frideswide? Her mortal remains are in the shrine above us. Were we to disinter her body, God forbid, we would find it as fresh today as the day she crossed over.'

'Yes, yes, of course.' Chaucer fumbled in his purse. He had never seen anyone pocket cash faster than the prior of St Frideswide– and the prior didn't even have pockets.

'Er … Hal?'

'Indeed.' The prior lit a large candle, as the crypt was completely windowless and it wasn't possible to see your hand in front of your face. Chaucer waited for a request for a shilling for candles, but the prior didn't seem to have thought of this revenue stream and they proceeded down the narrow aisle.

Hal Golightly lay under a shroud that had been tied at his head and feet. His face was as grey and lifeless as the slab he rested on and someone had wiped blood, none too carefully, from his forehead and eyes. Bunches of herbs, laid in his hands folded across his chest under the linen, were beginning to lose their battle with the subtle sweetness of corruption.

'I should like to examine him,' Chaucer said, though his flesh rebelled at the thought. A promise was a promise, though, and there was nothing to be seen on this shrouded corpse that would help bring any comfort to the lad's family.

The intake of the prior's breath was like a sword slid from a scabbard. 'I understand,' he said, 'that such things happen in the darker corners of the world; that some men even do it to, as they put it, "advance scientia", but I will not tolerate such an abomination in God's house, sir. I must ask you to leave.'

'Master Prior …'

The man held up his hand. 'That is the end of the matter,' he snapped. 'Make what arrangements you will for the body, but while it is under my roof, it will not be touched.'

Chapter 3

Meals at Merton were taken in silence, except for dinner, when, judging by the hum and noise and eruptions of laughter, it could easily pass for any Ordinary in London. In his travelling houppelande as he was, completely unaware where his other clothes had gone and still grimy from the trip upriver, Chaucer felt decidedly under-dressed at the high table. To his right sat the warden, resplendent in his university robes and hood, thrown back onto his shoulders. To his left …

'Richard Congleton.' The man held out his hand.

'Geoffrey Chaucer.' The comptroller shook it.

Congleton beamed. 'May I say what an honour …?'

'Master Congleton …' Chaucer began.

'Dick, please.'

'Dick, the Warden has already been effusive in his praise of me, but, honestly, I'm just a hack writer.'

'Geoffrey … may I?

Chaucer nodded.

'There is nothing hack about a man who writes like you. Your *Troilus and Cressida*…'

'You've read *Troilus and Cressida*, Dick?' Chaucer was astounded. 'It's not even published yet. How …?'

Congleton put a conspiratorial finger alongside his aquiline nose and looked out of the corner of his eye at Chaucer. 'John Gower.'

'You know John?'

'Lord, yes. We go back years. I hope you don't mind his sharing your opus.'

'Er … no, not at all.'

'Tell me, what brings you to Oxford? Looking for poetic inspiration?'

'Sadly, no.' Chaucer was hard pressed to imagine what possible inspiration he could be expected to extract from some rather dank passageways and a couple of building sites, but every man had his own view of where he lived and rose-coloured spectacles were not unknown, even in academe. 'Sorrow, I fear. The ward of a friend of mine was killed some days ago, right here in Merton.'

Congleton's smile vanished. 'Hal. Yes, I heard about that. Sorrow indeed.'

'Did you know him?'

'In the Trivium, yes, when he first arrived. Bright lad. Able. I'd rather lost track of him recently.'

'He was studying in the Quadrivium.'

'Right. Music. You'd need to talk to Quentin about him, then.'

'Quentin?'

'Quentin Selham, Master of Music.' He scanned the high table. 'That's him, at the end, the one with the squint. Strabo Selham, the scholars call him, but that's the price you pay for deformity, I'm afraid.'

The Warden stood up and rang a bell until the hubbub in the room subsided. 'Time for grace, gentlemen,' he said and looked beyond Chaucer to a large man in squirrel-fur robes. 'Master Frisby.'

The man stood up and in a broad Devon accent bellowed, '*Benedictus Benedicet.*'

There were 'amens' all around, but especially so from one corner of the room, where a particularly rowdy group of scholars were rolling their 'r's exuberantly. Frisby frowned, looking around in a fury. Congleton stifled his giggles. 'Poor Frisby,' he whispered to Chaucer. 'If there's anything scholars find funnier than a turned eye, it's an appalling accent. You should hear him trying to read Augustine in Greek.'

At some time, Chaucer was sure, he had been told that meals in colleges in Oxford were meagre affairs, slop and water just barely enough to keep body and soul together. As a stream of flunkeys began to troop in, carrying steaming dishes aloft, he could only assume he had remembered that conversation wrongly or the person who told him didn't know what he was talking about. Because this was no meagre repast designed solely to stave off starvation. This was food such as Chaucer had seldom seen before, even when he was sharing the king's table. There were swans, there were whole boar, there were piles of vegetables glazed in honey. There were crystallised fruits of every kind, including some that Chaucer was hard-pressed to identify. And wine, of course, wine of every hue from clear as spring water to as black as sin.

Chaucer looked around the table and saw little sign of abstemious behaviour from the men gathered around. Greasy chins wagged as they gossiped and plotted, greasy fingers dug into dishes and waved down the board to have something even more delicious passed their way. After over a week on the river eating elderly bread and dubious bacon, Chaucer was overwhelmed by it all and found that just a spoonful here and there was as much as he needed. Congleton, seeing his almost unsullied plate, waved a potted lark at him and enquired whether he was quite well.

'Indeed,' Chaucer assured him. 'I have just had an amplitude, thank you.' He patted his still ample stomach, little altered by his week of near fasting.

'Because if not, I was just going to point out the Master of Medicine to you. There he is, look. Down the table to your right. The one with half a blanc mange on his plate. Roger Allard is his name. Pleasant enough chap, if sometimes a trifle dour. But I suppose rummaging around in innards and such will keep a man close to his humanity.'

'Does he do that?' Chaucer was shocked. 'Rummage in innards?'

'Metaphorically,' Congleton said, peeling off a perfectly-cooked breast from his lark and popping it into his mouth. 'Metaphorically only, but that's enough, don't you think? Worth chatting to him, anyway. As I said, pleasant chap. And a wealth of anecdotes, should your stomach be unusually strong.' He leaned down the table and picked up a platter, proffering it to Chaucer. 'Dormouse?'

The gargantuan meal finally dragged itself to a close, leaving almost everyone slumped in their seats in a daze. Chaucer had asked Congleton– before his eyes had glazed over and he had started staring down at his own thumbs, twirling ever slower in his lap– what the occasion was. Congleton had looked at him with bleary eyes.

'Occasion?' he said, puzzled.

'For all this food.'

Congleton burped and managed to lift his head a little higher. 'No occasion. Just … Wednesday, is it? Something like that … no, not Wednesday. We don't have dormouse on a Wednesday unless there's some need eating up.' And his head had dropped again, along with his eyelids this time. An enormous snore was all Chaucer would get from him for hours.

So, he had pushed his chair back and made his way round the tables until he found a spare chair next to the Master of Medicine, who, he had noticed, had been a little more abstemious, blanc mange notwithstanding.

Allard pushed his hood back to have a better view of his new table companion and also to get it out of the way of the wine. 'Roger Allard,' he said. 'And you are Geoffrey Chaucer, or so I have been told by almost everyone in this room. Poet or something, I gather.'

Chaucer was relieved to be in the company of someone who didn't know his work. He liked a bit of lionising, who didn't, but it could quickly become rather wearing. 'I am,' he said, in answer to both remarks. 'And you are the Master of Medicine.'

'Well, that depends.' Allard smiled and topped up Chaucer's cup. 'On what?'

'On whether you're the sort of man who starts listing his ailments as soon as he knows he's in the company of a doctor of physic.'

'No, no, I assure you,' Chaucer chuckled. 'I wouldn't presume to bore you. Fit as a flea, me.'

Allard raised an eyebrow. 'Really? Tell me, Master Chaucer, when were you born? The month, I mean.'

'May,' Chaucer said.

'Ah, the bull.' Allard sipped his wine. 'Do you know the time?'

Chaucer craned his neck but there was no sign of a clock anywhere. Such things were expensive and probably a little new-fangled for Oxford. 'Not a clue,' he said.

'No, I mean, what time were you born?'

'Ah, I see. Well, my sainted mother always told me I was born a little before cock-shut, as the sun was going down.'

'Hmm.' Allard suddenly grabbed Chaucer's hand and held it up to his nose. 'Phlegm,' he said, sniffing. He let the hand go. 'Fat, great and short.'

'I say, steady on.' Chaucer was a little offended.

'Generalities, dear boy,' Allard said. 'But we have to start some-where. Any deformities? Mormals? Anything ...' he glanced below the table 'crooked?'

'I don't think so,' Chaucer bridled. 'I have had no complaints.' He couldn't remember when he had last had occasion for complaint or compliment, but he saw no need to share that information with a man he had only just met.

'How many fingers am I holding up?' the doctor wanted to know.

'Er ... two.'

'Excellent.' Allard snapped them together and a lackey hove into view carrying more wine. 'Have another cup of this, Master Chaucer, and you'll be right as rain in the morning.'

'I'm right as rain now,' the comptroller insisted, 'but I was hoping to pick your brains.'

'Ah,' Allard let his finger rise up the outside of his goblet and the lackey poured accordingly. 'That'll be a consultation, I'm afraid.' He rubbed his fingers together.

'It's about the dead scholar, Hal Golightly.'

'Ah, yes. Bad show, that. A nice lad, by all accounts.'

'You examined the body?'

'Forgive me, Master Chaucer, but I didn't take you for a ghoul. What is your interest?'

'Forgive *me,* Doctor,' the comptroller said, 'I am in *loco parentis* for the lad. His patron, Nicholas Brembre, has sent me to collect his body.'

'Hmm. If memory serves,' Allard was sniffing the wine now, 'he had a blow or blows to the head.'

'Blows?' Chaucer queried. 'In the plural?'

Allard closed to him. 'I know what you're thinking,' he said. 'Two blows makes it murder.'

'The thought had occurred.'

Allard leaned back. 'It had to me, too,' he muttered, 'but it's hardly my place to say so.'

'Really?' Chaucer looked at the man. 'Why not?'

The doctor closed in again, having checked to right and left that Merton's walls did not have ears. 'I owe a portion of my income to this college, Master Chaucer. Unlike the riffraff who patrol the Cherwell, you would surely not expect me to rock any boats, so to speak.'

'No,' Chaucer said, 'but I would expect you to tell the truth.'

Allard suddenly stood up and threw his napkin onto the table. He shot Chaucer a withering look, then spun on his heel. 'Forgive me, Warden,' he said loudly as he passed John Bloxham, 'I appear to have lost my appetite.' And he left.

Richard Congleton rose from his food-induced stupor, beckoned to Chaucer across the board and leaned closer. 'Don't tell me you found his fees a little salty,' he laughed.

But Chaucer wasn't laughing. 'I don't think fees were the issue,' he said. 'I wonder what is.'

Darkness had descended on Oxford by the time Geoffrey Chaucer left Merton. The streets were narrow and black as pitch as he wandered past Oriel with his knapsack on his shoulder. He was grateful that the shipman had limited his luggage. Dragging a trunk with a couple of weeks' worth of clothes would not have made for comfortable walking, especially after the wines of Merton. Somewhere a dog barked and a couple of scholars, clearly the worse for wear and gabbling in Greek, bade him goodnight. They were as surprised as he was when he answered them in the same language.

Around the corner, it was obvious where they had come from. Chaucer had no idea of the town's regulations as to opening hours, but if his own dear London was any yardstick, such rules were widely ignored anyway. The landlord of the Polychronicon was just putting up his shutters as Chaucer waddled past him.

'One for the road, Master,' he called, still in his apron and rolled sleeves.

'A little late for me, Master Publican,' Chaucer said. 'But you might tell me if I'm going in the right direction for St Frideswide Grange.'

'Oh, friend of Hattie's, eh? Yes. Past Oriel's walls, then left before you reach the High. Grosteste Lane. Can't miss it.'

But he did. Twice. On his third pass a rather large woman in a broad riding hat suddenly stood in front of him. 'Geoffrey Chaucer?' she asked.

'The same, madam.' He touched his liripipe.

'I'm Hattie Dalton. Come in. I've been expecting you. In fact, having been tripping over your luggage this past four days, I feel as if we know each other already.'

Chaucer gave a wan smile. He had feared that Alice would have gone all out as usual – she could never simply pack for the occasion but had to include clothes for eventualities which would never arise. Once, on a two-day visit to his sister three miles away, he had been startled to find that Alice had thoughtfully packed his shroud, complete with rosemary to keep it fresh. That had led to a spirited conversation when he got home and she had never repeated that particular item of clothing, but sometimes the contents of his trunk were a little surprising.

'I'm sorry about that,' he began. 'Sometimes my maidservant can be a little overzealous.' He crossed his fingers behind his back. If Alice ever heard him call her that, he would get a tongue lashing that would last him a lifetime.

'Goodness me,' she said, clapping him on the back and almost dislocating his shoulder. 'Everyone travels with luggage. It was just my little joke.'

She led him under a low archway and up a twisted wooden staircase to a landing. There were doors along the wall to the left and a solitary candle glowing in a sconce halfway down. Hattie fumbled in her plackets for a bunch of keys and unlocked the last door, next to the gable end. 'I hope this will serve, Master Chaucer,' she said. 'It's the one I usually give to my passing guests.'

The room was square, with a solid-looking tester in one corner, a large cupboard and a table next to the bed. Chaucer's trunk was pushed under the little latticed window and, all in all, it reminded him of his little eyrie above the Aldgate. 'Lovely,' he said.

'I assume you've eaten,' she said.

'Oh, yes,' Chaucer said, patting his stomach. 'Merton's high table.'

She snorted. 'Wednesday,' she said. 'So, it would be swan, I suppose. And left-over dormice. Dick tells me the cook there has no imagination at all. Same food, week in, week out.'

'Dick?' Chaucer didn't want to put his foot in it by assuming it was Richard Congleton – there were probably other Dicks in Oxford, after all.

'Richard Congleton. Serjeant at Law. He's my brother.'

'Serjeant at Law?' Chaucer was confused. 'I understood he was Master of Logic.'

'That too,' she laughed. 'Lecturing at Oxford is hardly a living wage, Master Chaucer. No, Dick makes his money in the courts. He's often in London, but at the moment he's got a big one coming up here in Oxford. King's bench, no less. The circuit.'

'Fascinating,' was all Chaucer could think to say.

'Well, it is,' she said, 'at least for the pig in question.'

Chaucer blinked. 'The ... er ...?'

'No, no,' she trilled, holding up her hand. 'I've said too much already. The boys take breakfast at seven, Master Chaucer. Will you join them?'

'Er ... yes, thank you,' he said. 'Have you been running the hall for long, Mistress Dalton?'

'Too long,' she grunted. 'But I mustn't grumble. The boys are reading for their Quadrivium, so they're grown men, really.' She closed to him. 'Some of them *fully* grown, if you get my meaning.'

Again, the comptroller had no meaningful answer, so he just chuckled. Hattie hauled back the bed covers and plumped his cushion. 'There's reading in the cupboard,' she said and winked at him. 'Ovid, if he's to your taste.'

'Ah, I'm more your Augustine man, myself,' Chaucer lied.

'Really?' she closed to him again, flicking a crumb off his houppelande. 'I *am* surprised to hear that.' She lingered for a moment, then made for the door. 'Goodnight, Master Chaucer. Don't let the bed bugs bite.'

And she was gone, leaving him alone with a stump of candle and his thoughts.

It had been a long and completely fruitless day and Chaucer was no wiser now as to the details of the death of Hal Golightly than he had been when Nicholas Brembre had enlisted his services in the first place. It seemed hardly credible that only this morning William Zouche had been tying up the *Madeleine* and fending off the Safety Committee. Chaucer sat on the bed and found it pleasingly lump-free. He did, out of curiosity, dip into the guest copy of Ovid, noting the fact that someone had underlined the juiciest bits with a thick nib and a trembling hand. Then he hauled off his travelling clothes and lifted the lid of his trunk to find his nightshirt folded on top, with just a sprinkling of lavender. Almost overwhelmed with homesickness, he fell into bed and a deep sleep.

It must have been soon after midnight that he heard it, a scrabbling that sounded like rats in the wainscotting. Except that it was more determined than that and at least one rat was muttering oaths under its breath. For a while he put up with it, then, exasperated, he threw the covers off and marched for the door.

In the passageway outside, a scholar was trying to get his key into the lock of the room next door and was not having much luck. He was steadying himself with his left hand on the doorframe and frowning at the metal in his right. He couldn't understand why he seemed to have three keys and why not a single one of them would slot into place.

Chaucer had once been that lad, albeit not in a university hall. He patted the boy's shoulder and took the key off him. The scholar frowned up at him from his crouching position.

After several attempts, involving pursed lips and some guttural sounds, he asked, 'Who are you?'

'A passing guest,' Chaucer told him. 'There.' He pushed the door open. The lad stood there, as if his next step, into a darkened room, was impossible to take. Chaucer took him by the arm and led him inside, leaving the door ajar so that the candlelight still flickered. The bed was in the same place as Chaucer's so the comptroller helped the scholar onto it and let him flop back. Then, he took pity on the lad and hauled off his shoes. The soft thud as they hit the floor woke the boy up and he suddenly sat upright in bed. He clawed at Chaucer's sleeve.

'You won't tell them, will you?' he whispered.

'Tell who what?' Chaucer was confused.

'The calculators. The Sand Reckoner. About me.' He waved in the general direction of himself. 'This.'

'No, no,' Chaucer patted the boy and laid him down again. 'Don't worry, I won't say a word.'

But the lad was already out of this world, snoring like an old bellows.

Chaucer felt completely at home the next morning, sitting on the hard oak of St Frideswide's Grange benches, munching on bread and cheese. Oxford ale wasn't *quite* up to Doggett's back home, but it would have to do. Around him, a dozen or so Quadrivium scholars were scoffing heartily, preparing for their day. In polite society, of course, anyone who was anyone didn't eat until midday, but these lads wouldn't see a square meal until suppertime, when the Devonian tones of Dr Frisby would unleash an avalanche of food which would stun a hungry ox. And back home, Chaucer had got used to Alice Doggett bringing him delicious things and porridge as he scratched his arse looking out of his window at cock-rise. Long days on the river and the dry bread and bacon were behind him now for a while and he tied a knot at the end of his liripipe tail to remind him to take his own food for the voyage back.

'Bless your breeches and your very balls!' a voice shouted.

All eyes turned to the door and a jovial-looking man stood there in fashionable liripipe and houppelande. 'Geoffrey Chaucer, you old comptroller!'

Chaucer was on his feet in seconds, something he wasn't always able to achieve these days. 'Ralph Strode, you old logician! What are you doing here?'

'Don't you remember?' Strode asked, clasping the man to him. 'This is my *alma mater*. Once a Merton man, always a Merton man. You?'

They sat down.

'It's a long story,' Chaucer said. 'And about to get longer. The ward of a friend of mine was killed recently, in Merton, as a matter of fact.'

'Ah, town versus gown,' Strode nodded. 'There were running battles back in my day.'

Chaucer looked at him. 'You mean a townsman could have killed him?'

'There's no "could" about it, dear boy. Now, tell me,' he leaned in to his old friend, 'has Hattie tried it on with you yet?'

'It?' Chaucer repeated.

Strode frowned. 'I don't remember you being such a prude, Geoff. It. The beast with two backs, making hay whether the sun is shining or not. What would they call it here? *Coitus*. A bit of how's your father ... I'm running out of euphemisms here, Geoff.'

'Yes, I do understand, Ralph,' Chaucer said. 'It's just that ... well, Hattie is a sort of university mother, isn't she? *In loco matris*, so to speak.'

'Matris, yes,' Strode sniggered. 'But not the spelling you mean.'

'But surely she wasn't running the Grange when you were here?'

'How old do you think I am, for God's sake? But no, she wasn't. I have met her since, you might say, not necessarily in the Biblical sense. Are you going to eat that?'

'Er … no.' Chaucer looked down at the rather delicious half loaf on his trencher. 'Feel free.'

'I'm staying at Tackley's in the High. Excellent fare, but they don't serve breakfast and my stomach thinks my throat's been cut. How's Philippa? It's been ages.'

'Oh, she's well. Very well.'

'Still away at …'

'Yes, yes. We write regularly, you know.'

'And the children. Little Thomas must be rather large by now.'

'Fifteen, when I saw him last,' Chaucer said.

'And he's at …'

'Absolutely. So, are you teaching at Merton?' Chaucer asked.

'Lord, no. I doubt old Bloxham would have me.'

'Author of the *Logica*? Come on, Ralph, you'd be a huge feather in his cap.'

'Well, that's as maybe, but at the moment …' he looked around him and dropped his voice almost to inaudibility for the rest of the sentence. 'I'm doing a spot of teaching at the Other Place. Peterhouse, specifically. Actually,' and he leaned in closer, 'I'm glad I bumped into you, really.'

'Oh?'

'An old sparring partner of mine, John Wyclif.'

'Ah.'

Strode frowned. 'What have you heard?'

'Well, nothing, really. Except that he's rather upset the old liturgical applecart. What does he bang on about? Corruption in the Church? All rather old cardinal's hat, surely?'

'No.' Strode's bonhomie had vanished. 'It's more serious than that. He's talking about predestination.'

'Er … pre …'

'That God has a plan for us all and there is nothing we can do to change it.'

Chaucer looked blank.

'Well, don't you see, Geoffrey? Taken to extremes, it means that some people are chosen, an elect if you will, to get to Heaven. Others aren't.'

'I see.'

'So, in theory, even if someone is a sinner, he can get into Heaven all the same.'

'Really?'

'So, your friend's ward, should it be said that he was murdered … his killer could still well meet St Peter because God had already ordained it.'

'But would God be so blinkered?' Chaucer asked. 'I mean, in the scheme of things, He must know His murderers and His rapists from His saints.'

Strode was horrified. 'Careful, Geoffrey,' he said. 'That's heresy in its own right, right there.'

'Is it?' Chaucer blinked. 'Sorry.'

'The fact is,' Strode was into his stride again, 'Wyclif is facing an ecclesiastical court in London in a few weeks. A Synod, no less, with the Archbishop of Canterbury in the chair. And he has followers.'

'The Archbishop?'

'Wyclif. His people call themselves Lollards.'

'Grumblers,' Chaucer nodded.

'You know about them?'

'I've heard the odd rumour. I know the derivation of the name because, wearing my Comptroller of Woollens hat, a lot of my clients are Flemings – it's a Dutch word.'

45

'Well, there you have it.' Strode spread his arms. 'Heretics *and* foreigners. I'm here to do a bit of quiet snooping. Like me, Wyclif was a Merton man and we need to know the extent of his malevolence. Oxford is a hotbed. Oops – and, talking of which …' the man was on his feet. 'Time I wasn't here.' And he made for the door.

A large woman in a broad hat had bustled in through a side door. 'Ralphie!' she trilled, grinning at him.

'Hattie!' he called from the safety of the far doorway. 'Must dash. Catch up with you later.'

'I wasn't quite straight with you, Zouche.'

Geoffrey Chaucer thought it was time to come clean. He had extricated himself from the questioning of Hattie Dalton, anxious to know how he knew Ralph Strode and he was determined to make progress.

'Oh?'

The shipman was oiling the tiller of the *Madeleine*, half-hidden as she was in the willows that edged the Thames.

'When I said I had come to collect the body of a scholar …'

'No body?'

'Oh, there's a body, all right, but I can't get to it.'

'What?' Zouche broke off from his work. 'They won't let you have possession?'

'It's not that,' Chaucer said, easing himself down amidships. 'I need to examine it *in situ*.'

'Where?'

'Here.'

'Why?'

Chaucer sighed. 'Because I think the boy was murdered,' he said, 'and I don't intend to leave Oxford until I've brought his murderer to book.'

'Don't tell me,' Zouche took a swig of ale from his goatskin bag, 'the university's clamming up.'

'That's right,' Chaucer said.

'Same in the Port of London,' Zouche shrugged. 'Along all the wharves. Nobody sees, hears or knows a damned thing. Funny, that, isn't it?'

'The only two people who might have been able to help – the prior of St Frideswide and the doctor of physic at Merton – I've managed to offend. So ...'

'So, we'll have to do it ourselves, then?'

'Do what?' Chaucer blinked.

'Have a look at the body. Where is it?'

'In the crypt at St Frideswide's Priory. Locked doors all the way.'

Zouche laughed. 'Locks were made for picking, Master Chaucer,' he said, and he pulled a set of small iron hooks out of his apron front. 'My extra fingers,' he said. 'Never been known to let me down.'

'Master Zouche,' Chaucer said, frowning. 'You may be able to get through the gates of Hell with those, but this is my problem, not yours. I couldn't let you ...'

Zouche handed over the faux keys. 'There you go, then,' he said. 'Don't forget to let me know how you get on.' He dipped his cloth back in the linseed oil and applied another coat with long, smooth strokes.

Chaucer looked at the bunch of iron in his hand. 'Er ...'

Zouche laughed again. 'Look, Master Chaucer,' he said, taking them back. 'There's only so much linseeding a knarre can stand, if I'm honest. We'll need darkness, though. Can you find your way back to the crypt in question?'

'I think so,' Chaucer said.

'Tonight, then.' The shipman gave the tiller one last polish and moved on to the rowlocks, stepping past Chaucer without making the *Madeleine* so much as rock at her moorings. 'Shall we say about midnight? I'll see you at Carfax. Have you got something to do until then?'

'Oh, yes,' Chaucer said. 'I've got to see a man about some books.'

Chapter 4

There's something about a library, at least if you're Geoffrey Chaucer. The books he dealt with on a daily basis were tedious ledgers, referring to the hides and woollens that passed through the customs house with predictable regularity. The books he loved, like those in the great library of Merton College, were something else altogether.

It was late morning as he wandered the room, the spring sunlight filtering through the tracery and flashing on the gilt lettering on the spines of the tomes. Gargoyles growing out of the oak leered at him as he walked below them and now and then the chains that held the books rattled as a draught came from nowhere, whispering around old vellum like the breath of God Himself.

Chaucer barely knew where to start. Thomas Aquinas? He knew it backwards. Vegetius? A bit martial for a Thursday morning. What about the *Seven Sagas of Rome*? No. He was just toying with *The Sayings of the Four Philosophers* when a voice hissed in his ear.

'Put that down!'

He spun around to see a venomous face scowling at him, rather pinker, perhaps, but just as unpleasant as any of the gargoyles in the fan vaulting.

'Have you washed your hands?' The face almost spat.

'Er … not since …'

'Come with me.' The large monk led Chaucer, now without the book he had been obliged to leave on a table, down a small flight of stairs to a niche in the wall. There was a bowl of water here that the comptroller had seen on the way up, but had ignored. 'Wash,' the monk ordered. And wash Geoffrey Chaucer did. There was no napkin, so the man who was the court poet wiped his hands down his houppelande.

'Right,' the monk said. 'Now suppose you tell me who you are and what you are doing in my library.'

'Certainly,' the comptroller said. 'I am Geoffrey Chaucer, court poet.' He thought that title might cut more ice with this objectionable book-keeper than that of customs official.

'Oh,' the monk's harsh voice softened to an oily purring, as though he had just poured honey over his tongue. 'Master Chaucer, forgive me. I heard you were in Merton. Please … I interrupted you. *The Four Philosophers* is a rattling good read, I have to say. Shall we?' And he ushered Chaucer back up the stairs to the man library.

'This is marvellous,' he said, 'Father …'

'Brother,' the man corrected him. 'Anselm. Librarian and *Defensor Libri* of the House of Scholars of Merton.' He bowed. 'At your service.'

'A little bird told me,' Chaucer said, 'that you have Ptolemy's *Geographia Cosmographia* here.'

Anselm positively glowed. 'Indeed, we have,' he beamed. 'Would you like to see it?'

'I certainly would,' Chaucer enthused. The big man led the way, filling the space as he padded along the walkway with its Persian carpets and up a small flight of stone steps to a door. This he unlocked with a huge key dangling from his waist and let Chaucer in. The room was tiny and Anselm lit a candle which he placed on a high lectern. He ferreted behind a velvet arras and staggered out with a huge book, bound in rich, tooled leather with brass mounts and clasps. He laid it on the lectern and carefully opened it up, 'Ptolemy's *Geographica Cosmographia*,' he announced proudly, 'drawn and written by the great man about one hundred and fifty *anno domini*.'

Chaucer marvelled at the thing, perhaps the only copy in the world. God's breath rippled the sea on the title page and terrifying monsters lurked in the deep, threatening to overturn the caravels churning through the foam. Earth lay, as was proper, in the centre of the universe and around it, the stars of God's firmament twinkled in all their majesty. Orion was there and the great bull, the seven sisters and the twins. Instinctively, Chaucer reached out to touch it and leaped backwards at a scream from Brother Anselm.

'I'm sorry,' the monk gasped, clutching his throat. 'It's just that no-one is allowed to handle this book except myself and, once he has gone to the confessional, Warden Bloxham. It is not possible to put a price on a volume such as this.'

'Indeed,' Chaucer said. 'Is that why the books downstairs are chained?'

'Lord, no.' Anselm slammed Ptolemy's clasps with something less than the usual awe, Chaucer thought, and put the book away again. 'That's to prevent those pilfering bastards of the Quadrivium from helping themselves.'

'The Quadrivium?' Chaucer repeated. 'Are they a particular problem?'

Anselm led the man out of the little room, blowing out the candle and locking the door. Then they were down the steps and in the main library again. 'Yes,' the monk said. 'Yes, they are. It's odd, really. It doesn't usually happen.'

'What doesn't?'

'Well … are you a university man, Master Chaucer?'

'Sadly, no.'

'Well, it isn't for everybody. Can you imagine a world in which half its population goes to university?' He shuddered.

'Impossible,' Chaucer agreed. 'Unthinkable.'

'No, most of our boys of the Trivium are from Winchester, a smattering from Eton. Good boys, they are, by and large, loyal and respectful.'

'And?'

'And so they stay, even after their first degrees. Until recently, the Quadrivium scholars have been more of the same, except that their voices have broken.'

'The sopranos are the tenors, eh?'

'Quite so.' His face darkened. 'But this lot! I won't name names and I doubt they'd mean much to you if I did, but they're arrogant this year, above their station.'

'Is there a reason for that?'

Anselm looked at Chaucer. 'It would not be appropriate for me to speculate,' he said.

'There is one student of the Quadrivium I would have known, at least by name. Hal Golightly.'

Anselm scowled anew. 'May I ask how you knew him?'

'He was the ward of a friend of mine,' Chaucer told him. 'I came to take him home, but I gather there are … shall we say, complications.'

'Complications?'

'Do you know what happened to him, Brother?' Chaucer asked. 'What caused his death?'

The monk shrugged. 'Falling masonry, I understand. You know there is much building going on around the grounds at the moment.'

'Indeed. Tell me, a moment ago, I got the impression you didn't care much for Hal Golightly.'

'It's not for me to speak ill of the dead, Master Chaucer. I'm afraid I didn't trust that young man entirely. He was one of the most arrogant of an arrogant bunch. And ... and it pains me to say it ... I think he was trying to steal the *Cosmographia*.'

'Ptolemy's?'

'The same.'

'Why?'

'For the money, I suppose. It's worth a fortune, man, a king's ransom. He must have heard about it in his lectures, although its existence is common knowledge amongst all the scholars.'

'What makes you think he was a thief?'

'He already had a copy of Sir John Mandeville's *Travels* in his satchel when I caught him sneaking out of here a few weeks ago.

'Mandeville?'

'Oh, not his real name, of course. Some Frenchman who claims to have found the Great Cham in the far east. People with faces in their chests who pass water upside down – you know the sort of thing.'

'What happened?'

'Well, I took Golightly to task. It was one of the unchained books so he hadn't much difficulty in slipping it into his bag. But he didn't reckon with old eagle-eyes Anselm here. I stopped him at the door and took it off him. Know what he said?'

'No.'

'*Mea culpa*. At first. Then he said that such trivia as Mandeville shouldn't be in a library anyway and that pretty soon, all the volumes herein would have to be torn up and thrown away.'

'What did he mean?'

Anselm dismissed it. 'Nothing, I don't suppose. Like all his generation, they're flakes of snow. He'd got caught and he was being juvenile about it rather than take his punishment like a man.'

'And was he punished?'

'Indeed he was. I felt it my duty to report the matter to Warden Bloxham who had him flogged by the proctors in Mob Quad. Not only could Hal Golightly not sit down for a week, he stole nothing else for the rest of his life. As it turned out.'

'Well, thank you, Brother Anselm, for the tour – and for what you've told me. So far, I've had the impression that young Hal was something of a saint. I'll have to revise that now. As for the library, well,' he smiled and threw his arms wide in admiration, 'it makes my own seem rather feeble by comparison.'

'Really?' Anselm smirked. 'How many volumes do you possess?'

'Sixty, at the last count.'

'Sixty?' The monk was astonished.

'Yes.' Chaucer noticed the gaping mouth. 'How many does Merton have?'

'Forty-three,' he said.

'Heigh ho,' Chaucer called as he pattered down the stairs. Then he felt bad and turned back. 'But I haven't got *Geographica Cosmographia*, have I?'

And he patted his houppelande, just to double check.

'Master Mason!' Chaucer was having to yell with all his might to be heard over the hammering and sawing.

A scrawny man in a rather expensive-looking houppelande clattered down the ladder from the buttress overhead. In the building trade, he'd been shouting at everybody for years, but there was something about the seriousness on the face of his visitor that made him talk to the man face-to-face rather than swinging on a crane.

'Geoffrey Chaucer.' The comptroller held out his hand.

'Arthur Perry. It's not the noise, is it? Warden Bloxham's already had a word, but, as I said to him, you can't make a posset without breaking a few eggs. Not much of a chef, isn't the Warden, but I think he understood the analogy.' An oaf shambled past and Perry caught him a nasty one around the head. 'You'll never get beyond apprentice carrying a bucket like that, lad,' he growled. 'Tuppence ha'penny a day I pay you and I expect better.'

Chaucer knew for a fact that the mason got four shillings, but he wasn't one to judge. 'No, no, Master Perry, I'm sure the noise goes with the territory. I wanted to talk to you about the accident the other day.'

'Which one?' Perry asked.

'The one in which the scholar was killed. Hal Golightly.'

'Oh, that one. I thought you were talking about the bedder who caught her tits in ... oh, no, that was the Balliol site.'

He turned away from Chaucer and cupped his hands around his mouth. 'Morrison!' he yelled. 'Here. Now.'

A giant of a man with a belt dangling with awls came shambling down the ladder that rattled and flexed with his weight. 'This gentleman wants to know about the lad.'

The giant looked vague.

'You know the one. You found him.'

'Oh, ar.' The giant looked at Chaucer, recognised quality when he saw it and tugged off his cap.

'Can we go in there?' Chaucer asked, pointing to an entry off the quad. 'Rather more private.'

The trio walked into the shadow of the archway. 'You found the body?' Chaucer asked Morrison.

'I did, sir.'

'Where was this?'

''E was lying on the ground, sir. Over there.' Morrison pointed to a corner of the quad. 'Early morning, it was. I was first on.'

'First on gets an extra ha'penny a day,' Perry explained to the comptroller, as if the fact had any relevance.

'Did you touch him at all?' Chaucer asked. 'The body, I mean.'

'I did, sir. Just to see if he were still breathin'.'

'And were … was he?'

'No, sir. Dead as a nit.'

'With head wounds?'

'Yessir. Blood everywhere, there was.'

Chaucer popped out into the sunshine. Above the spot where Golightly had been found, there was no scaffolding, and no windows, as yet, from which the boy might have fallen.

''E were dragged,' Morrison went on.

'How do you know?' Chaucer asked.

'Blood trail. From yonder.' The builder pointed to the next entry.

'Where does that lead to?' the comptroller wanted to know.

'See for yourself.' Perry led the way and the three ducked into the shadows again to emerge onto rough ground.

'Oh,' was Chaucer's only comment.

'That's the town wall, Master Chaucer,' the man said, pointing to the stonework ahead. 'When my lads have finished, it'll be all one with Merton College, but at the moment, there's this inconvenient gap. As you can see, half the town dumps their shit along here. You'd have thought the mayor would have cleaned it up.'

'Tell me, Master Mason,' Chaucer said. 'Are these walls patrolled?'

'You'll have to ask the mayor that.'

'Patrolled, Master Chaucer? Patrolled? Do you imagine Oxenford is *made* of money?' Jack Treddler was not having a good day.

'It was only a civil question, Master Mayor,' the comptroller was standing in the man's chambers but at no point was he asked to sit down or offered so much as a cup of wine.

'Civic, rather than civil,' the mayor snapped. 'You tell me you are making enquiries into the unfortunate death of a scholar and you seem to be implying that it is somehow the town's fault; nay, *my* fault.'

Chaucer knew already that paranoia went hand-in-glove with local government, but this was taking things to extremes. 'No, I …'

'Back in the day,' the mayor interrupted, 'when there was serious trouble between town and gown, we had a town guard; nay, militia, stout men all. Then came the Pestilence, a decline in the wool trade and that wretched business with the peasants last year. Oh, we didn't have the trouble you people faced in London, I grant you, but it was not pleasant. Half the militia resigned. And now, I can't afford to pay those who are left. So, no, Master Chaucer, no one would have been patrolling the walls so no-one would have seen anything untoward going on behind Merton College. And that, can I remind you, is a matter for the university, not for us. If there's nothing else, I'm a busy man.'

'I can see that,' Chaucer said. 'It must be a full-time job, haranguing royal officials. Don't look for promotion, Master Mayor; there isn't going to be any.' And he left.

When the door had stopped quivering on its hinges, a dark figure emerged from an arras behind the mayor's chair. 'Was that him?' the mayor asked. 'The man you saw on the *Madeleine*?'

'That's him,' the man said. 'I thought the Commission should know.'

'Right and proper, Marriot.'

'What did he want? I missed most of the conversation.' He sat down and helped himself to the mayor's Rhenish.

'He's poking his nose into the death of that Merton scholar. I don't trust these London people.'

'Nothing to do with us ... is it, Jack?'

Jack Treddler leaned back in his chair. 'You tell me, Marriot,' he said. 'You're the military wing of the Commission.'

'No,' Marriot told him. 'It's not us. That broken arm in Oriel Street – that was us. Oh, and the lead vanishing mysteriously from New College roof. Definitely us, that. As you know, Jack, we usually steer clear of actual murder.'

'Glad to hear it,' the mayor said. 'Keep an eye on Chaucer, though. God knows what he might turn up if he keeps asking questions. Your boys might have to step in.'

Marriot smiled. 'That'll be our positive pleasure,' he said.

Had anyone asked Geoffrey Chaucer if he knew the way from St Frideswide's Grange to Carfax, he would have given a merry laugh and said 'Of course!' However, this would have been far from the truth, so he erred on the side of caution and slipped out of a side door as a distant bell was chiming eleven. He was wrapped in his darkest clothing which, given Alice's proclivities to dress him as brightly as she could, meant a dark green cloak over a crimson houppelande and breeches. He had chosen to wear his indoor shoes, the ones with no fashionable moss in the toes. They were of the thinnest Cordovan leather and he knew he would feel every cobble, but he also knew there would be moments when the soles of his feet would be his only sense and he could step as silently as a cat in these old friends, which moulded to him like his own skin.

He arrived in the shadow of the tower of St Martin of Tours well before midnight. Even the curfew-free town of Oxenford was beginning to quieten down now, though the hub at which he stood was still home to some revellers and some ladies of the night more determined than their sisters to make a few extra pence. Chaucer was not sure whether to be pleased or not that he had not had to rebuff a single one of them as he made his way to his trysting place. He sighed. Time was – and not that long ago – that he would have been beating them off with a stick. He leant on the cold stones and contemplated the passing of those times.

He may even have dozed a little, standing there in the chill of a spring midnight when a stirring of the darkness told him he was no longer alone.

'Master Chaucer,' Zouche breathed almost in his ear. 'You are punctual almost to a fault. Have you been waiting long?'

'No,' Chaucer lied. 'Punctuality is the politeness of princes.'

'Indeed it is,' Zouche said. 'Shall we go and have a look at this stiff, then?'

'Can we have just a little decorum, Master Zouche?' Chaucer said, crisply. 'I suspect that the lad has been done to death horribly, let's not insult him further.'

Zouche's teeth glinted in the faint moonlight. 'My apologies, Master Chaucer and ... remind me of the lad's name.'

'Hal Golightly.'

'My apologies, Master Chaucer and Hal. I will try to be more respectful. Which brings me to something I meant to say before. I think it would be a good idea, when we are speaking to each other and we don't know who may be listening, to use less formality. There are probably other Wills and Geoffs in Oxford, but unlikely to be more than one Chaucer or Zouche. It would be a shame if busy ears should be our downfall.'

Chaucer considered it for a moment. He had never been one to stand on ceremony and it seemed a sensible plan.

'I agree, Will,' he said. 'And let's not keep it for when idle ears are flapping. We are about to desecrate a corpse. If that doesn't put us on first name terms, I don't know what does.'

The two stood in the shadows with their thoughts for a moment and then Zouche touched the comptroller on the shoulder.

'Let's not lose our resolve, Geoff,' he said, in a whisper. 'Lead on.'

'Lead on?' Chaucer was a little disconcerted. His day vision was not exactly perfect; his night vision was much worse. And his almost total lack of a sense of direction didn't help things one bit. 'I had hoped … you know … a navigator like you …'

Zouche let him bumble himself to a stop and then risked a quiet chuckle. 'Don't get your subjaculum in a bunch. I came into town earlier and have worked out the best route. Important if we might need to make a run for it, after all.'

'A run for it?' Chaucer lost a little more resolve from his diminishing store.

'I couldn't tell what they might have by way of men guarding the body,' Zouche said. 'I suspect none, but we are bound to be there during a service, unless we are really quick. And if they see a light …

well, you see why I have made contingency plans. At a comfortable trot, we are five minutes from the *Madeleine*.' He looked dubiously at Chaucer. 'Can you do a comfortable trot, Geoff?'

Chaucer sucked in his belly as best he could. 'I can trot,' he said, sulkily. It was the comfortable and five minutes he wasn't at all sure of.

'Well,' Zouche said, to comfort them both, 'it hopefully won't come to that.'

He led them at a smart walking pace through small alleys and pathways which Chaucer had a fleeting memory of and suddenly, they were against the walls of the church of St Frideswide, her uncorrupted body lying silently within. A single candle burning at the altar sent a gentle glow through a window just above their heads and he pointed to his left, to where the outer stair wound down into the pitch blackness of the crypt.

The two men sidled along the wall, feeling their way carefully. There were small memorials set partly into the stone and after his fourth stubbed toe Chaucer didn't even bother with the indrawn breath; his feet were almost numb anyway. After what seemed a lifetime, he felt the topmost stair under his foot and they descended into the dark. Once through the thick oaken door at the bottom, standing ankle deep in damp leaves blown down through the winter and only now starting to dry a little, they risked a small light, brought into being by Zouche's tinder and his unerring thumb.

The body still lay in the middle of the cold, shadow-filled room and they approached it, one going to each side. They stood, heads bowed, for a brief moment, each with his own thoughts. Though their lives had been so different, they had both known loss and they considered it and mortality before untying the shroud where it was gathered above the boy's head.

As the linen fell away, the stench of decay grew stronger, over-whelming the herbs at his breast. Even the icy cold of the crypt of St Frideswide's could not stop death's touch forever and black marks were appearing on the body, marring the boy's otherwise perfect skin. Underneath, the blood had sunk and the discoloration made it look as though he lay in a bath of ink. The ends of his fingers were blackening, the nails beginning to come loose. Some strands of hair lay in the shroud and as Zouche brought the small rushlight nearer, it could clearly be seen that they were held together by fragments of skin, dried blood and shards of bone.

Zouche pointed this out to Chaucer, who, to his distress, had to lean across the boy; had there been breath to feel, he would have felt it on his cheek. Leaning back as soon as he could, he stepped away, fighting down an urge to vomit. As he did so, he saw something which made his stomach lurch even more and he gestured to Zouche to join him with his light.

Under the hair on Chaucer's side of the body, something was moving, with a rippling motion like a slug making its way across a damp paving slab on an evening much warmer than this. Zouche put the light nearer, too near and some hairs sizzled briefly before going out leaving a singeing smell behind which for a moment overlaid the sick sweetness of death. In a deep wound almost under the boy's head as it lay there, a silent roar of maggots writhed in protest at their disturbance. On the shroud, some shells of pupae born and flown lay brown and discarded, along with a few of their brothers, fallen from the nest they had made of the boy's skull.

Zouche stood back and extinguished the light. Neither man would ever forget the sight, but plunging it now into darkness would help a little. The shipman could hear his companion heaving and gave him a little space to recover. Then, he whispered, 'You know what this means, don't you?'

'Yes,' Chaucer replied, his voice croaking with the sudden dryness of his throat.

'Two wounds. One to disable, one to kill. This boy was murdered, beyond a shadow of a doubt.'

'But who by?' Chaucer said.

'Someone taller,' Zouche said, 'judging by the angle. Someone strong. And ...'

'And?'

'Someone evil.'

Chapter 5

After the night he'd had, Geoffrey Chaucer couldn't face sleeping on the hard, unforgiving planking of the *Madeleine*'s decks. Warm during the day, it was unseasonably chilly at night along the river and damp with it. On the other hand, he couldn't be sure that Hattie Dalton's establishment would not be locked and barred. He knew already that there was no curfew in the town and no night watch worthy of the name, so no one would notice a well-dressed middle-aged man sneaking along the wall in the small hours.

Wrong.

'Hello, hello,' a rough voice grated in the darkness. 'What have we here?'

There were two of them, carrying wooden staves and wearing attitudes.

'Who goes?' one of them wanted to know.

'Geoffrey Chaucer,' he said. 'Comptroller of the King's Woollens.'

'Yes, and I'm John of Gaunt,' the other one chuckled.

Chaucer peered closer. 'No, you're not,' he said. 'The Duke of Lancaster is half a head taller than you.' He stepped back. 'And you can't smell him coming.'

'You what?' The man barged forward, his stick raised.

'Now, then, Tom, let's not be too hasty. Do you have any proof you're who you say you are?'

Chaucer flicked the golden hart from his purse. 'You know the king's crest?' he asked.

Tom peered at it and his friend smiled. 'Would you mind telling us, Master Chaucer, why you are wandering the streets at this unholy hour?'

'I'd left something on my boat,' Chaucer lied.

'Oh? What might that be?'

As luck would have it, the comptroller had a pocket edition of *Piers Plowman* in his purse and he held it up. 'My companion of a mile,' he said. 'I had lent it to my boatman.' He hoped Zouche would never hear of it; his edition was far superior and the use of the 'b' word was anathema, as Chaucer knew only too well. 'You know my name. What's yours?'

'Civis,' the man said.

'Citizen,' Chaucer translated. 'Very generic. Did the mayor teach you that one?'

'We're the Safety Commission, squire,' Tom sneered.

'Keeping our streets safe,' his friend hardly needed to add.

'Delighted to hear it,' Chaucer smiled.

'Mind how you go then, sir.' And the pair watched Chaucer go. 'Remember that, Tom. The cocky old bastard was travelling in an easterly direction a little before Lauds. He was armed and in possession of a book.'

'Got it,' Tom grunted, although he'd have been happier if he'd been able to put one on the cocky old bastard for good measure.

* * *

As he made his way back to his borrowed room at the Grange, Chaucer mulled over whether, on a scale of one to ten, this was the worst night of his life. He had lived through some interesting times, pestilence, war and revolt, but this would still score a solid nine and a half. If the door he had slipped out by was locked now he was here, it would immediately escalate to eleven, but no, it was still open to his touch and he crept upstairs in his soft cordovans. He hadn't been in his room much, but it felt like home now and the chest under the window had his nightshirt folded in it at the top, where he had placed it himself only that morning, though it seemed a lifetime ago. He stripped off his clothes. The crimson houppelande was going to the Poor Clares or whoever was in charge of charity in this godforsaken town – although Zouche told him he was imagining it, to Chaucer it would forever stink of corruption where the shoulder had brushed against Hal Golightly's cheek. His undershirt would do for another week or so of wear, and his hose and subjaculum seemed untainted by anything untoward so, with a quick sniff to check their freshness, he folded them roughly and threw them on the chest. He opened the window a touch – he liked fresh air when he could get it – and then closed it again against the barrage of birdsong which seemed to be coming from just inches away. Yawning and stretching, he walked the few steps across the room to his bed, which he knew from the night before was as soft as a caress, with crisp linen sheets tucked in as tight as a gnat's arse. He folded back the counterpane and slid his legs down the bed, which was warm as a …

Warm?

He sat up and felt with his right hand across to the other side of the bed, which should have been empty but was in fact full of rather generous mounds of his landlady. It had to be her. No other woman in the place had as much flesh on her as did Mistress Hattie Dalton. All in the right places, as she herself said to anyone who would listen. She was also of the opinion that most men with any wick in their candle liked a little something to grab ahold of.

'Mistress Dalton!' Chaucer's voice was a squeak. 'Have I mistaken my room?' He knew he hadn't, but he was a gentleman after all and didn't want to make a mountain out of a molehill if there was a polite way of getting out of the situation.

Hattie Dalton could move like lightning when she wanted to and she wanted to now. She was out of bed and pressed against Chaucer before he could do so much as move a step backwards. She had him in a wrestler's grip and he immediately knew that resistance was useless.

'Master Chaucer,' she breathed. 'Or may I call you Geoffrey?'

He found himself nodding.

'Geoffrey, Geoff, you are so kind to pretend you had made a mistake but surely you knew that you would find me in your bed sooner or later? I just decided to make it sooner.' She gave a sort of sinuous wriggle that made Chaucer wince. 'And I detect, Geoff,' she moved her mouth closer to his ear, so that her breath tickled, 'that you are not sorry that I am here.'

'Oh, that.' In the darkness, Chaucer blushed, 'that's my purse. I wear it constantly.'

'Your *purse?*' she murmured, loosening the grip of one arm to investigate. 'If that's your purse, Geoff, then you are a richer man than I had assumed.' She rummaged around and got her hand under his nightshirt. 'What an unusual design,' she whispered. 'I don't believe I …'

'*Madam!*' Chaucer hissed, shaking her off and standing back against the wall, his hands crossed in front of him. 'I am shocked.'

Her chuckle froze his blood. 'Shocked, Geoff?' she said. 'At what? I don't think I have ever pretended to be anything I am not. All the scholars here – or at least, those who have come to learn about everything, instead of stupid numbers and space – know what I am. And now, you will, too.'

'I don't need to know more, madam,' Chaucer said, closing his eyes and realising at once that he had made a major mistake, because she was on him like a snake on a toad.

'Oh, but you *do*,' she said. 'You're not young, Geoff, I'll give you that, but neither am I. And there's many a good tune played on an old fiddle.' She thought for a moment. 'Not that I am old and …' and she reached under his nightshirt again with unerring aim 'I *do* like a good fiddle.' Chaucer's back was against the wall in more ways than one and he had nowhere to go. 'Do *you* like a good fiddle, Geoff?'

'Really, madam, I …'

'I could always scream, Geoff,' she pouted. 'It's one of my specialities, as it happens and many of the gentlemen rather like it. But in this case, it could be misconstrued. Me, a lone, lorn widow, taken advantage of by the big man from London. What would people think?'

In the early dawn light through the window, she could see he looked stricken.

'Just joking, Geoff. There's not a man or woman in Oxenford who would believe that. I am a widow, that much is true. Some widows are bereaved, some relieved. I am of the latter kind. Dalton never did me a good turn if he could help it, though to be fair to him, he was hung like a mule.' Her grip under his nightshirt tightened. 'Not unlike your good self, Geoff, if you don't mind my expert opinion.'

'I have had rather a difficult night, madam,' Chaucer said, but he had stopped trying to get away.

'Nothing like a half an hour with Hattie to make bad memories go away, Geoff,' she purred, licking his neck. 'Tell you what, if you don't like it, you can always say stop, how does that sound?'

Chaucer hesitated, and was lost. 'You'll stop if I say so?' he checked, letting her draw him back towards the bed.

'Oooh, yes,' she muttered, falling back on the soft mattress, dragging him with her. 'Bound to. Eventually.'

Carfax had rarely seen anything like it. All four roads that led to it were choked with people that Friday, jostling, laughing, shouting. Chaucer had been on the way to the *Madeleine*, to talk to Zouche about what they intended to do next, but the common serjeant of England had other ideas.

'What's going on?' the comptroller asked a pieman trying to sell his wares.

'Bless you, sir. You can't be local.'

'No, I'm just passing through,' Chaucer said.

'You'll be lucky,' the pieman said. 'It's the judge and his party, beginning the assize. They'll be processing soon. You don't wanna miss that. More nobs in one place than you'll ever see in your life. First case is a marvel, sir.'

'Is it?'

'Attempted murder.' The man closed to Chaucer. 'And, as it happens, I've seen the victim's wounds.'

'Have you?'

'A very nasty laceration to the head which turned even nastier and led to the owner's near death.'

'They caught someone, I assume.'

'They did indeed and there's another four counts to be taken into consideration against him.'

'Something of a tearaway, this culprit,' Chaucer commented.

'You might say that. Nearly had my head off when I tried to give him a carrot.'

Chaucer frowned. 'That seems ungrateful.'

'Well, you'd hardly expect much civility from a pig, would you?'

'A …?' Chaucer stood there, mouth open.

'Now, then,' the pieman beamed. 'There's a mouth just drooling for a nice veal pie.' He closed to the man. 'But keep it quiet, 'cos it's Friday.'

'God, I'd forgotten how appalling the Assize was.' Ralph Strode was at Chaucer's elbow. 'Keep your hand on your purse, Geoffrey. A stroll along the Cheap will seem like the primrose path by comparison with this lot.' He nudged his old friend. 'And it's not just the lawyers I'm talking about. Oh, look, there's old Inglis, the Common Serjeant himself; he must be a hundred.'

Strode was perhaps a *little* unkind, but certainly the old duffer being carried on a litter towards the law courts would never see seventy again.

'Fancy a little peek at how the other half earn their money? It says here,' and he peered closer at a handbill he had found somewhere, 'Serjeant at Law Congleton is up first, prosecuting a pig.'

Chaucer stepped back to look at him. 'Yes,' he said slowly, 'some knarre selling pies just told me about that. I assumed it was some kind of complex marketing plan at first. Tell me, Ralph, you *are* a philosopher, am I right?'

'So they tell me,' Strode shrugged.

'And Master Congleton *is* a Master of Logic, yes?'

'Apparently so,' Strode agreed.

'And I am a royal customs officer and the king's poet. And yet we're all going to see a trial in which a member of the porcine community is being accused of attempted murder.'

'Come on, Geoffrey,' Strode chuckled. 'This is John of Gaunt's England; the hurling time. The king is a pimply child and there are people in this great country of ours who think the world is round. Set all that against a murderous porker and it suddenly doesn't seem all that preposterous, does it?'

There was a lot of bowing and scraping as the dignitaries took their places in the crowded courtroom. The riffraff were standing shoulder to shoulder behind the appropriately named rood screen, craning their necks to see the action. Sir Peter Inglis looked like God himself in his scarlet robes lined with ermine, glaring at the counsel who sat, hemmed in by clerks, all armed with quills and parchment and inkwells.

The crowd was getting restive by half past *nones*, since all the learned discussion so far had been in Latin.

'May it please the court.' Richard Congleton suddenly broke into the vernacular. From the look on his face, it didn't seem that anything would please the Common Serjeant, but Congleton had come before the old gargoyle before, many times, and knew just how far to push him. 'May we follow our business in English?'

Congleton asked. A raised eyebrow from Inglis was the judge's sign to continue.

'Does the pig have no classical education?' he asked, smirking at his own levity. The lawyers, along with Strode, Chaucer and a few others, joined in.

'Oh, very good, my lord,' the prosecutor gushed. 'I was hoping that the hoi-polloi,' he waved to the peasants beyond the screen and some of the simpler ones waved back gaily, 'would learn from today's proceedings, lest any of them have a murderous *sus domesticus* in their possession. Oh, I beg your pardon. Domestic pig, perhaps I should say in the interests of staying in the vernacular.'

'I must object to the word "murderous", my lord.' The counsel for the defence was on his feet. 'That is surely the question before us today and a matter for the court.'

Strode leaned in to Chaucer, high in their gallery perches. 'Goes by the name of Whittaker,' he murmured. 'Cambridge man. No chance.'

Chaucer nodded. What with the defence being from the 'other place' and the haughty attitude of the judge, the poet couldn't see a hope in hell for the pig. The beast in question was brought in, lashed and harnessed between two burly ushers, whips and goads dangling from their belts; these were not because their prisoner was a pig, they carried them constantly, but even so, it made things look rather more serious for the animal. Murder was clearly in the eye of the beholder. All Chaucer saw was an average porker, somewhat long-haired and pot-bellied, that promised some good bacon when all this was over. But clearly, not everybody saw it that way.

'There he is!' someone screamed from the gallery to Strode's right. 'There's the bastard! I'd know him anywhere!'

Inglis's gavel thudded down on his lectern and the youngest clerk, terrified, spilled his ink.

'I shall clear the court!' the Common Serjeant promised. 'Master Whittaker, has that loud-mouthed miscreant anything to do with you?'

Defence counsel scanned the heads in the gallery looking down at him. 'I think not, my lord,' he said.

'I am very glad to hear it,' the judge leaned forward. 'Under English law, *any* of God's creatures has a right to a fair hearing. No one will pre-empt the verdict of this court by outspoken interruptions. Proceed, Master Congleton.'

The man sitting alongside the woman who had been responsible for the outburst caught Strode's eye and felt he ought to offer an explanation.

'Sorry for the missus,' he hissed, a weather eye on Inglis who had hearing like a bat. 'Her mother was scared by a pig when she was having her and she's never been right about them. We've never shared a sausage in all our married life ...'

Strode raised an eyebrow and turned back to the events in the well of the court. There didn't seem much to add to that particular conversation.

'Members of the jury,' Congleton had crossed the court and was prowling in front of them. 'Look well at the prisoner at the bar.'

Everyone obediently looked at the pig, who refused to make eye contact. He kept his head down, snuffling around on the floor in a vain search for food, a long strand of drool hanging from his chin. 'That,' the prosecutor almost spat with contempt, 'was once a little piglet, the cutest of the animals of the farm, descendant of the original breeding pair that went aboard with Noah. What changed that innocent into the malevolent monster you see before you, I cannot tell. And that is neither your concern nor mine. Suffice it to say, as you will hear in sworn testimony, that the ravening beast before you lacerated the hand of its keeper, drawing blood with malice aforethought. Had it not been for God's good grace and the timely intervention of my good friend, Dr Allard ...' he paused while the doctor of physic stood up and took a bow, 'were it not for him, we would be discussing the capital crime of cold-blooded murder here today.'

There were cheers and roars from the crowd beyond the screen. Clearly, no one was rooting for the pig today.

'Classic, Dick.' Ralph Strode raised his cup to the man. 'Whittaker never got off the ground.'

The top table at Merton was groaning with goodies once again. In the centre was the body of a huge pig, an apple in its mouth and its ears singed from the spit. Everybody had an ample portion of today's accused on their plates.

'I take no credit.' Congleton clinked his cup with Strode's. 'Open and shut case, after all. And of course, the pig didn't help his case by pissing on Inglis's feet like that. What did you think, Geoffrey? Was I a little harsh on our porcine friend?'

Since Chaucer had a mouthful of said friend at the time, it was hardly his place to comment. He swallowed and wiped some grease from his chin. 'I always think,' he said, 'that if animals had the brains and opposable thumbs that we have, we'd all have to look to our laurels.'

Congleton laughed. 'From the man who is writing *The Parliament of Fowls*,' he said, 'I take that as a compliment.'

Chaucer would really have to have a word with their mutual friend,

John Gower. The poet couldn't fart without Gower reporting it. He turned to the dinner companion on his right. 'Thank you, Roger, for your medical input today.'

'Don't mention it, dear boy,' Allard smiled. 'All in a day's work. Usual fee, of course. By Monday, if you wouldn't mind.'

'Monday it is,' Congleton said. He turned back to Strode and Chaucer. 'Tell me, Geoffrey, this little case of yours …'

'Case?' Chaucer accepted the addition of more Romonye to his cup.

'That scholar … what was his name? Jollity?'

'Golightly,' Chaucer corrected him, 'although I'll grant you the g, h and second l are silent.'

'Damn silly language, English,' Strode commented, even though both he and Chaucer made a living from it.

'Golightly, yes,' Congleton went on. 'Are you getting anywhere?'

'I know it was murder,' Chaucer said flatly.

'Steady on,' Strode murmured. 'I don't think Johnny Bloxham will want that to get about.'

Instinctively, they all looked along the table to where the Warden of Merton was holding forth on something Aristotelian. Congleton snorted.

'But in reality, Dick,' Chaucer went on, 'I'm not much further forward than I was when I got here. I thought foul play was involved and I am convinced of it now.'

'So, what's your next step?' Congleton asked.

'I was hoping to talk to Master Frisby tonight,' Chaucer told him. 'In charge of the Quadrivium as he is.'

'Friday,' Allard chimed in from his seat several places along. He seemed to have forgotten his frosty parting of company from Chaucer the night before and was clearly speaking to the man again. 'Frisby doesn't do Fridays.' And he and Congleton laughed.

'Am I missing something?' Chaucer asked.

'I don't know, Geoffrey,' Congleton sniggered. 'It all depends on how well you're getting on with your landlady.'

Chapter 6

As things turned out, Geoffrey Chaucer wasn't getting along with Hattie Dalton at all. That was because she was getting on with somebody else. Chaucer guessed that from the squeak of the tester and the thud of the headboard against the wall. He felt a little awkward in the passageway at Frideswide Grange with a candle in his hand and vaguely realised that he might be forming part of an invisible queue, one that discreetly waited on Mistress Dalton most nights, but especially, it seemed, on Fridays.

Then he heard laughter beyond the door, blew out his candle and slid inside an archway. Suddenly, he realised he was between the devil and the deep. A scholarly figure was backing out of Hattie's room, blowing her kisses and another one, much younger, was padding along the corridor, candle bobbing. Just as suddenly, the young man ducked into the darkness and collided with Chaucer, his candle going out with a smell of tallow and singeing wool. Chaucer was resigned – he had never liked that houppelande anyway, though it was one of Alice's favourites. In a flurry of hissed confusion, the lad said, 'Sorry, sir. I didn't see you there. Are you next?'

'What?'

The lad jerked his head towards Hattie's door. 'Mistress Dalton. I thought I was her ten o'clock.'

'I'm sure you are,' Chaucer said. 'I was looking for Dr Frisby.'

'Oh,' the young man stopped short. 'Oh, I see.' He thanked God and the darkness that Chaucer couldn't see him blushing in the shadows. Man of the world though he was, his education from the monks of Glastonbury had not prepared him for moments like this. Not even the Greek bits.

Chaucer lurched out from the shadows and tapped the retreating Master of Mathematics on the shoulder. Frisby spun round, the glinting blade of a misericorde tickling Chaucer's stomach. 'Ah, Chaucer,' he mumbled. 'Sorry about that.' He slipped the blade away. 'Can't be too careful with some of these whippersnappers about.'

'Whippersnappers?' Chaucer repeated.

'West Country word,' Frisby said, canting his walk towards the front door. 'Scholars. Of the Quadrivium in particular.'

'Do you have rooms here, Dr Frisby?' Chaucer asked, all innocence.

'Er … no. I was returning a paper – er … on Euclid. To a scholar.'

'A particularly skilled one, I assume.' Chaucer was keeping pace with the man and they were set to collide in the doorway.

'Skilled?' Frisby put his head down and charged at the door like a thing possessed.

'I was just judging by your leave taking of the whippersnapper in question,' Chaucer said, sticking out a foot and bringing Frisby to a halt in a series of hops, skips and jumps. 'The … the kisses, you know. Not a very common thing between scholar and tutor, I would imagine.'

'Ha!' If Frisby thought that the sound could pass for a laugh he was sadly mistaken. 'A poor child missing his mother. It soothes him. One feels a fool doing it but … well, I promised. You know how it is. *In loco parentis* and all that.'

'I see.' Chaucer was now in front of Frisby and was barring his exit. Over the scholarly shoulder, he could see Hattie's ten o'clock slipping in through her door. 'Kind of you. I was expecting to see you at dinner.'

'Oh, I never do Fridays. As a good Christian I cannot demean myself to eat at all on the day of our Lord's suffering. Most people eat fish, but I …'

'It was hog roast at Warden Bloxham's table tonight. The miscreant pig, you know.'

Frisby looked horrified. 'Well, there you are. It gives me no pleasure to tell you, Master Chaucer, that most of my colleagues are blaspheming hypocrites.' He glanced back briefly at Hattie Dalton's door, now firmly closed on the shenanigans within. 'Did you want something?'

'Hal Golightly,' Chaucer said. 'I want to know how he died.'

By some sleight of body, Frisby was now outside and making a good attempt to evade Chaucer, but the poet was nippier than he looked and the scholar soon gave up, slumping down dejectedly on a low wall.

'Have you ever been in love, Chaucer?' he asked, plaintively.

'I'm a married man, Master Frisby!' Chaucer was outraged.

'Does that answer my question?' Frisby said and put his head in his hands.

Chaucer was confused. 'Are you trying to tell me that you were in love with Hal Golightly?' He knew it went on, of course, but still – it seemed to him that Frisby was being unusually frank.

The scholar looked up, his brows knitted. 'What?'

'Well,' Chaucer sat beside him, wincing as the cold stone struck through his hose, 'you did throw kisses to a boy who misses his mother, and then when I mentioned Golightly you said ...'

Frisby looked at him aghast, realising where a lie could get a person if he wasn't careful. 'I wasn't throwing kisses to a *boy*, Master Chaucer. It was Hattie Dalton. And I wasn't talking about that reprobate Golightly when I talked of love ...' He sighed and slumped forward.

Chaucer waited patiently. He had a feeling that he was going to discover a lot of things he didn't want to know about Dr Frisby before the night was out, but if he also discovered things about Hal Golightly, it was a price worth paying.

Finally, Frisby raised his head and squared his shoulders. He gave a mighty sniff and said, 'Shall we go to my rooms? It's getting chilly sitting here and I have a bottle of jenever – purely medicinal, of course – which will warm us up, I think.'

He got up and stretched his legs then his arms. He looked like a man about to tell all and Chaucer fell into step beside him. He had never learned to love jenever, though many a bottle had been broached over the years. The size of the headache the next day had never really seemed worthwhile but needs must, when the devil drives.

Frisby's rooms were cosily tucked under the eaves in one of the older buildings in Merton, and they showed the usual mix of squalor and luxury that all scholars' rooms display. A quill lay across a half-completed page of closely-written text, the writing crabbed and uneven. There were diagrams that made no sense. It seemed to have been thrown down in a hurry, with no thought to where the ink would fall. Chaucer guessed – correctly – that Frisby had suddenly become aware of the time and had fled across town to his love's bed.

Once the door was closed and the candles lit, Frisby reached behind a book leaning rakishly against the chimney piece, alone on a shelf which in Chaucer's rooms held thirty books. The bottle of jenever was not full; if it were for medicinal purposes only, Frisby was not a well man at all. He poured two hefty cups full and raised one to Chaucer, sitting down in a chair filled with cushions moulded to his form.

'A health unto his Grace and Aristarchus,' he said, knocking back most of the cup's contents in one go.

'Indeed.' Chaucer sat in a harder chair opposite and took a sip. He hadn't a clue who Aristarchus was, but this was better than the usual rotgut which posed as genuine jenever and his face showed it.

'Good stuff, isn't it? Frisby said. 'I brought it back myself from Haarlem when I attended a conference there to discuss ... well, we're not here to talk religion, are we?'

'No,' Chaucer agreed. 'What can you tell me about Ha ...?'

'Hattie? Well, what isn't there to say?' Frisby's eyes grew moist and he reached up for the jenever bottle. 'She's a wonderful woman, isn't she, Chaucer? So generous. So giving.' He sighed. 'She worries about me, you know. She doesn't want me to get into difficulties with the Warden, so she only lets me visit on a Friday, when I can explain my absence from table.' He shook his head, wonderingly. 'She is a wonder.'

Chaucer wondered if he looked as flummoxed as he felt. He made an effort to close his mouth and to look intelligent. Frisby seemed lost in thought, so he tried again. 'I was really talking more about Hal Golightly,' he said.

'Golightly?' Frisby said. 'Repellent youth. Light fingered as all get out and as dishonest as the day is long. Flaky character. Untrustworthy. Do you know,' he drew closer, 'he tried to tell me that he and my Hattie ...' he closed his eyes in horror and tightened his mouth with distaste, 'that he and my Hattie had done ... things. Things I didn't even want to think about. To think that my Hattie would soil herself by ...' He shook himself and opened his eyes, staring piercingly at Chaucer. 'Lies, of course. A thief and a liar, that's your Hal Golightly.'

Chaucer, thinking of Golightly's family, was half inclined to believe it. Nicholas Brembre had never met an illegal opportunity he didn't like, and so it wasn't that much out of the question that his nephew would be much the same. Even so, it seemed a little sweeping and a little harsh to speak so of a boy lying dead not that far away. '*De mortuis nil nisi bonum*, Doctor Frisby,' he said.

The scholar snorted. 'There is nothing good to say about Hal Golightly,' he said, shortly. 'He cheated in his work, he stole books and anything not nailed down, he borrowed money hither and yon and I have yet to hear of any he paid back. He drank, that I do know. And, of course, along with many others, he spoke untruths about ...'

'Your Hattie,' Chaucer sighed. 'Yes, you did mention that. Did he have any special friends?'

Frisby thought for a moment. 'Not that many. Herbert, the lad sneaking down the corridor this evening. I don't know if you saw him. Out after curfew, I expect. And Firth, though you don't see much of him around the place. He is usually in his room, working. Almost unhealthily attached to his studies, that one. My Hattie says that he … well, perhaps I shouldn't say what she thinks he does in there, on his own.' A fatuous grin appeared on his face. 'My Hattie can be a little …' he searched for a word that would not tarnish his beloved's name, 'outspoken.'

There were many things that Chaucer would say about Hattie Dalton, but outspoken would not have been first on the list. He made a mental note to track down Herbert and Firth the next day. Frisby meanwhile was pouring another libation and was gesturing at Chaucer with the bottle. The comptroller put his hand over the top of his cup and shook his head.

'Do you think that there may have been something strange about Hal Golightly's death?' Chaucer asked. He had decided that there was nothing to be gained by beating around the bush. Frisby was a hairsbreadth from being unconscious on the floor, so he needed to glean what he could, quickly.

Frisby considered. 'I can't say it's common for scholars here to be hit on the head by falling masonry,' he said, eventually. 'But I wasn't surprised. He was always poking around where he shouldn't be and the masons here are as careless a bunch of oafs as you would wish to meet in a day's march. Stupid handshakes and carving arcane symbols when they should be doing a day's work.' He hiccupped and covered his mouth prissily. 'I beg your pardon, Master Chaucer.'

Chaucer emptied his goblet and stood up. 'Thank you, Doctor Frisby,' he said, 'for your hospitality.'

Frisby leaned back and looked at him with eyes wide. 'Don't go, Master Chaucer,' he said, with a tremble in his voice. 'I haven't told you of my love, yet. I …' and to Chaucer's discomfiture, a tear rolled down his cheek. 'I can speak of her so seldom. A stranger to our town who has more than one thought in his head is so rare and I …'

Chaucer was a kind man and had had his share of *coup de foudre*. He looked at the scholar sitting there, about as dejected a creature as he had ever met. His hair was thin and scurfy, his nose pointed and red at the end with incipient weeping. His eyes were so close together that in the guttering candlelight they looked like one, perched over the bony bridge of his nose. His chin ran into his neck with no discernible ridge to show that he had a lower jaw at all. Taken all together, he was not the finest figure of a man there had ever been walking on the face of the earth. But he was in love and the fact that he was in love with the woman with quite possibly the loosest morals in the county, if not the country, did not diminish it. So, the Comptroller of Woollens and the king's poet sat back down again and held out his cup for a refill. He had a feeling it was going to be a long, long night.

'Master Chaucer, may I have a word?'

'Of course, Warden Bloxham.'

The warden was walking through the little garden he had made his own, neatly edged with rosemary bushes, that Sunday. The chapel bell was tolling solemnly, along with all the bells from the other colleges and the town's churches. Chaucer's head had just about cleared after his all-night Friday session with Frisby but even so, he closed his eyes when the sound reached its full cacophony, hoping the warden wouldn't notice.

'Tomorrow night,' Bloxham said, 'is the Great Debate. We hold it to honour the founding of our college in 1264.'

'Good year,' Chaucer nodded.

'Indeed,' Bloxham enthused. 'As we are constantly reminded in our daily lives, "He who fears God shall do good".'

'Amen,' Chaucer smiled. He hadn't got Bloxham down as a religious maniac; perhaps it was his age. Perhaps as and when the Comptroller of Woollens (and Hides) reached his dotage, he too would be fiddling with his rosary and muttering Biblical platitudes.

'And to that end,' the warden suddenly sat down on a stone misericorde which jutted out from the wall, 'I was wondering if you would do us the honour of speaking against the motion.'

'Me?' Chaucer was genuinely surprised, saw the expression on the warden's face and immediately changed his response to 'I?'

'You seem perfectly fitted,' Bloxham crawled.

Chaucer chuckled. 'As I told you, Warden, I am not a scholar ...'

'Come, come, Master Chaucer. You may not hold a university degree, but a scholar you most assuredly are.'

Chaucer thought for a moment, 'What is the motion?' he asked.

Bloxham looked a little pained. 'This house believes that the Earth is round.'

Chaucer burst out laughing.

'Yes, yes,' Bloxham was smiling too. 'But actually, it's no laughing matter, is it?'

'Well,' Chaucer spread his arms wide, 'God's church is broad, Warden. I may not know many scholars, but I know the youth of today. High spirits. Pushing the boundaries of what is acceptable. They'll grow up to be as boring as us ... er ... me.'

'That's a generous way of looking at things, Master Chaucer,' Bloxham said. There was concern etched on the man's face. 'But there are those who believe that God's house is built on sand. Nudge it just a little and it will collapse.'

'But you and I are men of the world, Warden,' Chaucer reassured the old man. 'We know that that is a myth.'

'Today's myth is tomorrow's reality, Master Chaucer,' Bloxham warned. 'Unless we kill such worms in the bud, who knows what heresy may grow?'

'That's as may be,' the comptroller said, 'but I am hardly …'

'You are a legend in your own lifetime, sir,' Bloxham gushed. 'In a way, you are right. A handful of adolescent idiots trying to shock is a not unfair description of the scholar body. But today's scholars are tomorrow's teachers; they are advisers to kings and popes, the movers and shakers of the future. Someone of your fame and gravitas can stop them in their tracks.'

'Well …'

'Please, Master Chaucer, for the sake of the college – and of reason.'

'Who will I be against?'

'The proposer is one Neville Cross, a Bachelor of Logic and one quite learned in the law. He is a protégé of Monachorum Frisby.'

Chaucer was startled.

'Oh, I'm sorry.' The warden smiled at the comptroller's expression. 'Had you not been introduced to Dr Frisby in all his pomp? He comes from the West Country, as you know. His father was an itinerant scholar and had many children and a very patient wife. His children were named after the place of their birth or …' the warden's colour rose as he steeled himself for the next revelation 'their conception. Poor Frisby was very unlucky, but perhaps less so than his sister Dunchideock. Nice woman, I met her once. Became a nun. Sister Anne.'

Chaucer nodded. 'I can see why she did that,' he murmured. 'Do his friends …?' He didn't want to fall victim to a solecism of that magnitude.

'No,' the warden assured him. 'We largely stick to Doctor, poor fellow. I became carried away. Do you find people often do that in your presence, Master Chaucer? You do have something of an air about you.'

Chaucer was beginning to be reminded of his last encounter with Hattie Dalton and edged away a little. He cleared his throat. 'So, young Cross is a protégé, you say? Does he share Dr Frisby's proclivities?' He remembered the young scholar slipping into Hattie Dalton's room the previous Friday.

'Proclivities?' Bloxham blinked. 'What have you heard?'

'Oh, nothing,' Chaucer said, perhaps a little too quickly. 'If Cross is a logician, he has clearly not followed Dr Frisby down the mathematical path; you know, the one paved with good intentions.'

Bloxham scowled for a moment, then broke into a chuckle that ended in a cough. 'You're quite right,' he said. 'Logic and mathematics are strange bedfellows, are they not? Tell me you'll do it, Master Chaucer.' He became serious again. 'Tell me you'll box young Cross's ears.'

Geoffrey Chaucer was not ready for the size and gravitas of his audience the next night. Since the previous day was Sunday and all the college libraries closed, he had had little time to consult chapter and verse for his argument. And all the time he had sat there, consulting every relevant tome he could find from Archimedes to Pomponius Mela, the ghost of Hal Golightly sat on his shoulder, tapping it now and then and whispering, 'What about me?'

But now there was no more time for fact-finding. The hall at Merton was crammed full, with the youngest scholars, pimply boys in outsize fustian, wedged between pews or squeezed onto steps.

It looked to Chaucer as if all five of the university colleges were represented, the Masters in their ermine and squirrel, their caps of coloured silk draped elegantly over their right shoulders. Chaucer was wearing his best houppelande, but he was aware that it was beginning to look a little the worse for wear. Alice did her best but he did have a distressing habit of drooling food down himself, especially when eating his favourite loseyns while reading at his desk. The stains were fainter but still there to see for those in the know. In the shadows at the back of the hall there was a familiar face and Chaucer nodded his head in acknowledgement. Although he hardly predicted a riot, he had quickly learned to feel safer when William Zouche was nearby. Zouche nodded back. Had Chaucer been nearer, he would have seen the smile on the shipman's face. He actually *did* predict a riot – he had seen that and more for lesser reasons than this.

By contrast with the young scholars, Neville Cross was tall and imposing, a mass of curly black hair under his cap and his scarlet bachelor's hood trailing at *just* the right angle from his shoulders. After the Warden had introduced the proceedings and prayers had been said by the ever-West Country Dr Frisby, the chairman rose to begin the debate. To Chaucer's annoyance, it was his old friend Ralph Strode, as glittering as any of the *academi* there. He introduced Chaucer, 'To speak against the motion,' he said, 'Master Geoffrey Chaucer, Comptroller of the King's Woollens and Hides, a poet of the first water and, if I may say so, my very good friend.'

'I trust, Master Chairman,' Neville Cross was on his feet, 'that that friendship will not colour your judgement in the debate to come.'

There was an inrush of breath. Warden Bloxham looked stricken and was about to intervene when Strode held up his hand.

'It will not, sir,' he smiled, 'but Master Chaucer is a stranger among us.' He looked at the hard faces of Cross's fellow scholars, glaring at him above a row of folded arms. 'He will, I fancy, need all the friends he can get.'

There were jeers and whistles and Chaucer realised at once that a morning jostling with the riffraff in the Cheap would have been a stroll in a cloister with Sister Anne, née Dunchideock Frisby, by comparison with this.

There was no doubt about it. Neville Cross was very good. He had an arrogance about him, a swagger that Chaucer had often met at court, but rarely anywhere else. The man was quoting from philosophers that the comptroller had never heard of and he was scoring point after point. As he held forth, Chaucer looked at the faces leering down like gargoyles from the raked benches. The scholars were loving this – their darling of debate was in full flow and it was only the Masters themselves who looked uncomfortable or downright dismayed. Old Bloxham had his head in his hands by the time he had finished and Chaucer heard his opponent end with a flourish, 'And so, gentlemen, the solution to centuries of doubt and angst is simple – follow the scientia!' And the hall exploded, caps being tossed into the air, feet thudding on the floorboards, fists pounding the woodwork.

Then, as it all subsided, the traditional moment's break to answer calls of nature before Chaucer gave his rebuttal.

'You'll have to go some to beat that, Geoffrey,' Strode murmured out of the corner of his mouth.

The warden looked on in agony and loss; had he been right to pin his hopes on a man who counted sheep hides for a living? Chaucer felt a firm hand on his shoulder.

'Give him hell, Geoffrey. We're counting on you. After all, you have right on your side.' It was Richard Congleton who had watched proceedings from a niche high in the fan-vaulted rafters. And the entourage resumed their seats.

'May it please the house,' Chaucer said when the hubbub had died down. 'I would ask for a moment's silence before I begin while we remember one of your number, a scholar of the Quadrivium recently taken from us – Hal Golightly.'

Cross was on his feet. 'Master Chairman,' he called in a silence that was almost painful. 'I have no wish to lessen the loss to this college of scholar Golightly, who was, in fact, a personal friend, but such a request from a speaker for the opposition is not in the spirit of Oxford debates.'

There were cheers and cries of 'Hear, hear!' from a scattering of scholars but the moment was muted.

'We can allow a little break in protocol,' Strode said. 'Stand, gentlemen. We will observe the silence.'

Everyone did as the chairman had commanded, but throughout the silent seconds that followed, Neville Cross proceeded to tap with an irritated quill nib on the lectern in front of him. Then, Chaucer cleared his throat at the nod from Strode. He held up a copy of the Bible with the arms of Merton engraved on the cover.

'Gentlemen,' he said, 'Master Chairman, Masters of the University and Scholars of the Quadrivium and Trivium, you have been urged by my worthy opponent to follow the scientia. Let me offer you an alternative.' He held the good book higher. 'An older, nay, a truer way. For he that believeth in this shall have ever-lasting life.' And he sat down.

For a moment, there was a stunned silence. Ralph Strode broke it. 'Is that *it*?' he asked, incredulous.

Chaucer nodded.

There were howls of laughter from all sides and gabbled voices reaching a crescendo of ridicule. Somehow, Strode restored order. Somehow, the seconds made their speeches, but the hapless scholar trying to support Chaucer had very little to work with. He muttered about Genesis, recounting the Creation that everybody knew off by heart. In the end, thoroughly discredited and through no fault of his own, he sat down.

Chaucer lost the debate. As Dr Allard swept past him out of the hall, he muttered, 'They made a monkey of you, sir,' and his stony face said it all. Dr Frisby, who had expected more after the frank exchange with the comptroller on Friday, wandered away, shaking his head. At last, as the hall emptied and the hollow laughter died away, Chaucer sat by himself in front of the lectern, the Bible that offered no comfort at all closed in front of him.

'Master Chaucer.' A quiet voice broke the silence.

The comptroller looked up to see a dishevelled scholar sitting to one side of the auditorium. It was the lad he had helped into his room at Frideswide Grange a few nights ago. 'Are you feeling better now?' Chaucer asked.

'Sir?' The lad got up and shambled over to him.

Chaucer smiled. 'When we last spoke, you were a little … unwell.'

'Was I?' the lad said. 'I'm sorry. I don't remember. I just wanted to thank you.'

'What for?' Chaucer asked. 'Not my performance, surely?' He was laughing.

'No. No, not that. For Hal. For Hal Golightly. He was a friend of mine. A dear friend. Thank you.'

And before Chaucer could think of anything else to say, the lad had gone.

Chapter 7

Like most towns with scholars in them, Oxford never really slept. The noise was not as raucous as London's perhaps. There were fewer food vendors crying their wares on street corners, the ladies of the night were a little less overt in their advertising, in that they tended not to hang out of upstairs windows with their breasts exposed, calling encouragement and offering special prices to the men walking along the road below. But the vendors were there and so were the ladies – they knew their audience and that they only had to wait, and they would come. Within an hour of the end of the debate, the last bit of toasted cheese had been scraped off the last grill and only old Cushie Brimmstun, toothless and practically bald, was without custom. And even she had had her moments, when the moon was behind a cloud.

William Zouche had not had to intervene, as he had expected to, in the riot that had never come. Chaucer had let everyone down, seemed to be the general view, but Zouche knew that he had taken the only possible path. To have vigorously defended that the Earth was flat would have pleased the powers that be in the university but would have enraged most of the scholars, who in general never met a mad rumour they didn't like. So, a simple statement and a quick sit down had been the safest course. Zouche smiled to himself as he swung in his easy stride back towards the *Madeleine*. Probably alone in the entire packed room, he knew for certain that the Earth was round, not that he would be saying it out loud any time soon. He had sailed so far in all directions and had never come close to falling off the edge. He had watched the sun, the moon and stars in their courses and it didn't take a genius to know that a globe was the only sensible shape for it. But it wasn't something he was going to die in a ditch over. When push came to shove, did it even matter? William Zouche had seen things most men only encountered in his nightmares and if there was one thing his life so far had taught him, it was not to meet trouble halfway.

He could get used to this life, the quiet life, daily retainers from Chaucer, who seemed nice enough, if a little slow. Zouche would have sorted out the death of Golightly days ago, by dint of banging a few heads together and shouting into the resulting dazed faces. But what did he know? He was only a shipman, after all. The thought made him smile. Shipman he may be, but he still owned more books than half the brains in the hall earlier – he was mulling that thought when he suddenly found himself flat on his face on the cobbles of Greyfriars Lane.

For a moment he lay there. Drink had not been taken, so it couldn't be that. The ground underfoot had not been slippery and there was no pain in the back of his head, so he had neither slipped nor been sandbagged by any of the Safety Commission louts. Deciding that there was no immediate danger, he turned over and looked behind him at what he had fallen over and scrambled to his knees when he saw what it was.

A boy lay there, a lad no more than nineteen at the very outside, by

Zouche's guess. Still on hands and knees, the shipman edged forward and looked into the boy's face, still and pale in the fitful moonlight.

Zouche had seen dead men before, many, more than any man should see, and some had looked like this. Peaceful and calm, eyes closed and lips together in an enigmatic smile of death. But none who looked like that had been lying on a pavement in the middle of the night – that usually was reserved for those whose faces looked as if the hounds of hell were after them which, metaphorically at least, they usually were.

Something was wrong. This peaceful boy shouldn't be lying here, shouldn't be dead. He should be in his bed, sleeping off the excesses of the night, not … Zouche pulled himself together. He had sons, he knew that. No one who had sailed as many seas as he had done had no sons. He had even met one, a doe-eyed child with hair as black as night and skin like a new laid egg, smooth and freckled as an orchid's throat. But that was in another country, and besides, the wench was dead. This boy lying there brought it all back and he blinked away an unexpected tear. He sat back on his heels and looked around, listening out as his eyes raked the nearby buildings for a closing door, an exhalation of breath that might tell where the murderer – because there was a murderer, of that he was in no doubt – where the murderer might be. But there was nothing.

He touched a gentle finger to the lad's throat, hoping even though he knew it was hopeless, to feel the flutter of life, but there was nothing. He was still warm, though, so he hadn't been here long, if that was any kind of comfort. Zouche scrambled to his feet and cupped his hands around his mouth.

'Hoo!' he bellowed, swinging his body from side to side to make the most of any listening ears behind the shuttered house fronts. 'Hoo!

Help out here, for the love of God!' Not a Godly man himself, he had nevertheless learned the efficacy of using the Almighty's name, when things were urgent. Just above his head, a shutter flew back and an angry voice yelled back at him.

'What's all the noise about? Don't you have no homes to go to? Do you know what time it is?'

Zouche had rarely heard such a splendid collection of rhetorical questions but now was not the time for debate. He looked up at the owner of the voice, a man of about his own age but rather more run to seed. He was wearing a nightshirt of almost indescribable decrepitude and a winding sheet about his head, which he had loosened slightly to make ranting easier.

Zouche touched his cap and the man's face began to look less petulant. 'I'm sorry, sir,' Zouche said, pleasantly. 'There's been an accident here, outside your house. Could your servant, perhaps …?' The shipman knew full well that the man had no servants, but a little flannel never went far amiss.

The householder looked down over the sill of his window and gasped. 'Is … is he … dead?'

Zouche stayed polite. 'I fear that he may be, sir, but if we could get him inside …?'

'Of course. Of course.' The shutters were left swinging as the man disappeared and footsteps and a plaintive female voice wafted down into the street. A moment later, bolts were drawn on the inside of the faded oaken door which was flung open with a flourish.

Zouche stepped back and the man from upstairs stepped gingerly onto the cobbles in his bare feet. 'Do you know him?' Zouche asked.

The man shook his head. 'Not to say *know* him,' he said. 'I've *seen* him, but that's not the same thing, is it?'

Zouche knew that more souls than the two of them were awake now, the others listening from behind their closed shutters. He asked himself quite what he had done in his life to warrant being landed with the philosophy king of Oxford in the middle of the night. He pinned on a smile. 'No, not at all the same thing,' he agreed. 'Where have you seen him, if I might ask?'

'I'm a buttonholer.'

Zouche waited for more, but there didn't seem to be anything, so he tried a small prompt. 'And so, because of that, you …'

'Well, I sew the buttonholes for Merkins the tailor.' He stopped again, expecting that would explain it all, then looked closely at the shipman. 'Furriner, are you?' he asked.

'I am not from here, no.' Zouche liked to think he came from everywhere and nowhere.

'Ah, well, then. Merkins the tailor has his shop just off the High. All the scholars come to us. Not expensive. Not tawdry. That's us. So this'n will have been in for sure.' He bent down and turned back the edge of the boy's jerkin. 'Yes. I thought so. That's my stitching there, look. I always finish off with a triple clove and a twist. It's my signature, you might say.'

Zouche nodded. Anything smaller than a canvas needle and quadruple twist hemp was something of a mystery to him. 'Shall we get him inside?' he suggested. 'It doesn't seem right to leave the poor boy out here in the street.'

The man stepped back and instantly regretted it as a cobblestone dug into the instep of his bare foot. 'In my house? The wife'll have my guts for her garters.'

'But …' Zouche spread his arms. 'Surely you don't want him out here, on your doorstep almost. People will say … what's your name?'

'Mollock, sir,' the buttonholer said. 'Mollock the Buttonholer, that's me.'

'Right.' Zouche almost felt sorry for the man and could only imagine what his name became when he and his friends had taken ale. 'Well, Master Mollock, people will say to each other, "Look at that poor dead child on Mollock's step. Either he's killed him himself or he has no soul to leave him there like that". Hmm?'

'But ... the wife. She likes to keep things nice.'

A glance at the man's nightshirt told the lie of that and Zouche put his head on one side and used his best fifty-mile stare on the buttonholer, who looked down, up, sideways, anywhere than at the dead boy. In the end, he relented and nodded his head, almost imperceptibly.

Zouche bent down and slid an arm under the lad's shoulders and the other under his knees, picking him up like a child.

'Well, I don't like it.' The woman's hard face was harder than ever, her mouth a gash of displeasure. 'I don't like it at all.'

'Madame,' Chaucer looked her squarely in the eye. 'We're none of us delirious. Every scholar's death diminishes us.'

'Ar, but that's the point, ain't it?' she persisted. 'He were a scholar. One of *them*. He's gown, not town. It's not right that he should be laid out in my house.' She caught sight of her husband, still in his nightshirt, hovering in the background. 'What's the matter with you, Mollock? Why did you allow this?'

'I didn't give him much choice, Madame,' Zouche loomed over them both and, given the man's size, Mistress Mollock saw his point.

Only half an hour ago, as the cryer had been going about his business proclaiming that all was well in Oxenford, the shipman had hot-footed it to Frideswide Grange to rout Geoffrey Chaucer from his slumbers. 'Slumbers' was the wrong word. Chaucer had still been awake after the debacle of the debate, idly thumbing through the Good Book by candlelight, searching vaguely for anything he could have used in his argument. Once again, the Vulgate had let him down. He was just wondering whether a Greek translation might shed any more light when Zouche's fist hammering on the oak drove all thoughts of academe from his mind.

And now, here they were, in the kitchen of a buttonhole-maker's hovel in Greyfriars Lane, looking at another corpse.

'I *know* this boy,' Chaucer realised as Zouche swung Mistress Mollock's candle nearer. 'He was the lad who thanked me after the debate.'

'Thanked you?' Zouche repeated. It didn't sound likely.

'For the minute's silence for Hal Golightly. They were friends, apparently.'

'They're back together now,' Zouche remarked.

'Hold that steady, Will.'

The shipman did. By the flickering light, Chaucer could make out the wounds to the back of the boy's head, his hair still sticky and matted with blood. 'Two blows,' the comptroller said, 'with parallel gashes. Just like Hal Golightly. What can have made those?'

Zouche leaned in. 'Wouldn't have known what hit him after the first one.'

'It wasn't just tonight I know him from, though,' Chaucer said. 'I saw this lad at Frideswide Grange. The first time he was drunk as a lord and I had to help him into his room. The second time he was part of a very discreet queue visiting Hattie Dalton.'

Mistress Mollock gave vent to a snort which would have shamed a herd of bullocks.

'Do you know …?' Chaucer continued, ignoring his temporary hostess.

'If she was the large lady who let me in tonight, yes, I do. In passing. But I assume this one knew her in the Biblical sense.'

'You know the trouble with assumptions, Will,' Chaucer said, hands on hips.

'Making an ass, you mean?' the shipman chuckled. 'Yes, I do.'

'Master Mollock, did I understand from Will here that you have stitched this boy's robes?'

Mollock hesitated, not wanting to be drawn any further into what was none of his business.

'Don't you say a word, Robbie Mollock,' his wife warned.

'On the contrary,' Chaucer snapped. 'You will say as many words as it takes. Do you know this boy?'

'He's a scholar,' the buttonholer folded his arms as if to end the conversation. 'They all looks alike to me.'

William Zouche pulled a massive iron-studded club from his belt and cradled it lovingly in his hand.

Mollock's gulp could be heard around the room and halfway down Greyfriars Lane. 'Master Merkin's your man,' he said. 'I don't deal with the scholars themselves. Master Merkin does. You'll have to talk to him.'

'Oh, we will,' Chaucer said. 'William, you've done stalwart service tonight, but can you do yet more? Get hold of the proctors at Merton. They'll need to get this young man into the priory of St Frideswide.' He looked at the Mollocks. 'But not until I've examined him first. If that bothers you, you can leave.'

Mistress Mollock knew her rights. They had been granted to her family by Aethelred Unraed, albeit rather a long time ago. She drew herself up to her full height. 'This is our house,' she said. 'You can't tell us what to do.' Since Zouche and his club were on their way out now, she felt herself on safer ground.

Chaucer drew himself up too. 'I am Comptroller of the King's Woollens and Hides, madame,' he said, holding up the gilded hart that flashed in the candlelight. 'And that's exactly what I can do.'

Perhaps it was because of his official calling that Geoffrey Chaucer tended to go to officialdom first. The Warden of Merton was having his tonsure neatened the next morning, in his private quarters at the college.

'Well, I'm appalled, of course,' Bloxham said as a lackey flitted about him with scissors and lather. The warden looked as if he had a blanc mange on his head. 'It's town, of course.'

'Town, Warden?' Chaucer was perching on a particularly unforgiving misericord, oak, carved with a Biblical scene of unusual limpness. The warden had been a little slow when it came to choosing one for his chambers and all the racy ones had already gone. No one knew who had snaffled Susannah and the Elders, but it had been hotly contested.

'Gervaise, you're not listening to any of this, are you?'

'Any of what, Warden?' the hairdresser asked.

'That's the spirit. I realise, Chaucer, that you are unfamiliar with the ways of Oxford.' The comptroller noted silently that the cloying adulation of a few days ago had been watered down somewhat to a mere surname. No doubt his lamentable showing at the debate was the cause of that. Bloxham swivelled his eyes to look at him. 'I have to concede,' he said, 'that in purely historical terms, town came first. There was a settlement here years – nay, centuries – before the university arrived. So the town, those ghastly burghers and their hoi-polloi, see us as interlopers. Never mind that we have raised the intellectual calibre to unprecedented heights, the riffraff can't see that. I was a clerk myself – Gervaise, you've missed a bit, there, look.' The warden raised an eyebrow and pointed to indicate the fault and the hairdresser looked at it dubiously, his head on one side. Everyone was a critic these days.

'I was a clerk myself, back in the day; the day being St Scholastica's. Three days of pitched battles between the colleges and the secular power. I've never seen myself as a violent man, Chaucer, but I scattered some teeth then, let me tell you.'

'And you think this boy's death is connected with all that?'

'It never goes away,' Bloxham sighed, leaning back and closing his eyes as Gervaise snipped and scraped. 'Where did you say the body was found?'

'Greyfriars Lane, Warden. My man Zouche literally fell over him.'

'And it couldn't be drink? College fever?' He crossed himself. 'Mother of God, not the Pestilence?'.

Gervaise and Chaucer did the same, the hairdresser letting fly some gobbets of soap which splattered on Chaucer's back. 'No, Warden,' Chaucer said, 'unless a crushed skull is a symptom of any of the above.'

'Where is the body now?'

'St Frideswide's priory.'

'Good. Good.' Bloxham's eyes were closed again. 'Best place for him. Let Roger Allard have a look at him; he knows his onions.'

The vegetable in question was probably all Allard did know, Chaucer thought. He'd probably claim that the lad's humours were out of balance and he died of a surfeit of black bile. Doctors, eh? You could never find one and when you did, they talked pure bollocks.

Bloxham suddenly sat upright, his finger raised to pause Gervaise's progress. 'Who did you say it was, again?'

'Alfred Herbert, the proctor told me.'

'Herbert? Oh, Lord, this is going to be awkward.'

'Why, Warden?'

The eyes swivelled again. 'Herbert senior is High Sheriff of the county. I wonder you haven't come across him in your capacity of sheep-counter. He's a force of nature is Herbert Herbert, and he doesn't take things lying down. He is also a major benefactor of the college; he'll want his money back, if I know anything.' He closed his eyes and clasped his hands across his chest, looking for all the world as if he was practising being laid out. 'Clip away, Gervaise, you old tonsurist. I have a lecture at eleven.'

The reaction to Alfred Herbert's death could not have been more different. Chaucer sat next to the comfortable shape of Hattie Dalton as she wailed her sorrow and let her tears soak into the comptroller's houppelande. After what seemed like most of the morning, she blew heartily into her veronica and sat upright. Her eyes were red and puffy and her lips trembled.

'You must compose yourself, Mistress Dalton.' Chaucer patted her.

She snorted. 'This *is* me composing myself,' she growled, then, softer, 'and that's still Hattie, by the way.'

'Tell me about him,' Chaucer said, 'young Herbert.'

A shuddering sigh escaped from Hattie's titanic bosom. She was twisting the veronica in her hands. 'He was a sweet boy,' she said. 'They all are.'

Remembering the howls of ridicule and the sneering at the

debate the other day, Chaucer doubted that. 'Did he have any enemies?' he asked.

'Oh, they all have their little squabbles,' she sniffed. 'Somebody called somebody else something or other. Somebody put a dead rat in somebody's bed; you know, the usual scholars' pranks.'

If dead rats were scholars' pranks, Chaucer was heartily glad he had never attended university.

'I had noticed …'

'What?'

Hattie wrestled with her inner thoughts. 'Well, Alfie was less cheerful than he had been. Oh, it can't have been much fun at home; you know his father's the High Sheriff?'

Chaucer did.

'Perfect bastard, by all accounts. Dick can't stand him.'

'Dick?'

'Richard Congelton, Serjeant at Law and Master of Logic up at the college. He's my brother; had you forgotten?'

'Oh, of course.' Chaucer was a literato of repute; his poems were known the length and breadth of Europe. When it came to ripostes, he was second to none.

'I know,' Hattie tutted. 'I'm not surprised you didn't remember. We're nothing alike, are we? And it must seem a bit incestuous to outsiders.'

Chaucer nodded, hoping she was speaking metaphorically, but with Hattie it was hard to know. 'So … Alfred was less cheerful.'

'Yes. When he first arrived, of course, he was only a child … what … fourteen? He'd been thrashed on a regular basis, to make a man of him or some such nonsense, but a term or two at Merton brought him out of himself. He did like a drink, of course.'

Chaucer could vouch for that.

'But ... well, since the death of Hal Golightly, I suppose, Alfie had become withdrawn again, morose. And he'd jump at his own shadow.'

'Would he?' Chaucer raised an eyebrow. 'Was there anyone in particular he was afraid of?'

Hattie shook her head. 'Not that I'm aware,' she said.

Then, Chaucer remembered something. 'A couple of nights ago,' he told her, 'young Alfie came in a little the worse for wear. You know, his room was just a couple down from mine.'

Hattie knew. She knew all the rooms at Frideswide Grange like the back of her hand.

'I've just remembered – and I didn't think anything of it at the time – he said, as I was putting him to bed, "You won't tell the calculators, will you? The Sand Reckoner?" What did he mean? Who are the calculators? What's a Sand Reckoner when it's at home?'

Hattie looked stricken. She stood up suddenly and gathered up her skirts. 'I'm sorry, Geoffrey,' she said. 'I have no idea.'

And she was gone.

'Most people, Master Chaucer,' the mayor said, 'have the grace to wait in an antechamber until they are summoned.'

'Most people, Master Treddler, are not trying to catch a murderer.'

'Oh, God.' The mayor tore off a hunk of bread and smiled paternally as his wolfhound snuffled among the crumbs. 'You're not still pestering everybody about that Golightly clerk?'

'No, sir. This is an altogether different clerk – Alfred Herbert.'

'Herbert?' Treddler looked up. 'Marriot, why wasn't I told?'

The military arm of the oxford Safety Commission was standing sullenly behind the mayor. 'Er ...'

'Are you telling me, Master Chaucer, that Alfred Herbert is dead?'

'As a nit, Mayor,' Chaucer said, 'and I mean nothing disparaging in that.'

'What happened?'

'I was hoping you could tell me.'

'What?'

'He was found last night along Greyfriars Lane. Someone had smashed in his skull.'

'Mother of God.' Chaucer didn't have the mayor down as a religious man, but he crossed himself now, more in fear of the living than the dead. 'You *do* know whose son he is ... was ... don't you?'

'The sheriff of the county; yes, I do. Does that make a difference?'

'Make a difference, Chaucer?' Treddler was on his feet, hauling the napkin from his collar. 'Make a difference? The last time I looked, this great county of ours operates under the feudal system, albeit somewhat bastardised.' He took a huge swig from his goblet. 'Which means that every man has his master. Mine happens to be the sheriff.'

'You *were* elected by the town council, Jack,' Marriot reminded him.

'Bugger the town council, Marriot!' Treddler screamed. 'As soon as this gets out, we'll have His High and Mightiness down here with a hundred heavies banging on doors and wanting answers.'

'As do I,' Chaucer reminded him.

Treddler took several deep breaths. 'Quite. Quite. Marriot, you're supposed to be the Safety Commission. Get out there, man. Find out what happened. Do you even know what safety means? Master Chaucer,' the mayor closed to the man, gripping his arm, 'I can assure you, no stone will be left unturned. In the meantime, you have carte blanche ...' he glanced at Marriot who was looking more than usually dense, 'a blank sheet. Do whatever you do. Investigate and things. Here,' he tore off a signet ring from his finger, wincing as it stuck briefly below the knuckle, 'my writ. It will open doors for you.'

In all the excitement, especially with the death of Alfie Herbert, Chaucer had forgotten all about their friend, the clerk Firth. He found him closeted in his attic under the eaves of Merton as the hammers rang below and the builders were whistling a lewd ditty, punctuating each verse with 'I adder, I adder, I adder.'

The boy was a scrawnier version of Herbert, his skin and hair the colour of dressed stone, his nails long and tapering. He had an air of death about him.

'I am looking into the deaths of your friends,' Chaucer said.

'They are past all help now,' Firth told him, with the air of a man without hope.

'I have reason to believe they were murdered.' The comptroller couldn't actually see anywhere to sit down.

Firth crossed himself. 'It's God's justice,' he muttered. 'We were warned.'

'What?' Chaucer frowned. 'Who warned you? About what?'

Firth looked terrified. 'Out there, Master Chaucer,' he said. 'In the quad. Is the sun shining? Only, I don't like the sun.' And he curled up into a ball, whimpering.

The comptroller had a boy, not much younger than this one but he hadn't seen him for years. His instinct nonetheless was to hold the lad, stroke his hair, soothe away his fears– but Robert Frith was somebody else's son, and Chaucer saw himself out.

The way to Richard Congleton's chamber was up a twisting staircase to the south of Mob Quad. From the slit windows on the stair's curve,

Chaucer could see the high walls of the castle a mellow grey in the afternoon sun. In the streets below, now that the Assize had gone, Oxford was business as usual. The fact that two students had died brutally in the space of a fortnight seemed to be irrelevant to virtually everybody, from Gervaise the tonsurist to the buttonholer Mollock and his wife, who wanted nothing to happen in their back yard. Only the mayor was perturbed and perhaps his minions were rushing about overturning stones. If they were, Chaucer didn't see them.

He knocked on the oak door.

'*Ave, Dominus* Chaucer.' Congleton had crossed the room to him. 'Oh, sorry. I've been lending a hand at the Ecclesiastical Court this morning. For a dead language, there's still an awful lot of Latin about. I admire you people using the vernacular. And,' he nudged Chaucer where he presumed his ribs were, 'it sells a lot more books, eh?'

'Well,' the poet smiled. 'It would if anybody could read.'

'Quite.' Congleton offered his guest a chair. 'I blame the universities, myself.' And they laughed. 'What brings you to my humble abode?'

'The murder of Alfred Herbert,' Chaucer said.

'Ah, yes,' Congleton said solemnly. 'Is it a little early for you?' He held up a bottle of Romonye.

'Never,' Chaucer said and the Serjeant at Law poured for them both.

'Yes, I heard about the boy this morning. Wretched business. You talked to the Warden?'

'I did.' Chaucer raised his cup. 'Beati Martini.'

'Beati, beati.' Congleton did likewise. 'Was he helpful?'

'The town did it,' Chaucer said. He looked around the study of the Master of Logic. Ancient tomes lined the walls, fewer than he himself had, it was true, but altogether of a different hue. He doubted very much whether the man had an original copy of

Quinquaginta Umbrae Ravi or *The Confessions of a Carmelite*, but he lived in hope.

'Yes,' Congleton ruminated. 'He would say that, wouldn't he? Still, between you and me, Geoffrey, the old boy has a point. We're like chalk and cheese, the colleges and the citizenry. The odd word spoken out of turn, a glance in the wrong direction; it doesn't take much.'

'The mayor's shitting himself.'

Congleton laughed. 'So, there is a God,' he said.

'What can you tell me about the late Herbert?'

'Not a lot, really,' Congleton shrugged. 'As you know, Frisby is in charge of the Quadrivium. My sister Hattie would know more.'

'I've already asked her. She's distraught.'

'Yes,' Congleton nodded. 'She would be. Oh … wait a minute … there was that business … oh, no, it's nothing.'

'Business, Dick?'

'Well, it was a couple of months ago, start of the Hilary Term, young Herbert and a clerk from Balliol. They had some sort of feud going on.'

'Feud?'

'Yes. Oh, it's probably an Italian thing. That's why we have schools.'

'Schools?'

'The schools are organised on a national basis, scattered through the colleges. French, German, Italian, that sort of thing.'

'I hadn't realised the university was so culturally broad,' Chaucer said.

'Warden Bloxham has introduced a new word for it, Geoffrey. *Inclusivity*. Oh, it's nonsense, of course. What it means is even more cash for the colleges. The Italians have made bickering a national pastime, constantly at each other's throats – and everybody else's – about something or other. Apparently, Herbert made a disparaging remark about the Pope.'

'Who is it, now?'

'Well, that's the stupid thing. It's Gregorius Undecimus. Gregory XI.'

'Stupid?'

'Well, the man's a Frenchman, from Limoges or some Godawful place. I'm amazed the French boys didn't get involved.'

'What happened?'

'Oh, Herbert and the Italian had a go at each other, egged on, of course, by the others.'

'Money changed hands.'

'Ah,' Congleton chuckled. 'You know your clerks, Geoffrey.'

'I know my human nature, Dick.'

'Well, the proctors parted them and both lads were thrashed. It's a fine old Oxford tradition. I wonder, though, in the scheme of things whether the Italian wasn't still harbouring a grudge.'

'Do you remember his name?'

'Ooh, now you have me. Luigi? Io Cicero? Lubilu? Something like that. Balliol, definitely.'

'Thank you,' Chaucer said. 'I'll find him. Now, Herbert senior. I haven't had the pleasure of the sheriff's acquaintance. Is he the tyrant everybody seems to believe he is?'

'Seems to believe he is, Geoffrey?' Congleton chuckled. 'Dear boy, you missed your calling when you weren't, in turn, called to the Bar. The man's a perfect arsehole. He'll certainly want his endowment back from the college, which means that fees will go up and we'll get richer, but even more moronic boys applying. I'm glad I've got my London practice. Talking of which,' he topped up Chaucer's cup, 'what do you know about the Lollards?'

110

'Ah,' Chaucer sipped and considered. 'John Wyclif.'

'The same. I have to be in London next month to try his case.'

'Prosecuting or defending?'

'Ah, I drew the short straw there. Defending, I'm afraid.'

'Is that a bad thing?' Chaucer asked.

Congleton leaned over his desk, as though the very walls of his chamber had ears. 'You and I, Geoffrey, know that dear old Mother Church is as bent as a Welsh longbow. Name me a crime – any crime you like – and I'll find you a monk, a friar, a nun or a bishop who's guilty of it. They flog fake relics, screw the populace with taxation and spout sanctimonious rubbish they don't believe in. That's Wyclif's argument and he's right. If I said so in open court, of course, I'd burn along with him.'

'It won't come to that, surely?' Chaucer said.

'Mark my words, Geoffrey,' Congleton leaned back. 'The Church is on the run. Today, it's Wyclif and his Lollards. Tomorrow … who knows? Some deranged German monk, I shouldn't wonder, upsetting everyone's apple cart. And there'll be blood, trust me. It'll make the death of the odd clerk of Oxenford look like child's play.'

Chapter 8

Chaucer was on his way back to his lodgings when he became vaguely aware of someone behind him. As he turned, he knew how ridiculous that was; along the High, half Oxford was behind him, scholars in their grey fustian, townsmen and women buying and selling, shouting their wares and haggling over prices. A mellow sun shone over it all, as if a bloodied corpse had never lain in a gutter three streets away; as if God was in His Heaven and all was right with the world.

One man in particular stood out. He was built like a garderobe and a livid white scar ran from his forehead to his left jaw. Days of stubble sprouted from his solid chin, that was the same colour as the prow of the *Madeleine* and nearly as big. Chaucer ducked to his left into an alleyway. Then he realised that it was dark and narrow, perfect for an ambush and he dodged right, back into the sunlight. Every time he turned, the large man did the same. Chaucer, in a series of what he hoped were surreptitious glances, took in the man's weaponry. He had a sword at his left hip strapped to a leather buckler and a dagger at his right. In his hand, he carried a staff, taller than he was and he looked as if he knew how to use it. Chaucer was a head shorter, ten years older and armed with a single poignard, which he couldn't actually see because his paunch got in the way. Nothing to trouble Doctor Allard with, but he could do with shedding a few pounds – though preferably not by having them sliced off by the monster following him.

The large man was gaining on him, his steady strides thudding on the Oxford cobbles, dust flying up from their feet. Chaucer felt panic rising in his throat. He was just about to break into what might pass for a run, when he all but collided with a harridan and her monstrous brood of children. They all shrieked as one and as Chaucer half turned, if only to avoid being trampled, he saw all five of the children leap onto his follower, tugging at his clothes and tangling their fingers in his hair. The large man was laughing, blowing raspberries into their faces and cuddling them to him. The harridan stepped back, hands on hips.

'What time do you call this, Tom Bickersneth?' she asked. 'I sent you out for a loaf of bread last Tuesday!' And they all collapsed in a heap, shrieking with laughter.

Chaucer's heart slipped gratefully from his mouth and he turned sharply to hit his nose against a man just as large as the one he'd just misread. Mercifully, this was one he knew. 'William Zouche!' he shouted, as if he hadn't seen the man for years. Relief does that to a man.

'Good afternoon, Geoff,' the shipman said. 'Any news of the late Herbert?'

The *Madeleine* rocked gently under the stars that night. An owl hooted from the tall elms to the south and sharper ears than Chaucer's could make out the scuffling of foxes and badgers.

The comptroller and the shipman sat amidships, enjoying the

Gascony that Chaucer had bought in the market that afternoon. Part of him wanted to be at Merton again, unable to move for the sumptuousness of the feast. But there again, there was the noise and the snide comments and the chill scowls from many and the need to extend bonhomie to the few. There was none of that with William Zouche, just an old salt who told it like it was.

'So,' Zouche said. 'In short, no progress.'

'Well,' Chaucer sighed, 'if I were to be writing a survey of a town, it would be perfect. The University blames the town, the town blames the University. Poor old Alfred Herbert falls between those two stools, I fear. I shall have to talk to the boys tomorrow.'

'Odd lot, clerks,' Zouche ruminated. 'Can't say I've ever had much to do with them. What sort of person becomes a clerk, Geoff?'

'I could be cruel and say, "Somebody who can't get a proper job", Will, but that would be unfair. Most of them see Oxford as a stepping-stone for the Church. And that means a bishop at the very least. Archbishop would be better, *legate a latere* not an impossibility.'

'Legate …?'

'Pope's right hand man in any given county.'

'We've never had an English pope, have we?' The shipman was out of his depth; he had always preferred to put his faith in wind, tides and good stout canvas rather than a God who often proved himself to be more than a little fickle.

'As a matter of fact, we have; one Nicholas Breakspear. Didn't go down a storm, I don't think. Before my time, really. Some of the Oxford clerks go into the law or medicine. Or they become disaffected curates in backwater villages who illicitly father families of ten. What they don't do,' he topped up Zouche's beaker, 'is sail ships or comptrol woollens. That's left to people like us.'

Zouche nodded. 'And they don't solve murders, either,' he said.

The Golden Cross was swarming the next night, as it was every night. Tonight was different, however, because Geoffrey Chaucer, the king's poet, was buying the drinks. Since it was all going on Nicholas Brembre's tab, Chaucer could afford a certain amount of largesse. The Cross was dark, with low oak beams that threatened to dent the skulls of taller men. The regulars quickly learned to duck as they entered and to stay seated while they supped.

Mine host's ale could not compete with London's fare, in Chaucer's opinion, but then he was not there to drink. On the contrary, he needed to keep a clear head. At his table sat a gaggle of the Quadrivium, unimpressed by Chaucer's rhetoric in debate but mightily impressed by the size of his purse.

'You lads must be devastated.' Chaucer had got round to the point of his generosity after what seemed an eternity of small talk. 'Two of your number in St Fridewide's crypt.'

'You know it's the town, of course, don't you?' one of the clerks said, nudging his elbow.

'Yes, I'd heard that, Master …?'

'Latimer,' the boy shook his hand. 'Harry Latimer.'

'Have there been other attacks, Master Latimer?'

'Well …' the lad was clearly the worse for wear, but he had the appearance of one who was about to tell all.

'Oh, shut up, Latimer,' another lad said. 'Look, Master Chaucer, we're not the children of the Trivium. We're men of the world.' And he nodded in the direction of a couple in the corner, a blonde girl writhing on the lap of a young Merton man who appeared to be trying to eat her neck.

Chaucer smiled. 'So I see, Master …'

'Temple. George Temple.' He shook the comptroller's hand. 'The point I'm making is that the Quadrivium, of any college, takes the rough with the smooth. Oh, some of us will go on to take the cloth and wear hairshirts …'

'Only the weird ones!' somebody else broke in and everybody laughed.

Temple went on, 'But most of us will go into the law or, God forbid, trade …' He narrowed his eyes at another lad who raised two fingers at him in the gesture of contempt of the Goddamns, the English archers who had made it their own. Everybody laughed again.

'Van der Gelder over there already owns three ships. His papa is something in the Hanse.'

Chaucer had met Van der Gelder senior. He knew that unless any of these boys became archbishop, Van der Gelder junior would be able to buy them out of existence.

'That's why we come here,' another boy said, raising his cup for a refill. 'Oh, the university's full of stuffed shirts and academic arseholes. Our dear lecturers think the world revolves around Aristotle and Euclid, knarres who've been dead for centuries. But this,' he slapped the rump of a passing waitress, 'is the real world. We're part of it.' And he belched loudly.

'Elegantly put, Fingle,' Latimer said, 'But he's right, Master Chaucer. Yes, we have trouble with the town from time to time, the odd rough-house, but we give as good as we get. See him over there, playing dice with that pardoner?'

Chaucer did.

'How many eyes has he got?'

'Er … one,' Chaucer counted.

'I had the other one,' Fingle said. 'Oh, not to keep, of course. It just sort of popped out during a fight.'

'He doesn't hold a grudge, though,' Latimer said. 'All's fair at the Cross– or any other tavern in the town, come to that.'

'So, it's not likely that one-eye would pay Hal Golightly or Alfred Herbert a visit, then, say at night, armed with a hammer?'

'Lord, no,' Latimer said. 'When we take on the town, it's in broad daylight, man to man. But what's your interest, Master Chaucer?'

'Hal Golightly was the ward of a friend of mine,' the comptroller told him. 'I'm trying to find out how he died.'

'Hmm,' Latimer sipped his ale thoughtfully. 'Rumour has it, it was an accident. All that scaffolding in Mob Quad.'

'Rumour has it wrong,' Chaucer told him. 'A hammer – or, indeed, any blunt object – doesn't fall twice in the same place.'

'Expert, are you,' Fingle asked, 'on head wounds?'

'Yes,' Chaucer said, flatly. Imperceptibly, the atmosphere in the inn had changed. The couple were still canoodling in the corner, her skirts pulled up even higher and the one-eyed one was still rolling his dice with the pardoner. But the lads around Chaucer, Merton men all, had withdrawn. They sat hunched over their beer, supping sullenly and not making eye contact.

Chaucer continued, cheerful as ever. 'Tell me,' he said to them all, 'who are the calculators? Who is the Sand Reckoner?'

Fingle dropped his cup and the hubbub around the table stopped at once. Out of nowhere a figure stood at Latimer's shoulder. It was Neville Cross, the champion of debate.

'Gentlemen,' he said. 'I don't have to remind you that tomorrow is

117

St Frideswide's Day. We all have to stir with the lark. Master Chaucer, good evening to you.'

'And to you, Master Cross.' The comptroller raised his cup. And suddenly, he was alone at the table, Fingle's cup still rolling gently on the uneven flagstone of the floor. In all his life, Geoffrey Chaucer had never seen a conversation stopped so quickly or so irrevocably.

The pounding in his head was drowned out by the pounding on his door. Chaucer had not had *that* much to drink at the Cross last night, but this row was not part of his dream, the recurring one in which half a dozen delicious novices from the Poor Clares were crawling all over him. And not even in his worst nightmares did he ever hear the repeated bellow of 'Fride! Fride! Fride!' to accompany the knock on wood.

It did his self-image no good at all when the first person to see him sitting up in bed, his spectacles dangling from one ear, was Hattie Dalton, up with the lark and dangling with ribbons.

'Sorry about that, Geoffrey,' she beamed at him. 'Fingle, will you stop doing that!' she bellowed down the passageway. 'St Frideswide's Day. *Tcha*!' and she tossed her head. 'Sorry, did no one tell you?' And she was gone.

Once the thudding of running feet had died down along the passage, Chaucer ventured out. He put his head around the door. The sun was bright already and perhaps summer had come to Oxford. He heard the thud of a drum and the rattling of tabours outside and opened a window latch. The street below was crammed with crowds cheering and whistling as a church procession made its solemn way behind a huge swaying statue of a saint. There were ribbons and streamers everywhere, children dodging in and out of the feet of tramping monks, cowls over their heads, mumbling something deep and Gregorian.

Chaucer doubled back into his inner sanctum and got dressed. He wondered if there was the remotest chance of breakfast with all this hullabaloo going on. Alongside this, the arrival of the Assize court seemed like a solemn vigil. In the refectory, the tables and benches were empty, the wood polished and worn by generations of graduate elbows and bums. At high table, however, a solitary figure sat sipping ale and munching bread.

'Ralph!' Chaucer hailed his old friend. 'Thank God! I thought I had gone mad.'

'Not ready for St Frideswide's Day, then?' Strode smiled, pushing the flagon across.

'I thought that was October,' Chaucer said.

'Oh, it is. The nineteenth, to be exact. But who wants a fair in October? It's always wet, usually freezing and it's only lashings of powder forte that keep a man going.'

'Powder forte?' Chaucer was pouring his ale. 'Is that an Oxford delicacy, particularly?'

'Lord, no. You've had it in Aldgate, presumably?'

'Not willingly,' Chaucer said. 'I don't usually need to cover up rancid meat. But I can see it has its place.'

'It does have a local ingredient added here in Oxford. Damned if I know what it is. A word of warning, though. Don't get it in your eyes. You'll go blind.'

'You don't believe that nonsense, do you, Strode? Surely to God.' Richard Congleton had swept in in a sumptuous robe edged with squirrel fur and yards of gold braid.

'Morning, Dick.' Strode passed the flagon to him.

'I assume you're explaining our local saint to Geoffrey here.'

'No, no,' Strode said. 'The going blind thing referred to powder forte. I was advising him against it.'

'Quite so. No, the story of St Frideswide is that she was pursued by an amorous suitor to whom she didn't take at all. She fled to a church here in the town, claiming sanctuary. Said suitor tried to elbow his way in and was instantly struck blind.'

'Like I said,' Strode nudged Chaucer. 'Too much powder forte.'

Congleton helped himself to the bread and cheese. 'I assume, too,' he smiled at Chaucer, 'from the rather bewildered look on your face that no one told you about St Frideswide's Day.'

'Indeed not,' Chaucer said. 'I hadn't a notion that anyone could just change the date of a saint's day because of the weather.'

Congleton and Strode shrugged.

'I presume it lasts all day?' Chaucer checked.

'And most of tomorrow,' Strode said.

'I wanted to talk to you both about young Alfred Herbert. I tried talking to the clerks, but I got nowhere. Young Firth's afraid of his shadow. The others clammed up.'

'No surprises there,' Congleton said. 'It's political, of course.'

'Really?' Chaucer hadn't heard this before. 'Not town related?'

'God, no.' Congleton dipped his bread into his ale. 'Oh, excuse me,' he said. 'Bad habit.'

The others excused him accordingly.

'No, look around you later,' the serjeant at law went on, 'in the streets. You'll find the townsfolk and the scholars arm in arm, drinking, feasting, dancing. Come nightfall, there'll be the usual fumblings in the back alleys.' He raised an eyebrow at Strode. 'Isn't that where you learned all about the birds and the bees, Ralphie?'

'God, yes.' Strode was grinning from ear to ear. 'Bessie Catchpole, her name was. Had an arse on her like a rouncey – not that I would share that piece of information with Mistress Strode, of course.'

'No,' Congleton went on, 'this town versus gown thing is mere folklore. The town doesn't like us as a bunch of pampered academics and clever-clogs. And we despise them as a crowd of inbred morons, but other than that, we get along famously. Half the babies born in any given year are half gown, anyway, by definition. No, Geoffrey, this one's about politics.'

'In what way?'

'Well, it *could* be that Italian school thing I told you about – the Balliol lad – but, equally …'

Strode leaned in. 'Herbert's old man,' he muttered.

'The High Sheriff,' Chaucer nodded. 'Yes, I know.'

'They don't come much higher,' Congleton said. 'I'm surprised you don't know him, Geoffrey – court circles and all that.'

'Just lucky, I suppose.' Chaucer took another bite of cheese.

'Well,' Strode leaned back from the table, 'you'll have that pleasure soon enough. He'll almost certainly be here tomorrow, if not today. Like you, Geoffrey, the High Sheriff will want some answers. Now,' he stood up and brushed crumbs off his front, 'I'm off to the fair. Dick?'

Congleton stood up too. 'I didn't get dressed up like this for nothing,' he said. 'Who's your money on, Ralph, for the college cup?'

'Queen's,' Strode said.

'You traitor!' Congleton laughed. 'Where's your loyalty, man? You're an old Mertonian!'

'Merton hasn't won the cup for fourteen years, Dick. And as I recall, that year the other teams all went down with the Pestilence

121

and couldn't compete. I can't speak for the urchins of the Trivium, but the Quadrivium aren't up to much.'

'Fingle's pretty handy,' Congleton said. 'And Van der Gelder – a dark horse if ever I saw one. Very muscular, your Fleming. Low centre of gravity.' Congleton flexed his knees, his arms out straight in front of him, then had to help himself up using the edge of the table.

'What's the cup for?' Chaucer asked.

'Best college with the quarter-staff,' Strode told him. 'Lots of dented skulls, bruised knuckles. And a lot of fun. By the way, Geoffrey; three things, by way of advice.'

'I'm all ears.'

'Don't get involved in quarter-staff warm-ups; you could be killed.'

'Got it.'

Congleton cut in. 'If anybody asks you to kiss St Frideswide, decline politely.'

'Got it.'

'And above all,' Strode went on, 'Stay away from the powder forte.'

'That,' smiled Chaucer, 'goes without saying.'

Congleton and Strode left the refectory, arms linked, heads together, whispering and chortling like a pair of five year olds. Chaucer watched them go and wished he could relax a little more, sometimes. With his position in court to consider, he had to always watch his behaviour and while he would be the last person on God's green Earth to deny that he had occasionally been held up as a bit of a spectacle, as a rule he was a fine, upstanding pillar of the community. The noise from outside had become even more raucous– if that were even possible– and he decided that the best way to stay out of trouble would be to go to his room and not come out until the fair was over.

In his room, he set out parchment and quill, then searched everywhere for his travelling inkwell, without which he never left home. He always said to Alice when she tried to leave it on the shelf, that you could never be sure when you might suddenly get an idea, a bolt from the blue, the line to end all lines, the plot line which would make him a household name. Or perhaps, and even just thinking it made him blush a bit, more of a household name. Because he had to admit, he was really rather famous.

After a thorough search, the inkwell was nowhere to be found, so he rolled the parchment and put it all to one side. He would just have to hope that inspiration wouldn't strike. He went to the window and, leaning on his trunk, lifted the latch and pushed the casement wide. The noise instantly increased exponentially and came into the room almost as a tangible thing, lifting what wisps of hair Chaucer kept on the crown of his head and making the bed head and springs hum in harmony.

With a sigh, Chaucer leaned out to pull the window closed again … and then it happened. In the blink of an eye, he was a boy again, running through St Bartholomew's fair with Dick Glanville at his heels, a saffron bun in his purse and a globe of spun sugar in his hand. Just one waft of caramel and mixed peel had taken him back and it was all he could do not to skip down the stairs in his hurry to get outside and join the throng. Just in time, he remembered what had happened when he skipped downstairs the last time, in the early days of his marriage – he was laid up for weeks, strapped to a board, not that that had stopped him and his Pippa. He sighed for those long-dead days, but not for long. He threw open the door and was immediately swept up in the throng.

As a Londoner through and through these days, Chaucer found

almost any other town or city hopelessly small and cramped, so he was staggered by the sheer numbers of people who had managed to squeeze themselves into Oxenford that day. There were stalls selling every conceivable thing from live geese honking desolately as they hung upside down from poles to love philtres, sold discreetly packed in glass phials in small hessian bags, the whole transaction completed in a mutter and a few coins slipped covertly from hand to hand. There were buns and Chaucer couldn't resist buying some for later. There was dried fruit, sugared and glistening. There were clothes of every colour, fluttering from the sides of carts and from the arms of laughing girls. He bought Alice a new apron, sprigged with apple blossom embroidery across the bosom, and grandly had the package sent back to Friedeswide Grange in the arms of a little boy, all for nothing because on the day of the fair, everyone loved their fellow man.

Over the noise and the smells of food both cooked, raw and still alive, came the sound of bells. Every church and college in the town had teams of ringers, so the bells would never fall silent. Only the church of St Frideswide was silent, but the steeple there had other fish to fry.

At first, the level of noise had been very disorienting but Chaucer found after he had wound his way down a few lanes and out onto the High that he became quite used to it and it lulled him, as rain on a roof in a downpour will. So, he jumped a little when he heard his name.

'Try your hand, Master Chaucer?' Neville Cross stood in the centre of Carfax, the stone cross behind him, twirling a quarter-staff.

The comptroller laughed. 'I am a little too long in the tooth for all that, Master Cross,' he said.

'Nonsense!' a voice boomed at his elbow. It was Quentin Selham, Merton's Master of Music; the man was a walking alliteration.

'He bested you in the debate,' another voice hissed in his ear. 'This is your chance for revenge.' It was Roger Allard, Master of Medicine. 'And anyway, if necessary, I'll patch you up. Free of charge.'

'Go on, Master Chaucer,' Selham urged. He leaned in to his man, his roving eye peering over the bridge of his nose. 'Between you and me, young Cross over there has grown too big for his sollerets. Take him down a peg or two.'

'It's only a friendly, Master Chaucer,' Cross called. 'Bit of a warm-up for the real thing this afternoon.'

Chaucer had four hands slapping his back, nudging him forward, whistles and cheers assailed his ears. The last person he expected to see in that melee was Warden Bloxham, and yet there he was.

'Come on, Master Chaucer,' he beamed, positively tribal in his college finery. 'Show them that a man does not have to have a university education.'

That was something of an admission from John Bloxham and Chaucer fell for it. He felt a quarter-staff thrust into his hands, six feet of polished oak, hard as iron. The cheers and the whistles grew louder.

'I'm hardly dressed …' Chaucer began, but Cross's staff punctuated his sentence, bouncing off his left shoulder and the crowd roared with delight. A ring had formed around the cross at the centre of Carfax and people were crowding in from the stalls along the High. All thoughts of St Frideswide, the town's virgin patroness, had vanished. Now, it was all about blood and somebody else's teeth.

'Hold your poignard and purse, Master Chaucer?' Allard held out his hand. Chaucer obliged; if you couldn't trust a doctor of physic, who could you trust?

He saw Cross lunge at him out of the corner of his eye and jerked sideways. The scholar recovered instantly and prowled the open space, passing his staff from hand to hand, grinning at Chaucer like a cat with a mouse. Cross was twenty years the comptroller's junior, a head taller and fast with it. Even so …

Chaucer parried the next two blows, the crack of wood drowned out by the roar of the crowd. He left a buzz shoot right up his left arm and lost his footing, feeling the breeze of Cross's staff as he went down.

'Aha, Master Chaucer,' Cross shouted. 'Your defence is fine.' There were loud guffaws. 'But have you no attack?'

A red mist was beginning to affect Chaucer's vision.

'Get him low, Chaucer,' Selham hissed as the comptroller rolled at his feet. 'Knees. Shins. It hurts like hell.'

Chaucer knew that, but actually being able to reach those knees and shins was another matter altogether. He feinted with his right hand, then twirled the staff and thrust with his left. The wood bounced off Cross's thigh and he cursed, falling back.

'Good move!' Roger Allard shouted, waving Chaucer's dagger in the air.

Cross drew back. This meant war. It was one thing to tease an old dodderer, a rank outsider who had had the temerity to impose himself upon the sanctity of an Oxford college; it was entirely another to be bruised by the bastard. He came for Chaucer, bashing left and right against his opponent, driving him back to the edge of the crowd. Now, the comptroller was parrying for dear life, the staffs cracking together like nuts bursting in a fire. Chaucer had nowhere else to go, so he took his chance and ducked, throwing himself forward and tripping Cross with his body weight. Both men went down in the dust and the crowd surged in, anxious not to miss anything at close quarters.

'Kill him, Cross,' Chaucer heard, along with any number of oaths. 'Remember you're a royal servant!' That was Warden Bloxham.

In the scuffle on the ground, it was Neville Cross who found his feet first. As Chaucer knelt up, he swung his staff horizontally with both hands. There was a sickening thud as it collided with the comptroller's skull.

For Chaucer, the rest was blackness.

Chapter 9

'For God's sake, keep still!' Roger Allard was winding the bandage around Chaucer's head. For a while, the comptroller wasn't sure where he was but he was too much of a writer to come out with the old cliché, 'Where am I?' still less, 'What are you doing here?'

What Allard was doing was obvious enough. He had wiped the blood from Chaucer's head and was applying a poultice with a revolting smell to the jagged wound. 'There,' the doctor said, 'that'll take the swelling down.' He pulled Chaucer's eyelid up to see the white of his eye. 'Hmm. Touch of yellow bile there, if I'm not mistaken. I should take it easy for the rest of the day.'

Through the open door, Chaucer could see the crowds in the bright sunlight and could hear the crack and thud of quarter-staffs as another 'friendly' was taking place.

'I'm sorry to have put you to so much trouble, Doctor,' he said, moving his jaw gently.

'Not at all,' Allard said. 'Your purse and your poignard.' He handed them back to the comptroller. 'No,' he threw an angel into the air and caught it expertly. 'You've entertained us royally this morning – and I've made a groat or two into the bargain.'

Chaucer was horrified. 'You were betting on me?' he asked.

'Good Lord, no,' Allard laughed. 'I was betting *against* you.'

Chaucer finally felt well enough to walk. At first, a straight line was a little tricky, but once he got the hang of looking out of alternate eyes, the one not in use being reduced to a slit, it got easier and by the time he ran into the back of the crowd surrounding St Frideswide's church, he was as near to back to normal as he expected to be for a day or so. The back he cannoned into was warm and soft and there was something familiar about it.

'Master Chaucer!' The shrill cry went through his head like a hot knife through butter and he recoiled a little.

'Mistress Dalton ... Hattie,' he said, keeping his teeth as near to clenched as was compatible with reasonably clear diction. 'I didn't see you there. What's going on?'

'Oh, Master Chaucer ... whatever is that awful smell?' She stepped back, her hand over her nose.

'Oh, I'm sorry,' Chaucer said, also stepping back. 'It's me, I'm afraid. Or rather, my poultice. I ...' he put a tentative hand up to his head 'I came off rather the worst in a quarter-staff contest.'

'Quarter-staff? At your age? Are you insane?' As comforting words went, Chaucer had heard better.

'It was just a bit of fun,' he said, with a careful smile.

'Goodness me. As long as you're all right.' She closed back in, smell or no smell and dropped her voice. 'It is just the head, is it? Nothing else ... *hors de combat*? Only, I usually like to see ... special friends ... on fair nights.'

Chaucer gulped and looked around but no one took any notice of anything that Hattie Dalton said, or stroked, as was the case here.

'Madam!' he said, moving her hand. 'Everything is in perfect working order, thank you, but tonight I think I am very likely to have a headache.' If it was a tenth as bad as it currently was, it was going to be disabling to say the least.

She smiled, lowering her eyelids. 'If you can't be helpful to a friend tonight,' she said, 'perhaps you could help me now. My poor little cat is stuck up the steeple. Look.' And she pointed to the topmost point of the church to show that, sure enough, a cat was clinging, its frantic meowing not audible from the ground.

'How in the name of all that's holy did it get up there?' Chaucer asked, shielding his aching eyes from the glare of the sky.

'She.'

'What?'

'She. She's a girl cat. Her name is Poppy.' Hattie Dalton looked soppily at Chaucer, as cat owners will.

'How did she get up there, then? Surely, it isn't normal cat behaviour?'

'She got a bit scared by the crowd, I expect.' Hattie wasn't interested in details, she just wanted to rescue Poppy. 'She doesn't usually come out, but ... well, call me a softie, but I brought her with me, in a basket, and she ... she got out and next thing I know, she's up the steeple.'

Chaucer looked at the woman in disbelief. He knew she had her failings and like many men in Oxford had not been ungrateful for the most obvious one, but ... take a cat in a basket to the St Frideswide's Day Fair? She had to be certifiably insane.

'I've asked and asked,' Hattie said, 'and no one will get her down.'

'I'm not surprised!' Chaucer was horrified. 'If she got herself up there, she can get herself down.'

'Of course she can't,' the cat's bereft owner said. 'Look at the height of the thing. She's terrified!'

'She is only a cat,' Chaucer said and immediately found himself surrounded by angry faces.

An old woman directly in front of him poked him savagely in the midriff with her walking stick. 'That cat is as much one of God's creatures as you, you loathsome article,' she said. She sniffed. 'And I would imagine she smells a lot better than you. What *is* that?'

'Herbs,' Chaucer said, shortly. 'I meant no offence. But really …'

He looked around and could see that he was going to have no peace until he climbed the tower, rescued the cat and fell to lie writhing in indescribable pain for minutes before death took him. He had often worried about the future, how he would die and when, and in a way it was quite comforting to suddenly know it all. And without that long to wait either. He turned to Hattie.

'Before I do this insane thing, I need to know something. Are you seriously asking me, a man very much past his prime, with a head injury, to climb the steeple of that church, to rescue a cat? Because, when St Peter is standing before me, twirling his keys in disbelief, I want to know that I am telling him the right thing. He's been known to get testy.'

Hattie's eyes swivelled to the left and then back to Chaucer. 'If you don't mind, Geoffrey,' she said. 'She is a dear little cat.'

Chaucer sighed. 'How do I get up as far as the leads?' he asked.

A man standing nearby leaned in. 'The sacristan will let you in and you can go up the tower inside, of course. Then, there's a sort of trapdoor effort, onto a ledge that goes all the way round. You follow that and there's a ladder. Well, you might not call it a ladder, as such …' He looked round and heads shook and nodded. 'It's steps, attached to a sort of pole. Anyway, there's that, all the way to the top. So, it isn't climbing a steeple, so much as going up some steps.'

'You sound very familiar with it,' Chaucer observed. 'Why don't you go?'

'Can't abide cats, nor them me,' the man said. 'I'd scare it.'

'Cats don't like me either,' Chaucer said.

'Nonsense,' Hattie said, clapping him on the back and instantly patting him instead when he nearly fell over. 'Little Poppy loves you. Look how she ...'

The look in Chaucer's eye stopped her in her tracks.

'Mistress Dalton,' he said, 'ladies, gentlemen, boys and girls and any other sentient being who may be watching, birds, beasts and reptiles. I want you to bear witness to this. I know I go to my death, but I do not go in fear. If I can, I will return Poppy to her mistress. But if I fail, then *ave atque vale*.' And with as much dignity as he could muster, he stalked off towards the door of the church. Then, suddenly remembering, he turned.

'Can I have the basket?' he called.

Hattie looked puzzled. 'The what?'

'The basket? The basket you bought Poppy in.'

'Oh, the *basket*. I don't seem to have it.'

'No,' Chaucer said. 'No, I don't expect you do.'

The sacristan was waiting just inside the church and greeted Chaucer by name, instantly becoming covered in confusion.

'Well, I say Master Chaucer,' he hedged. 'If so be that's your name. It might be something else. It might be as how you're called Master ...'

Chaucer was too exhausted by now to play the game that he had privately called 'Kill Geoffrey Chaucer By Any Means To Hand' and just patted the man on the arm. 'Just take me up the tower and show me the trapdoor,' he said. 'And, if you don't mind my asking, seeing as it is highly likely that you will be the last human soul on Earth I will speak to, then can we do it in silence? I would just like to tell you that I attach no blame, but if you fancy confessing you led Geoff Chaucer to his doom, then do please, be my guest.'

The sacristan gave him a sideways look and led the way through a door so low that even Chaucer had to dip his head. Immediately inside the door, in almost total blackness, a spiral stair disappeared upwards, a faint gleam from the first slit window making it look as though it led into a silvered Heaven. Chaucer hadn't climbed more than one flight of stairs in years, but put his head down and took one step at a time. At first he counted, then he stopped – after one hundred and fifty, it was just depressing. Eventually, just as his thigh muscles were beginning to scream in silent pain, the pair stopped on a small landing. At an angle to his left, a trapdoor led out onto the slates. The sacristan silently pointed, laid a comforting hand on Chaucer's shoulder and bowed his head for a moment. Chaucer's heart jumped as he realised he was the subject of the man's silent prayer. And then, suddenly, he was alone.

He pushed the trapdoor open and it crashed back against a low parapet before bouncing back and fetching him a nasty one on the shoulder. But by this point, he hardly cared. He heard a gasp from the crowd below in response to the crash and had a little chuckle when he thought how they would react when he fell off the steeple. He could almost hear the rattle of Peter's keys.

Up here on the roof, the sun was even hotter than down below in the press of bodies of the fair. He could smell roasting pork wafting up and the faint cries of the pickled onion seller, who didn't seem to be doing a very good trade. With one hand on the hot slate and one on the parapet, he walked gingerly round widdershins to where the ladder reached up to the top of the steeple. He could hear the cat meowing now and had to admit that she did sound rather disgruntled.

He had walked past the ladder before he even realised that it was there. It was just a halved tree trunk leaning on the slates, with roundels of branches nailed on on opposite sides, added by a man with far longer legs than Chaucer's. The bottom of the trunk was wedged against the parapet by two logs – it was these that had made Chaucer realise the ladder was there as he had almost fallen over them. He looked up and up. The small clouds scudding by seemed to make the steeple sway and his head wound gave him a sudden twinge. He rocked backwards and heard another gasp from the crowd. Looking down, hanging on for grim death to the warm stone, he saw for the first time a man standing off in a shaded corner, a heavy bag hanging from his waist and a chalked board propped on a trestle. There was a queue of men – and a few women, including Hattie Dalton – all with their purses out.

'You bastards!' he shouted, but no one looked up. 'You're taking bets on me!' It can't be whether I will fall, he thought to himself, because that's odds on. It's probably what rung I'll fall from. Anger gave him strength and he put his foot on the first tread and heaved himself up.

At the beginning, it didn't seem to be too bad. Then he realised that there was a small flat platform at the top, so that was even better. He would at least have somewhere to sit for a moment before he died. Hand over hand, foot after foot he climbed and surprised himself even more than those on the ground when he got to the top.

As he turned round gingerly and sat with his legs dangling over the side, he saw more than half the crowd turn away from the man with the fat purse in disgust. One or two looked up and shook their fists at Chaucer. He rightly identified them as those who had backed him for a fall on the way up. The others looked smug; they still had a chance to see a nice return on their money. The cat's meows had stopped now and she was unaccountably purring. He turned as well as he could without losing his balance and saw to his horror that someone had tied her to a statue, worn and weathered, which took up a good two thirds of the tiny balcony.

'St Frideswide, I presume,' he said, squinting into the weathered stone face. 'I'll be chatting to your Boss, soon. Do you have a message you want me to convey?' He gave a little chuckle and surprised himself – this didn't really seem the time for levity and he assumed it was a mix of panic, exhaustion and a mighty ding to the head. The cat had struggled in her bonds and had made a veritable cradle of it. He looked for the end and finally found it, soggy with cat spittle where the poor creature had tried to gnaw herself free. He was about to tug on it when he realised that if he did, she could quite easily jump for it and although cats were said to land on their feet, this did seem a bit far, even for a feline. He opened the front of his houppelande and put the cat inside, then began the untangling.

After the first time it dug all eighteen claws into his naked chest, he jumped but after that, it was just one more thing to ignore. The last few rounds of wool – he was sure he had seen a stocking frame with just the same colour on it in Hattie Dalton's bedroom – were particularly well wound but once they were off, the cat relaxed and even seemed to be grateful, settling in against Chaucer's paunch where the belt pulled the houppelande tight. He did up the laces, cooing to the creature as he did so and finally was ready for the descent. This was where he would be meeting St Peter and he apologised to the cat.

'I'm sorry, Poppy,' he said, pulling the neck out so he could peer down. All he could see was some goat-eyes looking back at him, trusting as any animal about to be thrown from a high building could be. 'I'll try not to land on you. If you land on me, you might stand a chance.' He turned, taking tiny steps as he did so and hanging on to St Frideswide. Her lichened face looked blandly into his and he held onto the folds of her robes as he stepped carefully backwards towards the ladder.

'Thank you, St Frideswide,' he said. 'Excuse me if I hold onto anything untoward. As you see, I have little choice.' And he leaned forward and kissed her. 'No offence,' he said. It just would have seemed churlish not to. He barely heard the muted cheers from the ground.

Once he was on the ladder, his problems really began. On the way up, he had been able to see where to put his feet, his hands. On the way down, he had to feel for every step and he was discovering the hard way that they had not been added at exactly the same distance apart. There were a few heart-stopping moments when he had missed his footing and one particular one which had excited a night-soil man very much – who had a bet on that very step – when he found himself with one leg in mid-air and the other bent in such a way that his thigh muscle couldn't straighten it. He had no choice but to clamber hand over hand, taking his body weight on his arms, until he had his foot on a step and his leg could be extricated. He lay there for a moment then, with his forehead against the slate and his heart thumping so hard it was a wonder they couldn't hear it below. Poppy chose that moment to give vent to her frustrations with a stream of panic-stricken shit which trickled down between his belt and his skin and soaked into his hose. Everyone would blame him, he knew, but really – what else could they expect?

After that incident, the rest of the journey down seemed relatively easy. He got to the leads, he walked clockwise round to the trapdoor and eased himself gently down onto the cool, footworn steps. He let himself down one by one, sliding a buttock at a time over the edge and slipping slowly downwards, trying not to let the tears run down his face. By the time he got to the bottom, his backside was numb, his chest was clawed to ribbons by Poppy who had had enough of it now, his poultice had slipped but even so, he found the energy to get down on his knees and kiss the lovely, the solid, the blessed ground.

The sacristan had to help him up and by the time he had tottered out of the church into the fresh air, the crowd and the man with the fat purse – now thin – had gone. Only Hattie Dalton was there, with open arms. Chaucer fished Poppy out and handed her over.

'My precious,' she cooed. 'And you of course, Geoffrey. Actually,' she jingled the bag of coins at her hip, 'I have had something of a windfall.'

'How so?' Chaucer's mouth was dry and he could hardly croak.

'I was the only one who bet on you coming back down. I had a side bet that you'd have the cat.' She leaned in and kissed him on the cheek, then recoiled. 'No, really, Geoff, what *is* that smell?'

Chaucer leaned against a wall in a quiet alley as the fair wound its way to its natural conclusion around him. It would have been a perfect world if he could have just turned a corner and found his temporary home just a hand's breadth away, but it wasn't. He knew he smelt horrible; it was hard to know whether his disintegrating poultice or the cat shit was worse, and finally decided that it was in the sum of their parts that they really made their mark. So, he waited while the crowds thinned and finally ventured forth, heading for the river and

William Zouche. He could dunk off the side of the *Madeleine* while Zouche went for some clean clothes. He could dine off … no, he thought. No food. He wasn't really hungry. Then, he realised he was. Perhaps cheating certain death did that to a man. He could smell the remnants of the roast pig and followed his nose.

The cook was finishing up, scraping the last shreds of flesh from the bones and putting them in a bowl made of crackling. He didn't eat pork himself – it gave him wind – but his dogs loved it and there was more than enough for them there.

'Do you have anything left?' Chaucer's voice was weak but the man turned and looked him up and down.

'No,' he said, wiping his hands down the seat of his hose. ''Ere, wait a minute. You're that knarre what climbed the steeple, ain't ya?'

Chaucer inclined his head. 'I am indeed that knarre,' he said. 'Geoffrey Chaucer's the name.'

'You're famous, ain't ya?'

'Mildly so, perhaps,' Chaucer said, smiling. 'I write … well, I dabble …'

'No, you're that knarre what got his head stove in by that jumped up clerk. What's his name? Cross? What were you thinking? Homi-bloody-cidal he is, no mistake.'

'Yes, so it seems. Ummm … do you really have nothing left?' Chaucer looked hungrily at the pork lying in its crackling nest.

The cook followed his gaze. 'Well, this is for the dogs, really,' he said. 'But … look, you've given a lot of people a lot of fun today. I don't remember when I enjoyed a St Frideswide's day more. And it's given people an appetite, too. Tell you what I'll do. You can have this on the house. And a helping of powder forte as well. I'm at the bottom of the pot, so it might be a bit strong. Are you going to manage that all right?'

Chaucer nodded. The cook upended a cylindrical pot over the pork and tossed it expertly in the air, to coat every glistening fibre.

'You'll need a drink with that.'

'No, I'll be fine. I'm going towards the river and my friend there will have a drink for me.' Chaucer reached out and took the crunchy bowl from the man and took a huge pinch of greasy meat between thumb and fingers and tossed it into his mouth. The cook watched, his own mouth agape. The smell of the powder forte had just hit him and it was almost entirely mace. That happened at the bottom of the pot – he always forgot to keep mixing it during the day. He grabbed his knives and skewers and turned to go.

'Can't stop. Late already.'

'You're very kind,' Chaucer mumbled around the meat.

'No, no, not at all. Any time.' The man broke into a trot and the last thing Chaucer saw of his benefactor was a clean pair of heels.

The pork was delicious and stayed delicious until the last greasy bit of crunchy crackling had followed the first mouthful. Chaucer thought of the homicidal pig from the Assize and started to giggle. Something was striking him as hilariously funny but he was finding it difficult to put his finger on it. Was it the thought of a pig murdering someone? He pulled a solemn face and wagged his finger at the pig sitting cross-legged in front of him. No. *Nonononono*. Murder was never funny. So, was it … he looked at the sky, not such a bright blue, now that evening was coming on. Bright blue. That was a funny thing. Bright blue. Why was it bright blue? Could you have bright black? The pig thought not and took up its knitting. 'That's odd,' Chaucer said, after a few false starts. 'Isn't it usually sheep who knit?' The pig shrugged – that was such a speciesist remark it wanted no truck with it. Chaucer nodded. He wasn't one to argue. For all he knew ... for all he knew ...

The wall he was sitting on was warm, but he was afraid he might fall off. Because, after all, the ground looked a long way off. His tiny feet on his long legs were still his, he could tell, because when he waggled his toes, the tiny toes waggled back. The pig had obligingly put down its knitting and had moved over to sit next to him on the wall. He leaned against its bristly shoulder and snuggled in. The pig was reading a book and every now and then gave Chaucer a trotter to lick, so it could turn the page without disturbing him. It was peaceful there in the fading sun, with just the gentle murmur of the pig reading the difficult words syllable by syllable under its breath. Chaucer licked his lips to get the last of the pork from his moustache and apologised to the pig, who told him he was welcome.

Chaucer slept.

The pig seemed to have lost all patience, all of a sudden, and was shaking him by the shoulder and was shouting in his face. Chaucer shook himself and stood up suddenly, his legs the right length, his feet the right size. He blinked and tried to focus. A face was close to his and seemed concerned. At least, he *thought* it seemed concerned. He didn't seem to be doing too well at emotions at the moment. He suddenly felt like crying.

'Geoff,' the pig was saying, remarkably clearly for a pig. 'Geoffrey. Master Chaucer!' The pig gave him a none-too-gentle smack around the face and Chaucer's tears fell.

'Don't,' he whimpered. 'I didn't mean to eat you.'

'Geoff.' William Zouche had seen this before, on many a voyage. The local 'seasoning' that could send a stranger off his head while the locals stayed perfectly sane. 'Geoff, what have you eaten? Or is it drink? Have you been drinking?'

'No,' Chaucer said, suddenly outraged. 'No, I haven't been drinking. And I am thirsty, to tell the truth. Have *you* got anything to drink?'

Zouche offered him his water bottle and Chaucer upended it into his mouth, drinking greedily.

'Thank you,' he said, with a deep belch. 'Sorry. Pork always gives me wind.'

'Pork?' Zouche was suspicious and moved nearer. Over the smell of cat shit and poultice was another smell – mace. 'Geoff, have you had any powder forte?'

'Umm … do you know,' Chaucer said, poking him in the stomach or where he thought his stomach was, 'I did. Have some. I did have some. And very delicious it was, too. Not as strong as people say. I could hardly taste the ginger at all. And sometimes, you know, they put far too much ginger in. Yes.' He nodded his head once, very emphatically and then seemed unable to raise it again. Zouche did it for him, a finger underneath his chin.

'Was it the bottom of the pot? Don't nod, just say yes, if so.'

'Yes if so,' Chaucer said, obediently.

Zouche sighed. 'Have you been hallucinating at all?'

Chaucer was outraged. The thought that he, the Comptroller of the King's Woollens and Hides could be accused of hallucinating! He'd just check with the pig, but for some reason, the pig had moved on. That was a shame – he hadn't got to the end of the book and it had been quite a page turner.

'Geoff,' Zouche said, firmly, looking into as many as the man's eyes as were facing forward at any one time. 'I am going to pick you up and take you down to the *Madeleine*. It will be a sailor's lift, over my shoulder, so things will be upside down for a while, but don't worry. We'll soon have you back to rights.' He crossed his fingers behind his back. He had known men who, once they experienced the world to the left and down a bit from the real one never wanted to come back, so never did. 'Ready?'

Chaucer nodded and looked expectant. He had no idea at all what this man was talking about, but he was big and a bit bossy, so it was probably best to go along with his plans. He could ask his ferret later how to escape if necessary; it looked to be quite friendly, even if it did have glowing red eyes.

With a grunt and a heave, Zouche threw Chaucer over his shoulder and set off down to the river, trying not to inhale too much as the smell was quite overpowering. Never mind, a good dunk in the river would soon solve that and might bring the man to his senses a bit as well. This wasn't the St Frideswide's Night that Zouche had had in mind, but he couldn't leave the Comptroller of Woollens and Hides to his fate. And he could always add this as extra services to the final bill.

Suddenly, Chaucer's world was wet and green, roaring through his head on a tide of coldness and fear. He gasped and took in water and knew his life was over. Above his head, through the green glass ceiling, lights bobbed and dipped, a pink moon leaned over and he was hauled out into the air by a steel-hard hand. With a flop and a slither, he was over the side of the boat and threshing like a landed fish on the deck. Someone was crowing, desperate for breath, that person was. Surely, someone ought to do something about that. It sounded like someone dying, that was what it sounded like.

Chaucer was flopped over on his belly and he knew with sudden clarity that he was naked. Naked and very wet. Naked, very wet and not really breathing as he should. A sharp blow between his shoulders made him draw in a mighty breath and he was suddenly on his hands and knees, spewing river water with just a hint of pork onto the boards.

'Thank you, Geoff.' Zouche's voice from over his head was ironic. He threw a bucketful of river water across the deck and everything poured out through the drainage holes set along the *Madeleine*'s sides. Chaucer coughed another couple of times and then scrambled upright. From the gloom of the bank, there was a scream and he hurriedly turned round to face the river.

'I …' he looked around, just to make sure there was no pig. 'What happened?'

'Pork laced with powder forte happened,' Zouche said. 'Along with a blow to the head and a near death experience, from what I heard as I walked through the fair.'

Remembrance came to Chaucer like chilling waves of water flowing down his back and the goose pimples marked its passing. 'I do remember that,' he conceded. 'Some of it. I thought it might be a dream. Did I really scale the steeple of St Frideswide's?'

Zouche nodded. He didn't want to mention to Chaucer that he was totally naked, standing there in the middle of the *Madeleine*'s deck. Let that come to him gradually.

'Was there a pig, though?'

'No,' Zouche told him. 'Only the one you ate some of.'

'Ah. But not a whole one.'

'No.' Perhaps now was the time to tell him, but he was pacing the deck now and it wasn't quite right.

'I … I hadn't had anything to drink, though. So … why the pig?'

'Good question. And I can tell you the answer. You had some powder forte, I gather.'

143

'Yes. It was delicious.'

'Hmm. It was delicious because it was at the bottom of the pot, and that is always the bit most full of mace. And mace is what makes you see … well, whatever you see. In your case it was a pig?' Zouche made it into a question.

'Yes. It was knitting.'

'I see.' Zouche began to hunt around for a blanket. Chaucer would be realising any moment now.

'Pigs don't knit, though, do they?' Chaucer's brow was furrowed and he looked down. There seemed to be an awful lot of pink in his get-up today. He must have a word with Alice.

'Not often,' Zouche said, getting up. 'And when they do, they don't do it well. Geoff, would you just wrap this blanket round yourself. You look cold.' He forced himself not to look down.

Chaucer clutched at his buttocks. 'Will!' he said, horrified. 'I don't have any clothes on!' He grabbed the blanket and threw it round his shoulders before hunkering down in the shelter of the prow.

'Well, no, Geoff. You don't. You had quite a lot of cat shit on you, to be brutally frank. As well as rather a lot of pork fat. And your poultice had leaked down your back. You were rather smelly, to be brutally frank.'

Chaucer extended a hand from the blanket and sniffed. 'I smell all right now, though, don't I?' he asked, tremulously. The whole of the day – the worst day of his life, he had no hesitation in calling it – had suddenly spread itself before him for his delectation and delight and it was not pleasant viewing.

'A bit rivery,' Zouche reassured him. 'But there's nothing wrong with that.'

Chaucer looked about him, seeing the dim bank and the broad sweep of Orion overhead. He could hear the last carousings of the fair from the town and could feel the gentle flop and lollop of the *Madeleine* as she gave herself to the river. He backed further into the cushions which Zouche had put in the prow for him on their journey to Oxford and closed his eyes. It was nice, here in the dark, with no one poking at him or making him climb things. Zouche looked at him and he didn't have the heart to wake him. He looked up at the stars and decided to give him until Orion's belt touched the tip of St Frideswide's steeple.

Chapter 10

Chaucer woke again but stayed back on his pillows. Everything ached, but especially his thighs, which had done more work in the last twelve hours than in the last twelve months, give or take.

Zouche turned to him and saw that he had turned a corner. He was relieved because for some, mace intoxication made a permanent difference. But he could see flashes of the Comptroller of the King's Woollens looking out through anxious eyes.

'Do you feel well enough for me to take you home?' he asked.

'Can I stay here?' Chaucer asked. 'It's soft here, and safe.'

'You need to go back to the Grange,' Zouche said. 'For one thing, Hattie will worry. And for another, you'll be needed, surely, if the sheriff arrives.'

Chaucer sank further into the cushions. 'I don't really want to meet the sheriff,' he said. 'He sounds a bit ... a bit ...' He bit his lip and closed his eyes.

Zouche put out a consoling hand and Chaucer flinched from it. 'Geoffrey,' he said, patiently. 'You have been in the grip of powder forte and everyone recovers differently. You have had a fright. Several frights, in fact, so now you feel scared of your own shadow.'

Chaucer looked hurriedly over his shoulder. He had no idea that his shadow was frightening. Now there was another thing to be scared of.

'But that will pass. You're much better already than when I found you. You were talking to a pig.' As soon as he spoke, he knew that was a mistake.

'Thank the Lord for that,' Chaucer said. 'I thought I had imagined it.'

'You did.' Zouche was a patient man but was coming to the end of his tether. 'Geoff, I have an idea. What if I show you my treasure? Tell you some old seadog stories, eh? Take your mind off things. And then, we'll see how you feel about going home to sleep. Does that sound like a good idea?'

Chaucer gave it some thought and then nodded.

'I'll have to ask you to close your eyes so you don't see my hiding place. It isn't that I don't trust you, but I never let anyone see where I hide it.'

Chaucer closed his eyes like an obedient child and Zouche lifted two planks amidships and pulled out an oak chest, much stained with seawater and time.

'You can open your eyes now,' the shipman said. 'Come and sit over here and we can have a look through. I haven't had this out in years.' He pulled out a golden chalice which in the half-light still twinkled.

Chaucer's eyes widened and he leaned forward. 'William! Where did you get that?' He was entranced and reached his hand out to touch it.

'Do you know, I don't really remember,' Zouche said. 'It might have been when I was in the Golden Horn … it certainly brings back memories of a seraglio, anyway.' He chuckled and dipped again into the box. 'Now, this,' he held up a dagger, stuck forever in a leather sheath, 'this little devil has got me out of some tight spaces.' He hefted it in his hand. 'I think I'll let her lie, though. She's done her work.'

Chaucer craned over and peered inside. 'What's that?' he asked, pointing to some dull brass wedged in a corner.

'That?' Zouche pulled it out, dislodging a jewel encrusted bracelet to do so, 'That is my astrolabe. It has got me out of almost as many tight corners as this poignard,' he said. He held it up, with its curves and engravings glowing in the moonlight. 'I don't suppose you come across many of these in the Aldgate.'

'No,' Chaucer said. 'My rooms don't need much navigation. But I have seen them, of course, when I deal with merchants on their ships. I just don't know how they work.'

Zouche smiled. 'Yes,' he said, 'it used to be Greek to me, too.'

'They invented it, didn't they?' Chaucer ran his finger over the tooled brass, 'the ancient Greeks?'

'I believe they did,' Zouche said, 'but whether you accept Hipparchus or Apollonius is up to you. Here, see these markings?' He pointed to various squiggles around the astrolabe's rim, 'Arcturus, the bear. The plough. The seven sisters. There's Orion. Hold it up to your eye – no, the good ... the better one. That's it.'

Chaucer was still having difficulty with his vision, so that the stars overhead twinkled more mistily – and mysteriously – than ever. Now, line up with ... the plough.' Chaucer felt his head and the astrolabe tilted gently to the left. 'Look at the reading.' Zouche pointed to the brass. 'That gives you the height of the stars and the compass point.'

'That's why it's called the star-taker.' Chaucer tried to click his fingers, but it wasn't a success.

'The Mohammedans use it to find their holy city, Mecca. We don't need that. Jerusalem's over there,' he pointed to the south-east, 'and a seasoned pilgrim like you'll know exactly where Canterbury is. They work out their prayer times with it too, so every Mohammedan can pray to Allah at the same time.'

'Less noisy than our bells,' Chaucer nodded. 'What an amazing contraption.'

'On a river it is,' Zouche agreed, 'or on dry land. On a rough sea with a sou'wester blowing, not so much.'

'Can it calculate anything else, Will?' Chaucer asked

'Better ask your average doctor of physic that,' the shipman said. 'Times of birth, the star sign, the humours – it's all one, isn't it? Whether the day will come when a doctor can cure a leper with one of these or restore a man's sight or make him walk again, I don't know. There are more things in Heaven and Earth, Geoffrey.'

'There are indeed, William,' Chaucer nodded solemnly. 'Indeed, there are. You really should have been a scholar, Will,' Chaucer said. He had rarely learned so much in such a short space of time.

'I am, in my own way,' the shipman said.

'Yes, you are.' Chaucer looked down at his blanket. 'Do you think anyone would notice if I went back to St Frideswide's Grange dressed like this?'

'On fair night?' Zouche laughed. 'You'll see worse than this on your way home, believe me. I'll walk with you, don't worry. I might stop off at an inn on my way back. Wet the saint's head, that kind of thing.'

'Ooh …' Chaucer's eyes lit up.

'Oh, no, not for you. The mace will still be inside your head and there is no room for that and ale. No, come on, wrap your blanket tighter and we'll start. With no shoes, you'll find the cobbles a challenge, but bear up. You'll soon be under Hattie's roof and safe and sound.'

Zouche thought for a moment.

'As long as there's a bolt on the door, at any rate.'

And, with wandering steps and slow, to St Frideswide Grange they made their solitary way.

Oxford looked like a battlefield. The day after St Frideswide's Day was always the same; too many aching heads and not enough brooms. The town blamed the gown and the gown blamed the town; nobody took responsibility.

So it was that Sir Herbert Herbert clattered through the town gate from the north that morning with his entourage. The guard on the postern barely had time to leap aside before the bay thundered past him, foam flecking its shoulders and flanks. The High Sheriff glanced up to the battlements of the castle, sold and grey on its Norman motte. A couple of heads bobbed up to watch him. He half-turned to the minion at his back. 'Make a note, Vallender. Insufficient guardage on the ramparts; bugger all at the gate.'

'Yes, my lord,' the call came back and the job was done.

The cavalcade cantered along the High and swerved into the grounds of the mayor's chambers at the Guild Hall. Herbert threw his reins to a lackey and crashed through the doors that groaned and shuddered in his wake. 'Treddler!' he thundered, and the mayor's establishment jumped into life, early morning though it still was.

'My lord!' Jack Treddler was tying on his houppelande. He growled at the man stumbling behind him. 'Marriot, why wasn't I told? His lordship is a busy man.'

'Vallender,' Herbert grunted. 'Rank incompetence in the mayor's office.'

The minion swung a little wooden lectern across his chest, from its usual position across his shoulder blades. Out flipped an inkwell and quill and he stood there, beavering away. Treddler was impressed; he must get himself one of these, both man and gadget.

'May I say, my lord,' the mayor gushed, 'how sorry I am for your loss?'

'You may, Treddler,' Herbert snapped. 'Although it's an empty phrase and doesn't really touch the sides, does it? But I mustn't be morose. I have other sons.' He threw himself down in the largest chair in the room. 'Now, to business. I understand that Alfred was found dead in the street.'

'Yes, my lord; Greyfriars Lane.'

'As such, it's your responsibility.'

'Indeed, my lord.'

'So, what are you doing about it?'

'Geoffrey Chaucer is in charge of the investigation, my lord.'

'Chaucer?' Herbert blinked. 'Who the hell is he?'

'The court poet, my lord.' Treddler injected every ounce of shock and horror into the fact that the sheriff had to ask that question. 'Comptroller of the King's Woollens.'

'And Hides,' Vallender added, scribbling furiously.

'You've heard of this fellow, Vallender?' Herbert asked.

'I have, my lord. Lives over the Aldgate on a sinecure. He's well thought of, though, both in court and academic circles.'

'Mind like a bodkin,' Treddler added.

'What?' Herbert didn't like similes. Waste of good breath in his opinion and often clear as mud. 'Narrow and often lost down the back of the chair?'

'I was thinking sharp, but ...' Treddler was too slow. Herbert Herbert was still speaking.

'Can he catch murderers, though?'

'That must remain to be seen, my lord,' the mayor said. 'Although …'

'Yes?' Herbert raised his head.

'Well, this *is* a little tricky,' Treddler wheedled, 'but since your late son was a clerk of Merton College, the jurisdiction is rather … shall we say … ambiguous?'

'Shall we say *ambiguous*, Bloxham?' Sir Herbert Herbert was standing, arms folded and legs apart in the warden's inner sanctum. The second St Frideswide's Day it might have been, but the builders were back at work in Mob Quad, sawing and hammering. At least they were until Sir Herbert Herbert arrived and at that point, they stopped suddenly.

'My lord?' The Warden never felt comfortable in the presence of a maniac and wished he could have chosen a different college for his boy.

'The mayor effectively tells me my son's murder is your job. Are you now telling me that it's his?'

'Well, we *do* have Geoffrey Chaucer on it, my lord. He's …'

Herbert held up his hand. 'Yes, Bloxham, I know who Geoffrey Chaucer is. What I don't know is where to find him.'

For the life of him, Geoffrey Chaucer couldn't understand why a six-foot cat should be striding into his room at Frideswide Grange. The cat had a smaller one, slightly behind him, licking its paws. And what was even more disturbing, both of them were on their hind legs – he'd seen depictions of them on illuminated manuscripts. He comforted himself with the fact that at least they weren't pigs. That would surely have been a step too far.

'Good God!'

For a second or two, he thought that the cat was talking, then he realised that it was a man, as was the shadowy form behind him.

'I'm sorry …' Chaucer tried to get up, but what with his head spinning, his eyes barely opening and his legs refusing to move, he didn't make much of a stab at it.

'Are you Geoffrey Chaucer?' the man asked, hands on hips.

'I am,' the comptroller said. He would have added 'at your service' but he wasn't sure how much service he could possibly offer this morning. He became vaguely aware that his window was open and that Oxford was already babbling with the sound of trade overlaid with church bells.

'I am Herbert Herbert,' the visitor said. 'High Sheriff of Oxfordshire.'

'My lord.' Chaucer tried a half bow, but that didn't work either.

Herbert sat himself down in the corner chair and clicked his fingers. The second man had swung a lectern from the straps over his shoulders and stood poised with ink and parchment.

'I understand,' the sheriff said, 'that you are carrying out some sort of investigation into the death of my son.'

'After a fashion, my lord,' Chaucer said. All in all, given his situation this morning, it didn't seem likely. Herbert saw before him a wreck of a man, his head bound with a bandage, darkened to one side with blood. His eyes were mere slits, tears trickled down his cheeks. The fact that he was barely moving gave Herbert reason to believe that he was hopelessly crippled, like those ghastly wretches that scooted along streets on little carts, a menace to other road users.

'What fashion would that be?' the sheriff asked.

With his head buzzing as it was, Chaucer took the question too literally and he glanced at his houppelande and liripipe hanging on the peg. Zouche had picked out a fresh suit of clothes from his trunk because the clothes he had worn the day before were now soaking in lye at the laundry after the quarter-staff adventure, the climb to rescue the cat and whatever he had slopped down himself last night. He perhaps didn't have the eye for colour that Alice always displayed, so the bright red clashed somewhat with the orange. But when all was said and done, they *were* the finest work of Eden and Ravenspur, Haberdashers to His Grace the King *and* they passed muster at court.

When no answer was forthcoming, Herbert sailed on. 'Vallender here tells me you are court poet and some sort of customs official.'

'Woollens and hides,' Vallender confirmed out of the corner of his mouth.

'Whatever.' Herbert dismissed such extraneous knowledge with a wave of his glove. 'No qualifications in the law, then?'

'Er ... I was once enrolled at Lincoln's Inn,' Chaucer told him.

'Yes,' Herbert sighed. 'I went to Wisbech once. Didn't like it. The point is that both the mayor of this fair town and the Warden of Merton College have assured me that you are making progress.' He leaned forward and fixed the shambling wreck with a steely gaze. 'You *are* making progress?' he asked.

'My lord,' Chaucer struggled to sit up. 'Forgive me. I have not expressed my condolences. I have a son. It must be devastating.'

'I'm sure you mean well, Chaucer,' Herbert leaned back, 'but, with respect for – and in respect of – my boy, you are slightly changing the subject. What progress?'

Chaucer pulled himself together. 'Your son was found dead in Greyfriars Lane,' he said. 'Three ... no, two nights ago. His body is ...'

'I know where it is, Chaucer. I've just come from there. Some crawling sycophant of a prior enquired after my soul. Again, I'm sure he meant well, but I told him where to stick it. Say on.'

'I'd say that Alfred had been hit from behind. From what I remember,' and Chaucer tried not to sound too vague on that score, 'two blows with a heavy object, I am not sure what. Something with a hard edge, so not the normal club or cudgel you see in the belt of the general knarre in the street. And he's not the only one.'

'Ah,' Herbert sat upright, clicking his fingers at Vallender to put quill to parchment.

'A fellow clerk, Hal Golightly, died in similar circumstances days before.'

'Did he now?'

'Gollity ...?' Vallender was a stickler for accuracy.

Chaucer spelt it out for him and secretly felt rather proud of himself. 'The boys were friends,' he went on, 'in fact, your son made a point of identifying himself as such.'

'I assume this sort of rough-housing goes with the territory,' Herbert said. 'Young clerks carousing, letting off steam ... is that what they call it, Vallender? Vapoury stuff in kitchens?'

'It is, my lord,' the lackey nodded.

'No, my lord,' Chaucer said. 'This is more than that. Both these lads were murdered. This is not the random chance of scholarly violence.' He felt his head throb just at the thought of it. 'They were targeted, singled out – and, I'd say, by the same individual.'

'But who?' Herbert asked. 'And why?'

'Those are the two questions uppermost in my mind, my lord,' Chaucer said.

Looking at the man now, Herbert wondered whether the man had a mind at all. 'Look, don't take this the wrong way, Chaucer, but what *is* wrong with you?'

Chaucer managed a chuckle. 'St Frideswide's Day, my lord,' he said.

'Ah.' Herbert got to his feet. 'I must take my boy home,' he said. 'Arrange a funeral, set up a chantry, that sort of thing. I'll be back ... Vallender?'

'Week Tuesday, my lord.'

'Week Tuesday. I shall expect answers by then. Clear?'

'As a bell, my lord,' Chaucer said. And he was rather startled to see two very large cats being shown out of his bedroom by a pig, who closed the door behind them and went to sit on the edge of Chaucer's bed, companionably knitting.

Chaucer lay back, his eyes closed, the inflamed lids collapsing over the fevered, red-veined eyeballs with relief. His breathing stilled and he slept for a while, his hands calm on the coverlet, a small breeze from the open window soothing his hot cheeks.

'Geoffrey?' A soft hand shook his arm and he whimpered a little and shook it off. 'Geoffrey? I think it's time that you thought of getting up now, really, don't you?'

He opened his eyes a slit and looked at where the voice had come from and was a little surprised to find that the knitting pig had metamorphosed into Hattie Dalton, still knitting and smiling just as pleasantly.

'Hattie?' he croaked and coughed to clear his throat. 'Hattie? Is that you? Where's the pig?'

She tutted and laughed. 'Master Zouche warned me about the pig,' she said. 'I could tell you there is and was no pig, Geoff, but I know you won't believe me. Mace takes some people that way.'

Chaucer tutted and moved his head fretfully from side to side, wincing as it pulled on his damaged temple. 'People keep talking about mace,' he complained. 'I don't remember that.'

Hattie was fortunately a very patient woman, so decided not to hit him upside the head. 'Yesterday,' she said, 'you had the last portion of powder forte sprinkled in large quantities on some roast pork. Unless the cook keeps mixing powder forte, the mace tends to get left behind and you got a dose that would kill frailer men. But what doesn't kill you makes you see things in this case and because it was on pork – *voila*!' She clicked her fingers. 'You see pigs everywhere.'

Chaucer lay back and considered. It was true that the pigs – and the occasional cat – had begun to strike him as a little unlikely. But … he opened his eyes as best he could and nodded carefully. 'I do understand, Hattie, but … it seemed very real.'

'Yes, Geoff, that's the bugger of it. Otherwise, it wouldn't be much of an hallucination, would it?' She put her knitting aside and stood up, tightening her apron and looking ready for business. 'Now, let's get you out of bed, let's get those eyes washed – I expect you rubbed them with mace on your fingers, it's a wonder you're not stone blind – choose you some clothes which won't give everyone a headache and give you a nice cool sponge bath.'

Chaucer cowered into the mattress. 'I hate sponge baths,' he muttered. 'Don't want one.'

Hattie raised an eyebrow. 'But you've never had a sponge bath from me, have you, Geoffrey? Now, that's a very different proposition.' And with practised hands, she whipped off the bedclothes and pushed up her sleeves ready for action.

Chaucer still cowered, but a little less so than before. 'Just one thing?' he asked.

'What's that, Geoff?' Hattie was at the door, calling for the girl to bring the bowl and sponges.

'Can it be warm water?' Chaucer was a funny age and needed all the help he could get.

Hattie snorted. 'Warm water?' she laughed. 'Now, where's the fun in that?'

Looking a lot more human and feeling a little more human, Chaucer made his way down to the river. Oxford was also looking more her usual self as the day wore on and the drunks woke up and went home to nurse their aching heads in more comfort and the detritus was picked over or picked up and moved to a more suitable place. The sun shone and all seemed a little more right with the world, were it not for the two dead clerks. Finally, he arrived at the path along the bank and found the spot he needed.

'Is that a thing?' Chaucer asked, leaning out as far as he dared from the riverbank. His balance was still not exactly perfect and the glitter of the sun off the water didn't help.

'Is what a thing?' the clerk called back from the boat. The accent was right. The lad was more tanned than your average Oxford scholar. So far, so good.

'You're sitting in a boat,' Chaucer observed.

Antonio da Silva sighed. Ever since he had arrived at Oxford as a snivelling little Italian, he had known that the university was *streets* ahead of the hoi-polloi who had never attended. Even so, this was a new low. The man *looked* well dressed, seemed quite refined, if you ignored the somewhat puffy eyes and the bandage on the head. But you could never tell. Da Silva, though, came of a good– if large– family and he was polite, at least for now.

'I am,' he said. It paid to be careful, too. Occasionally, the odd madman broke out from Oxford's gaol and da Silva knew from his own pranks that the castle walls could be climbed.

'But you *are* a clerk, aren't you?' Chaucer checked. 'From Balliol college? Not a boatman or anything?'

'Si,' the Italian said. 'See?' and he pointed to the Balliol arms stitched to his shoulder.

Chaucer knew that many clerks struggled to make ends meet. The college fees were extortionate and not everyone was lucky enough to have sponsorship. 'Doubling as a boatman, then?'

Da Silva slammed his oars into the rowlocks as his boat rocked and wobbled at the water's edge. A couple of mallards took umbrage and flapped skywards out of the reeds, calling noisily. 'I am in training,' he said.

Chaucer toyed with squatting but that was a young man's game, so he sat on the grassy bank instead. 'Really? What for?'

'Look,' the clerk folded his arms and sat upright. 'I do not know who you are or what you want …'

'Oh, forgive me,' Chaucer held out a hand. Then he thought the lad might grab it and pull him in, so he withdrew it. 'My name is Geoffrey Chaucer. I am hoping you are Antonio da Silva.'

'All men live in hope,' the clerk said, as if to prove that he had been to the philosophy lectures.

'Indeed,' Chaucer said.

'Wait a minute!' da Silva clicked his fingers. 'I know you now. You were that knarre … er … that signor who kissed the saint at the top of her steeple.'

'I was,' Chaucer admitted, suddenly praying that this little fact would never leave Oxford.

'I watched you from the ground,' da Silva said. 'Why did you do it?'

'Oh,' Chaucer thought quickly. 'An old Oxford custom – you know how it is.'

'Yes,' the Italian said. 'I do. And thank you, by the way.'

'What for?'

'The money I made on my side bets. We Italians invented betting, you know.'

'Really?'

'*Si*. Just like we invented rowing.'

'Good heavens.'

'I am from Venezia,' da Silva told him. 'Hence and whence, the boat. As a bambino, I was brought up on the water. I was a little … how do you say it … dismayed? Dismayed to find that Oxford was so far inland. I used to race my boat against the gondoliers. We have feasts and celebrations, blessing the sea. And of course, we have no streets. Only waterways.'

'Indeed. When I was in Florence last …'

'Firenze? You have been to Firenze?'

'Oh, yes. A while ago now, of course, visiting my old friend Plutarch.'

'*Madre di Dio*! You know Plutarch?'

'Oh, we go way back. It was through him I met Bocaccio.'

'Bocaccio!' da Silva reached out, despite the wobbling skiff and hugged the man. 'Signor Chaucer, you are so much more than the man who climbs the spire.'

'Well, thank you for that,' Chaucer said. 'So, you're bringing your boating to Oxford, eh?'

'*Tcha*!' da Silva made an exasperated gesture that Chaucer had seen before, mostly aimed at him by Italians. 'I would like to see a day when the colleges race each other on the river. And the Isis *is* a fine river.'

'Yes.' Chaucer would believe it when he saw it. 'Important, are they, college rivalries?'

'Here, it is the life-blood,' da Silva said.

'Is that why you went head-to-head with Alfred Herbert?'

Da Silva frowned. 'Head-to-head?'

'*Mano a mano*,' Chaucer half-translated. 'Fisticuffs.'

'Fisti…?'

Chaucer almost resorted to '*Tcha*' but thought better of it. 'You had a fight with a Merton man, Alfred Herbert.'

'Ah, *si, si*. Herbie. I was sorry to hear of his death.'

'Were you?' Chaucer asked, scanning the lad's face carefully.

'Despite our little confrontation, he was a good man. I was teaching him to row. He would have been quite competent in two decades or so.'

'So what was the fight about?'

Da Silva spread his arms. 'Why does any man fight, Signor Chaucer? A woman? Land? Or something as silly as "My college is better than yours"? It was that, I am afraid. And, I regret to say, drink had been taken.' He wobbled his oars.

'And is Balliol better than Merton?' Chaucer asked. 'I speak as an impartial outsider, of course.'

Da Silva shrugged. 'Of course,' he said. 'Merton has these ridiculous clubs.'

'Clubs?'

'Societies. There is the Diogenes, named after the old Greek. The Bladder – challenging each other to drink more than anybody else before having a pee. Let me see … oh, yes, the Calcolatrici … er … the Queckorians … then there's …'

'Queck?' Chaucer's eyes lit up.

'*Si*. It is a silly English game.'

'I know it,' Chaucer laughed. 'Played in Suffolk, if I remember rightly. I once nearly lost my shirt on the outcome of a game of Queck.'

'Well, it is all childish,' da Silva said. 'Schoolboy games and mad ideas. That's what Herbie and I fought over. And I am very sorry for it now.'

There was a quiet moment between them. Then the Italian upped his oars and pushed away from the bank. 'I must finish my practice,' he said. 'It has been fun, Signor Chaucer – you are a very pleasant person. Unless you'd care to …?' He motioned to his boat.

'Thank you, no,' Chaucer chuckled, getting up gingerly. 'I prefer *terra firma*.'

'Ah, yes,' da Silva laughed, pulling away. 'The old English joke, eh? The more firmer, the less terror. *Ciao*.'

Chapter 11

'I am in something of a cleft stick, Geoffrey.' Ralph Strode was staring into his cup of Romonye that night.

Chaucer was not surprised. He and Strode went far back, to the days when the comptroller was a humble page, fetching and carrying for the great and the good. Strode was one of life's worriers; philosophers were, generally speaking. His manchet loaf always landed butter side down and at Christmastide, he tended to feel sorry for the geese. Never mind that the repellent grey things always travelled in a gaggle and spat at the very hand that fed them, Strode had a soft spot for them.

'What is it, Ralph?' Chaucer asked.

The philosopher looked from left to right and back again. It was a warm spring evening and the pair sat out under the stars in the garden of the Ridge and Furrow. There was nobody else about. 'The Lollards,' he said. 'Right here in Oxford.'

'You've found proof?'

Strode wiped the wine from his lips and ferreted in his scholar's satchel. 'Look at this.'

The light was not good, despite the guttering candle and the glow from inside the inn. 'Er …' Chaucer fumbled for his spectacles. Strode saw his predicament at once.

'It's a Lollard tract,' he whispered, 'almost certainly for a sermon. Written in Greek, so it's no rubbish.'

'What does it say?' Chaucer had given up his search for his glasses.

'Usual tosh. The Pope's the anti-Christ. The cardinals are in league with the Devil. Some of the bishops are lizards. But – and this is the interesting part – it tries to persuade the colleges and the townsfolk to refuse to pay Peter's pence.'

'I've often thought of that myself,' Chaucer shrugged. For a lackey of the state, he had always had something of the rebel in him.

'Yes, of course, we all have,' Strode agreed, 'but what you and I mutter in our cups is a world away from stoking rebellion. We know from last year's peasants that it doesn't take much to make the riffraff fire up their torches and march on the nearest bastion of officialdom. Turn that fire against the Church and God alone knows where it would end. It starts with not paying taxes, then it leads to smashing stained glass and hanging priests from their own steeples.'

'Where did you get this?' Chaucer asked.

'Well, that's the very devil of it,' Strode told him. 'As you know, I am here to root out this sort of thing. I was discussing Plato with Martin Frisby the other night and he nipped out to relieve himself.'

'As even Masters of Mathematics must,' Chaucer pointed out.

'Indeed. It might have been the suggestion of his going or too much Gascony or both, but I went as soon as he came back.'

'All this urinification is fascinating, Ralph,' Chaucer began, 'but …'

The philosopher cut him off. 'He's got rather an interesting garderobe as garderobes go,' Strode said. 'Very niche, you might say. Carved oak that holds your buttocks just so.'

'Ralph ...'

'But that's not the point. Frisby's interior décor is actually neither here nor there. But this,' he held up the tract, '*was* there, wedged between two slats of wood.'

'Bum roll,' Chaucer reasoned. 'Best use for it, surely?'

'Factoring in the cost of ink and vellum, Geoffrey,' Strode said, 'there are cheaper ways to wipe your arse. Rags, for instance ...'

'So, what are you saying?' Chaucer said.

'Well,' Strode huddled lower in his seat, as though the night air had ears. 'I think that all our talk rattled Frisby. Don't ask how Plato got us on to the Lollards, but it did. I didn't tell him why I'm here, of course, but I pulled no punches at all about my views on them. "Vermin, Frisby" I said.'

'And he saw your point?'

'Not at all. He said that I should be more liberal, more forgiving, more ... what's that ghastly word old Bloxham uses ... *diverse*. Then he went to the garderobe.'

'I see.'

'And as he did so, he paused in the anteroom. I couldn't see what he was doing from where I was sitting, but he appeared to pick something up. When he came back, of course, he had nothing in his hand.'

'And you think it was that tract?'

Strode nodded. 'He knew I was on to him, Geoff,' he said. 'And rather than have me catch him in flagrante, so to speak, he tried to destroy the evidence.'

'Why not throw it down the chute, then?' Chaucer said. 'The fishes of the Cherwell could have enjoyed it later.'

'I think he needed it again.' Strode murmured. 'Perhaps to pass to friends, to spread the word. Just didn't want me to see it.'

M. J. Trow

'Ralph, Ralph,' Chaucer calmed the man down. 'All this is circumstantial. Is that Frisby's handwriting?'

'No, I don't think so. But it was in his garderobe.'

'And is the aforementioned office for his use only? Or is it communal?'

'I believe his secretary uses it.'

'Anything known?' Chaucer asked.

'A rather vain and prissy chap. Highlights his tonsure with verjuice and sunlight, I have been told.'

'Could the tract be his?'

'It's possible,' Strode admitted. 'It's also possible that the secretary and Frisby are in it together. To think that my alma mater is a hot bed of Lollardy, a sink of iniquity.'

'You're reading too much into it, Ralph.'

'The thing is, I've caught them all unawares. With John Wyclif's trial in London next month, all the attention has gone south.'

'You know Richard Congleton's defending him, don't you?'

'Yes, I do,' Strode said sourly. 'We've had words. The trouble with the man is that he enjoys playing the Devil's advocate. Never met a handsome fee he doesn't like. Look, Geoff, I hate to ask you this, but ... well, could you have a word with Frisby? You're the one man in Oxford, save myself, whose opinion I trust. You're good at reading people.'

'I've already talked to him,' Chaucer said, 'about the murder of Hal Golightly.'

'And?'

'I found him a rather sad soul,' the comptroller said.

'Aha!' Strode clicked his finger. 'Guilt!'

'No; love,' Chaucer said. 'Without betraying confidences, Martin Frisby is rather in love with a certain lady, one whose interests, shall we say, lie elsewhere. And I do mean *lie* elsewhere.'

166

'Oh, Hattie Dalton,' Strode shrugged.

Chaucer slapped the man's shoulder. 'No wonder you're a philosopher,' he laughed.

'Try him again, Geoff,' Strode said. 'This time from the Lollard angle. Nobody expects the Holy Inquisition, but they certainly won't be expecting you. They know your quest is to get to the bottom of these murders. Their guard will be down.'

'Oh, I don't know, Ralph,' Chaucer dithered.

'And, of course,' the philosopher said, 'I wouldn't put murder past these people.'

'The Lollards?'

Strode nodded. 'I'm pretty reasonable about most people,' he said. 'The Flagellants for wandering about spreading the Pestilence; the French, for starting the current war ...'

'Er ... they didn't, Ralph,' Chaucer pointed out.

'Well, whatever,' the philosopher flustered. 'They might as well have done. But the Lollards? No, I can't forgive them. They must be stopped, Geoffrey. And here and now, in Oxford, you're the man to do it.'

Chaucer was quite familiar with the labyrinthic passages of Merton by now. Away from Mob Quad, where the cranes swung and the hammers rang, the quiet of academia dominated. It was etched into the fan-vaulting, had seeped into the blackened oak and it hung like a funeral pall over the bright heraldry of the college.

The Comptroller of Woollens and Hides padded along the well-worn planking. Something caught his eye as he turned a sharp corner, something hanging from a gargoyle that jutted out from a sheer wall. He poked his head out of the latticed window and realised what it was. Someone had hung an effigy of the pope below the buttress of the north wall. The rough hemp was tight around his neck and the papal crown had slipped to one side. Chaucer had never seen the current pope, but he was pretty sure that the face was not much of a likeness; surely, Gregory Undecimus didn't have three eyes and a nose the size of the White Tower?

So, Chaucer was not looking where he was going as he spun back to continue his journey. He collided with a clerk carrying an enormous pile of papers that scattered all over the floor. The comptroller muttered his apologies and helped the man collect his scrolls.

'Euclid, eh?' the clerk almost spat. 'That man will be the death of me one day.'

The man was wearing the Merton livery and sported a particularly bouffant tonsure; surely he knew that Master Euclid had died rather a long time ago.

'All right?' Chaucer checked that the man had a firm grip on the scrolls.

'Yes, thank you,' the clerk said. 'Can I help you? You're a stranger around … Oh, Mother of God!' He had caught sight of the twirling effigy that had caught Chaucer's eye and it made him drop his parchment again. 'What *is* that?' He was leaning out of the casement.

'Er … I believe it's supposed to be the Pope.'

The clerk crossed himself. 'Sacrilege!' he all but screamed. 'I must tell Dr Frisby.'

'You are …?'

'Absolutely appalled,' the clerk said, scrabbling on the floor for his scrolls again.

'No, I mean, what is your name?'

'Oh, Sylvester; I am Dr Frisby's secretary.'

'Geoffrey Chaucer,' the comptroller said, doing the honours once again with the parchment. He glanced up to see a pair of moss-stuffed toes padding towards him.

'Dr Frisby!' Sylvester wailed. 'Look!'

'Yes, I know that there are a lot of them, Sylvester, but you've carried piles of disputations before.'

'No, sir. The effigy.' The man was nodding frantically towards the window, unwilling to point in case he dropped his load *again*.

'Looks like a student prank, Dr Frisby,' Chaucer volunteered.

The Master of Mathematics poked his head out of the window and crossed himself. 'Sylvester. Put those things down. Yes, there, man, on the floor. As you were.'

The parchment hit the parquet for a third time. 'Find Warden Bloxham.' Frisby turned to Chaucer. 'This is not some ignorant clerk's idea of a joke, Master Chaucer,' he said. 'This is a blasphemous outrage!'

By midday, the word had spread throughout Oxford. Merton had gone mad. All the scholars had been found wherever they were, some skulking in the library, some lounging on the banks of the Cherwell, some sipping ale in their tavern of choice. One was being entertained by Hattie Dalton and he was the last to arrive, still fumbling with his points. The hollow square in Mob Quad looked impressive, the press of standing bodies in their college fustian hiding the piles of stones and panelling. The college staff were all there, in their full robes, and the schools' contingents stood under the banner of their respective countries – the limp fleur de lys of France, the snarling lion of Venetia, the ambling bear of Switzerland.

At the back of the student body, unusually silent in the spring sunshine, the proctors prowled ominously, their whips and clubs cradled in their arms.

Warden Bloxham walked out into the open space, like a general haranguing his army. He looked younger than his years, taller than his height, his robes bright in scarlet and gold.

'Scholars of Merton,' he called out in a strong, clear voice. 'It is my grim duty to tell you that a sacrilege has been committed within these very walls. But then, one or more of you knows that already.' He looked round at them all, his mouth set implacably, his eyes uncompromising. 'For those of you who do not, an effigy of His Holiness the Pope was hung from a buttress of the north wall.'

There was an inrush of breath and a rustle of fustian as some of the clerks crossed themselves.

'Proctor Simmons.'

'Warden?' A large man, bristling with weapons of correction, strode forward.

'We have a list of the boys of the Trivium whose rooms are on that landing?'

'Oh, yes, Warden,' Simmons said, his lips twisting into what passed for a smile. He passed a parchment to Bloxham, who read it quickly. 'See to it that these people learn what it is to insult the Papacy in this blasphemous way.'

'It will be my pleasure, Warden,' Simmons said.

Martin Frisby was the first to break ranks. From where he and Ralph Strode stood at the edge of the Quad, Chaucer saw the Master of Mathematics scuttle across to his own master. He couldn't hear what Frisby said but he heard Bloxham's reply and saw the contempt on his face.

'They are not children, Dr Frisby. And if they are not guilty, they allowed whoever is to hang the effigy from their windows. A price must be paid.'

Frisby tried again, but Warden Bloxham stopped him.

'Desist, sir,' he snapped. 'I will not have this college become a laughing stock.'

'Wouldn't think that his real concern was the Quadrivium, would you?' Richard Congleton whispered out of the corner of his mouth. 'All this bleating over the boys.'

'Whole thing leaves a nasty taste,' Dr Allard said, shaking his head. 'The youth of today.'

Chaucer was mildly astonished by what happened next. He had seen plenty of men – and women, too – flogged at the cart's tail. And he had felt the sting of the lash – what child had not? But it was the stoicism that surprised him. Nobody whined. Nobody moaned. The men of the Quadrivium, with Neville Cross in their centre, formed a line with arms folded. On their flanks, the staff in their finery; they had seen this countless times before. Six boys, all of them fourteen or a little younger, were led out by the proctors, their robes stripped off them and they were made to kneel facing the Warden. While the college chaplain chanted something deep and low, Bloxham gave the order.

'Proctor Simmons, do your duty.'

The whip hissed through the air, slapping the first boy across the back, ripping the skin. He winced and bit his lip. Then the second lash came and the third, a spray of scarlet flying through the air. Still no one moved. Simmons moved on to the second boy and one by one, all six were reduced to quivering wrecks, their flesh twitching, tears streaming down their cheeks.

Simmons folded his whip around his fist. 'Punishment carried out, Warden,' he said.

Bloxham nodded and stepped forward, a clerk scurrying beside him. One by one, each whimpering boy took the little pot the clerk gave him.

'Ointment,' the Warden said, soothingly. 'God's balm. Bravely borne, lads. But next time, look to your windows.' He ruffled the hair of the last boy, soaking with sweat as it was. Then he stood back, and in a loud voice called, 'And when the *real* culprit, he who has vilified God's house, has the spine to step forward and confess his guilt, these six shall aid the proctors in his punishment. Merton, dismiss.' And the staff swept out of the Quad.

'Well, Master Chaucer,' Quentin Selham raised his cup to the comptroller. 'How did you like Merton justice?'

'It's hardly for me to comment,' Chaucer said. 'That's more Dick's demesne.'

Congleton laughed. 'It's bugger all to do with the law,' he said. 'As for justice, well …'

'It's all about tradition, though, isn't it?' Roger Allard helped himself to another sweetmeat. 'This kind of indirect flogging's been going on at Merton since … well, since the foundation, I suppose.'

'More interestingly,' Congleton refreshed his Romonye, 'who *did* hang the Pope from the walls?'

'It's not anybody in the Trivium,' Selham said. 'They're children. They wouldn't know the Pope from their left testicle – if I may encroach on your discipline a little, Roger?'

The doctor snorted. 'Bollocks are common to all of us, Quentin. I can't claim any sovereignty there.'

'In other news, Geoffrey,' Congleton leaned back in the comfiest chair in Merton's solar, long appropriated as the Senior Common

Room, 'how goes your investigation? Hal Golightly and the Herbert boy.'

Chaucer sighed. 'Stone walls, Dick,' he said. 'Oxford seems to be fuller of them than most towns I have visited.'

'Indeed it does,' Selham said. 'And not a little brick creeping in here and there, too. Modern rubbish. It's all too depressing.'

'Has the mayor been helpful?' Congleton asked.

'Master Treddler fell over himself to be helpful as soon as he knew that the sheriff was on his way.'

'He's gone, surely?' Allard asked.

'For now,' Chaucer said. 'But he'll be back. I think he thinks I'll have some answers by then.'

'And will you?' Congleton looked at him.

'You know better than most, Dick,' Chaucer said, 'that I have no jurisdiction here. I am not even an officer of the law. I could use your help.'

'Mine?' Congleton raised an eyebrow.

'You not only know Oxford like the back of your hand, but you are also a Serjeant at Law. You must have handled dozens of murder cases.'

'A few,' the lawyer nodded. He sat upright. 'Very well, let me see. Gentlemen, I will have need of your cups – if you'd oblige?'

'Er … we will get them back?' Selham wanted assurance.

'Indeed. This will only take a moment. Geoffrey, this table is Oxford. North. South. East. West. Here we are, at Merton.' He placed his own goblet in the relevant place. 'Now, tell me, Geoffrey. Do you believe that both clerks were killed by the same person?'

'I do,' Chaucer said.

'Why?' Everyone thought it, but only Congleton said it out loud.

173

'Roger,' Chaucer knew he was treading dangerous ground, 'Hal Golightly had severe head wounds, didn't he? Parallel cuts made by something less sharp than a blade?'

Allard's mouth fell open. 'How did you …?'

'Call it intuition,' Chaucer said. He had no intention of admitting his visit to the crypt of St Frideswide in the early hours in the company of a shipman. 'Hal's body was found here,' Chaucer put his cup next to Congleton's. The lawyer nodded.

'The body of Alfred Herbert,' Chaucer went on, 'I saw for myself, in that it was my man Zouche who discovered it.'

'Where was that?' Congleton asked.

'Greyfriars Lane,' Chaucer told him.

'Quentin …' Congleton jerked his thumb towards the table.

The Master of Music placed his cup about a foot from the others.

'Forgive me, Dick,' Allard said, 'but what is the point of this little chess game?'

'If Geoffrey is right about one killer and two victims, we may be able to find a pattern.'

'A pattern?' Selham chuckled. 'Shame Martin isn't here. He's the geometry man.'

'What's the killer's motive, Geoffrey?' Congleton asked. 'Any idea?'

'Could be a disgruntled townsperson,' the comptroller said, 'renewing the old gown/town animosity.'

'I thought you said Treddler was on your side,' Congleton pointed out.

'The mayor, possibly,' Chaucer nodded, 'but can he speak for Oxford? I doubt it.'

'The man's a vegetable,' Allard grunted. 'I'm amazed he can speak at all.'

'There again,' Chaucer went on, 'both lads were Merton men.'

'Now, we're getting somewhere,' Congleton said.

'It's another college!' Selham clapped his hands, as musicians will. 'My money's on Balliol.'

'Balliol,' Allard said. 'Has to be Balliol. That bastard Muncaster.'

'Roger, Andrew Muncaster is eighty if he's a day,' Congleton pointed out. 'I can't see him stoving anybody's head in.'

'Ah, but he has people, Dick,' Allard reasoned. 'Toughs of the Quadrivium, proctors with shoulders like warships. There is no shortage of muscle.'

'Geoffrey?' Congleton brought the focus back to Chaucer or unfounded accusations would be flying all night.

'Go on with your pattern, Dick,' he said. 'I'm intrigued.'

'All right. Mind you, I am talking about a particular kind of murderer, one who kills compulsively.'

'Like the pig?' someone muttered and Congleton looked round with narrowed eyes, seeing only innocence on every face.

'He – and we must assume it is "he", for no woman kills like that – he, for whatever reason, is stalking his victim. Is it the lad's age? His height? The colour of his hair? Roger?'

Allard concentrated. 'Hal Golightly was … what, five foot eight, I'd guess. His hair was covered in blood, of course,' he glanced suspiciously at Chaucer, 'but it was dark. He was … what? Nineteen?'

'And Herbert?'

'Shorter,' Chaucer remembered. 'Mousy hair. The same age or rather younger.'

'Er … was there any evidence of what we in the courts call "interference"?' Congleton asked. 'Clothes disarranged, subjaculi rolled down? Anything like that?'

'Not that I recall,' Allard said.

'Nor I,' Chaucer agreed.

'Of course,' Selham interjected, 'A lot of that sort of thing goes on at Oxford. Hunnish practices. The sin of Sodom.'

The others looked at him.

'Just saying,' Selham shrugged.

'If my experience counts for anything,' Congleton went on,' our killer is not from Merton. Here,' he pointed to Chaucer's cup, 'the first murder. Body found in Mob Quad. Nobody, to use the vernacular, shits on his own doorstep. Here,' he pointed to Selham's cup, 'the second murder. Body found in Greyfriars Lane. So …' he crouched to line up the cups, 'if experience serves … our murderer lives … here.' And he put his cup down halfway between the two.

There was a murmur from the others. 'Off Carfax,' Allard said. 'So, it *is* a townsman!'

'If, God forbid, he should strike again,' Congleton said, 'we'd be able to pinpoint it exactly. My guess is that our elusive friend lives or works nearer to Balliol than to Merton.' He stood up and folded his arms. 'And my other guess, which has nothing to do with the murder map, is that he is a Lollard.'

Chapter 12

It was far into the watches of the night when Geoffrey Chaucer, Comptroller of Woollens and Hides, court poet and man about Oxford Town, said his farewells to the alumni of Merton. His mind was racing with Congleton's ingenious murder map; he had had no idea that a killer's mind worked that way. 'If, God forbid, he should strike again' – the words kept circling in Chaucer's brain. Why did these boys have to die? And might there be a third in the list? Whatever God's plan was, He wasn't sharing it with Geoffrey Chaucer.

He was making his way along the passageway that led to the library when he saw the flicker of candlelight in the gap under a study door. Unless he was mistaken, that was Martin Frisby's lair, the demesne of the Master of Mathematics. And Chaucer needed to talk to him.

He tapped lightly on the door and waited. There were muffled voices from inside and then the oak swung wide. A tall figure with a bouffant tonsure, gleaming with yellow highlights in the light, stood there, holding the candle aloft to see who knocked.

'Master Sylvester,' Chaucer nodded. 'I apologise for the lateness of the hour, but I was wondering if Dr Frisby ...'

'Come in, Chaucer, come in.' Martin Frisby was sitting cross-legged on the floor, a circle drawn around him and a pentagram within it, marked with strange symbols. Some of them Chaucer recognised – the ram was there, the twins, the great bear; others, he could only guess at.

'It's late, Doctor,' Chaucer said. 'Forgive me, but I saw a light under your door.' He smiled at the secretary. 'You keep long hours in Oxford,' he said.

'Needs must,' Frisby said. 'Sylvester, some wine for Master Chaucer. Or are you more of an ale man?'

'Wine would be fine,' Chaucer said and sat down in the chair that Frisby had pointed to.

'Excuse me if I continue,' Frisby said, swinging an arm to encompass his symbols. 'A spot of divination. We all do it here at Merton. Allard uses the cosmos to diagnose ailments. Selham doesn't break into song without consulting the stars. Even the Warden has been known to dabble. Except Congleton,' Frisby smiled. 'Dick is above such things. The law, he says, has no links with what he calls gobbledegook.'

Chaucer laughed. 'A good word,' he said. 'I can see you'd use this in mathematics. Angles, radians, circumferences and so on.'

'If the world were round, of course,' Frisby said, 'it would be invaluable.'

'If only,' Chaucer laughed again.

'But actually,' Frisby lowered his voice and became almost conspiratorial. 'I'm not doing this for any mathematical reason. I'm doing it to catch a killer.'

'Really?' Chaucer sat up to take his cup of wine from the secretary. Suddenly, everybody in the world – or at any rate, everybody at Merton, which was more or less the same thing – was a detective.

'Look here,' Frisby pointed to a symbol. 'Sylvester used to work for an apothecary. Tell him, Sylvester.'

The secretary knelt just outside the circle. 'The man I worked for was … well, I had better keep his real name out of it, but he was known in some circles as the Stargazer.'

'Ah.'

'He believed, as we all do, that our fates, our very lives, are in the stars, the revolving patterns of the planets.'

'The Greeks had a word for it,' Chaucer nodded.

'Bollocks!' Frisby snorted.

Chaucer looked at him. 'No, that wasn't it.'

'No, I mean the Greeks were mere beginners. We're far ahead of Aristarchus now. For instance, it's May, so … Gemini, the twins.'

'Right.' Chaucer had to admit that he wasn't impressed so far.

'The twins, right?' Frisby looked at him with a satisfied look on his face. 'Two. And how many murders do we have? Two. So, there we have it.'

'Er …'

'Tell him, Sylvester.'

'Everything in the universe,' the secretary went on, 'has an opposite, doesn't it?'

'Umm …'

'Here.' Frisby pointed. 'Scorpio. Opposite to the twins in the Heavens. So …' Frisby was endlessly patient. For years he had been dragging solutions out of his scholars; it was like drawing teeth – ask Roger Allard.

'So …' There was a reason that Chaucer had never attended university.

Frisby sighed. 'So, our killer was born under the sign of Scorpio. He's vicious with huge pincers and a poisonous sting, metaphorically, of course. I have yet to plot the charts of my fellow lecturers and those at Balliol, but I believe I have whittled it down.'

'You have?' Chaucer said. 'To whom?' Could it really be that simple?

'Ah, no,' the Master of Mathematics shook his head. 'Not until I'm sure. It's a dreadful thing, to accuse a fellow academic of taking another man's life. After blasphemy, the worst crime in the book.'

'Talking of which,' Chaucer saw his chance to broach what he had really come for, 'the hanging of the Pope ...'

Frisby crossed himself. 'Shocking,' he said. 'Shocking ...'

'Yet, you interceded on behalf of those scholars earlier today.'

'I did,' Frisby conceded. 'It's no good pointing a finger at someone just because their rooms are nearby. You might as well select half a dozen urchins from the town.'

'Dick Congleton thinks the Lollards are involved,' Chaucer told him, watching the man closely. Ralph Strode had found the Lollard text in Frisby's garderobe, yet the man had seemed genuinely appalled by the papal effigy.

'Undoubtedly,' Frisby agreed. 'And it embarrasses me to think that such Godless arseholes live under the same roof as the rest of us. Worse, I believe that those responsible for this are not actually under this roof as we speak, but at Frideswide Grange. They are among the men of my very own Quadrivium. When I think of that poor, dear, defenceless woman among such filth ...' Frisby hung his head, shaking it sadly in his despair.

Chaucer knew it was important to shake Frisby out of the slough of despond into which the merest thought of Hattie Dalton alone and vulnerable could send him. The fact that she was about as vulnerable as the walls of the castle was a fact Frisby could not fathom.

'Dick Congleton believes that the murders are the work of the Lollards too.'

'Ah, now, there I must demur,' Frisby said. 'Dick and I go back a long way and I have the highest respect for the man. But he's wrong about that. No, the killer is a Scorpion. Give me a day or two, Master Chaucer, and I'll prove it.'

Chaucer decided the next day that enough was enough. Everybody and his wife had an arcane, scholarly way to find a murderer, but there was a boy's body turning a nasty colour in St Frideswide's crypt and it was Chaucer's duty to see him buried. He had promised Nicholas Brembre to keep him informed, yet here he was, many days later, and news from the north came there none. Chaucer could not have known that the former mayor of London, richer than God as he was, had his own troubles which rather put the shade of Hal Golightly in the shade, so to speak. The Hanse were plotting against London again, insisting on petty bureaucracy, hard borders and searching ships' cargoes six miles off the coast of France. Brembre was busy.

Chaucer's soul was rather purer and he paid a small fortune, albeit of Brembre's money, for an elm coffin for the clerk, a cart suitably draped in black and a rouncey of the same colour. He had also hired an undertaker, complete with bells and ashes, and had stood solemnly by as Hal Golightly began his sorrowful journey out of the South Gate on the road to London. The comptroller even handed a purse of silver to the carrier, to have prayers said for the boy at various shrines along the road. He was somebody's scholar; somebody's son.

Finding a carrier willing to do it had not been easy. At first, he had thought to send the boy by river, but wiser words had prevailed. Zouche had pointed out that at some points the river was barely navigable and carrying a coffin over narrow tow paths and through undergrowth to re-join the Thames on its journey to the sea was not very reverent, in the scheme of things.

The first carriers along Grandpont he had approached had been keen to take a load to London for good, hard gold, but had backed away when they heard what they would be carrying.

''S' against the charter, see,' one had said.

'Charter?' Chaucer had cocked a dubious eyebrow. He knew that there was a charter for almost every activity these days but he hadn't heard of that one.

'Oh, yeah. Well known, that one. No carrying o' dead bodies on the King's Highway. Big fine for that, oh, yes. P'raps I could do it …' the carter sucked his teeth, 'for a consideration. In case I'm fined on the way, sort of thing.'

Chaucer had moved on, and on, and on along the row of carriers and their patient horses, lined up waiting for work along the Cherwell.

Finally, when he thought he was going to have to haul the boy back to London himself, a busy little sparrow of a woman had tugged his sleeve.

'We'll do it,' she said. 'I've got boys of my own and I wouldn't like to think of one of them lying unburied for want of someone to take him back to his mother.'

Chaucer had often seen carriers coming in through the Aldgate, husband and wife together on the bench in degrees of amity from total hatred to virtual copulation, but they were rare. He glanced up to see a rubicund face looking down at him, gappy teeth showing in a grin so wide as to be almost imbecilic. But the wife seemed sharp enough, so he listened to what she had to say.

'As a matter of fact, master, you would be helping us out. We have a load to bring back from Lunnon as soon as we can, but we can't afford to get there to fetch it. And we don't get the money until we fetch it ...'

Chaucer had also seen this, a bind into which so many working men fell. There was a job, but to get to the job, or to buy what was needed to do the job, they needed a job. 'What's your name, mistress?' he asked, reaching for his purse.

'Araminta Gosling,' she said. 'And I know yours already, Master Chaucer. The load we have to bring back is wool and I've seen your seal many a time. That's my husband up there. Emmanuel Gosling, but we all call him Nol. We'll take the boy back for decent burial and we'll pray for him ourselves, all the way.' Her big eyes in her little brown face filled with tears. 'My eldest is away in the Borders with Lord Greystoke and I hope someone will care for him if he falls to those Scots bastards.'

Chaucer smiled and she smiled back. They both had boys they rarely saw and both hoped the same. He gave her the coins that any of the carters would have had, and then two more for luck for her boy, away in the Borders.

'Thank you, Mistress Gosling,' he said. 'And may God go with you all.'

That day brought a change in the weather. Spring drew in its horns and retreated, to shelter, like everyone else, from the drumming, incessant rain. Chaucer had planned to spend some time with William Zouche on the river. He had come to welcome the gentle rocking of the *Madeleine* when another craft went by, the soft slap of the water on her planks and the erudite conversation of her master. But the rain was so incessant that Chaucer had a feeling that, if he waited in his room at Frideswide Grange, that the *Madeleine* might come to him.

There was of course a built-in problem with spending the day in his room and that problem had already tapped on his door twice. He pulled his hood over his head and toyed with putting some of the spare moss, which Alice had thoughtfully packed in his box, in his ears, but he decided against it – it was bad enough when a hidden insect got between his toes; into his ear didn't really bear thinking about.

After the third discreet tap, this time accompanied by a soft *coo-ee*, the fear of incipient pneumonia brought on by a chill caused in its turn by getting his feet wet was beaten into submission by the fear of having to spend the rest of the day until dinner entertaining Hattie Dalton. Because Hattie took a lot of entertaining and Chaucer was not as young as he was. Apart from the fact that he had a bad back. So, he delved into his clothes to see if Alice had packed him anything approaching waterproof and indeed, the dear woman had packed an oiled silk cloak, with hood and a generous lap-over at the front. He wished he had found that before seeing Hal Golightly off with the Goslings. He sent Alice good thoughts and, checking first that the landing was clear of landladies, wrapped himself in it and splashed his way down to the river.

When he got to the boat, he barely recognised her. Zouche had pulled across a tarred cloth, battened down all along the length by tying ropes to the rowlocks. It looked impregnable but also very cosy. Chaucer stood there, rain dripping from the edge of his cloak, not that it made that much difference – the rain coming up from the ground, bouncing with the unspent fury of Heaven, had made him wet all the way up to his subjaculum. What he wanted more than anything was to get in, into the dry. He began to feel quite bereft. The rain had made the whole world deaf and dumb. No birds sang and the few people out and about scurried past each other, heads down, not speaking. On days like this, even college libraries were popular.

Chaucer tapped tentatively on *Madeleine's* prow. Nothing happened, so he tapped again. After a moment, a tie was released just near where he was standing and the tarred cloth was lifted a scant inch. An eye peered out.

'Oh. Master Chaucer, it's you.' Zouche was not effusive at the best of times, but seemed to have become more taciturn still. Perhaps it was the rain.

'Will, thank goodness,' Chaucer began. 'I'm so glad to find you in. I'm soaked and ...'

'I'm entertaining, Master Chaucer,' Zouche said, in a half-whisper. He had to raise his voice a little more than he would have liked, to be heard over the drumming rain.

'Of course you are, Will,' Chaucer said, cheerily. 'I love your nautical stories. Untie another rope so I can squeeze through. I don't have your lissom thews.'

'Indeed you don't, Geoffrey,' Zouche said, through clenched teeth. 'And they're a bit busy, if you know what I mean.'

'Busy?' Chaucer was flummoxed. 'How can ...?' The groat dropped and Chaucer blushed under his hood. 'Oh, I see. You're enter*taining*. You have a lady in there.'

'Well, happily, she's not that much of a lady,' Zouche said, his eye crinkling as he smiled. 'But we're rubbing along all right, if you get my meaning?' There was a shriek of laughter from the darkness of the boat.

'I see.' Chaucer took a step back and the gap in the tarred cloth began to narrow and the rope was soon retied tightly. He bent down and raised his voice. 'I'll let you get on, then, shall I?'

'If you would,' Zouche's voice was hardly audible over the rain, but the female laugh rang out loud and clear.

'Where shall I go, though?' Chaucer's plaintive question was drowned out by the rain as was, fortunately for their friendship, Zouche's reply.

It was a long, wet slog back up into town and through the streaming streets back to Frideswide Grange. Chaucer now had to work out how to get back in without alerting Hattie and, perhaps a more important task, to get himself and his clothes dry without the help of either her or one of the maids. He eased up the latch and managed to do it without so much as a rattle. He crept up the stairs one at a time, remembering that the fifth one up squeaked if you trod on it towards the left-hand side. That safely negotiated, he just had the landing to conquer and then he would be home and wet. He took huge pains with the latch on this second door and held on to it, ostentatiously easing it closed by sliding round it and shutting it with both hands, again being careful with the latch.

It was therefore all the more heart-attack inducing when a voice from the direction of the bed said, 'Geoffrey Chaucer, you naughty man. Come here and let me get those wet clothes off of you. You'll catch your death! Come to Hattie!'

After leaning his forehead on the smooth oak of the door, Chaucer turned around and met his fate.

Not everyone in Oxford could make their own entertainment just because the Heavens had opened. The inns were still serving, the shops were still welcoming customers, albeit in smaller numbers. And in the library, Brother Anselm and Martin Frisby were entangled in some arithmetic so arcane that it was making their heads hurt.

The candles spat and guttered in the draught from the windows and their voices were underscored by the music of the water cascading out of gutters not built for an onslaught like this. Although it was only afternoon, it was like midnight here in the library and the men lost all sense of time.

'So,' Anselm said, rather testily and from a position of relative ignorance, 'if I understand you correctly …'

'Which I doubt,' Frisby snorted.

Anselm drew in a deep breath. He would truly love to punch this man on the nose but didn't think that his position of librarian would survive it. And being Merton's librarian was rather a soft number and he had no intention of relinquishing it. They would have to prise the library keys from his cold, dead hands. 'The axiomatic system,' he began again, 'seems to me to clarify the point in question, which is …' he pricked up his ears. 'Did I just hear a bell? Can it be the rain is getting less?'

Frisby pricked his ears up as well. 'You did; indeed you did. And it's time I wasn't here. I have a tutorial in a very few minutes. If I run, I might be on time. This rain, it makes the day so dark.' He smiled at Anselm. 'I didn't mean to be rude,' he said, clapping him on the shoulder. 'I should make allowances. I am sure there are some things you know more about than I do.'

And with that, he was gone, grabbing his cloak from the hook as he went. The door at the bottom of the winding stair slammed shut in the wind and the librarian was alone.

He sat there for a moment, then lit a taper from the candle, before dousing the wick with a snuffer. He wouldn't have any passing scholars today, not in this weather. He made his way across to the pegs hammered into the wall almost above his reach by some former, taller librarian.

He pulled the cloak down and let rip with a stream of profanities most of which he didn't even know he knew. Not only was Frisby a condescending arsehole, he had also taken his best cloak and left him with his, damp and – Anselm took a tentative sniff – smelling of a strange mixture of lavender … he sniffed again … damp wool and … the final insult… fart. He sighed. As a rule, he would have made his way back to his rooms without recourse to an outer garment. After all, it was only another layer much the same as the one he wore indoors. But it was too wet for that. So he kirtled up his robes, added the cloak and plunged out into the weather.

'Master Selham,' the Warden called in a clear voice. 'Since we do not have the accompaniment of Dr Frisby tonight, could you say grace?'

'Of course, Warden.' The Master of Music bowed his head at the far end of the top table and rumbled out the '*Benedictus Benedicat*'. The piss-taking scholars at the farthest end of the bench were furious. Without the West Country burr, there was absolutely point in rolling their 'r's for the 'Arrrrrmen'.

'It's not like Martin,' Bloxham said as everybody sat down. 'He invariably informs me if he's going to be late. Thank you,' he nodded to the scullion who placed the conger eel dressed with crayfish eggs on his trencher. He looked down at it and gave it a desultory poke with his knife. 'Cook knows I don't like conger,' he said plaintively, and clicked his fingers to the scullion. 'Can you take this back and bring me something else?' he asked.

The scullion shrugged. He was just about fed to the back teeth today with everybody wanting this and wanting that. There was people in this town, no, bugger it, people in this *building* who would give their eye teeth for a nice bit of conger. He picked up the trencher and stalked back to the kitchen with it.

'Oh, dear,' Bloxham said. 'He's cross now.'

Allard, sitting to his right, could only agree. As a medical man, he should warn Bloxham against eating the replacement, as being almost certainly full of something he wouldn't want to be eating, but he forbore and smiled encouragingly instead.

'And I *am* worried about Martin. Have you seen him, Roger?'

'No, Warden,' Allard said, sniffing the Romonye in his cup. He had read a treatise recently about the effects on yellow bile of various species of grape and as a medical man, he felt he could not be too careful. Then he raised an eyebrow. 'Perhaps something is keeping him at Frideswide Grange, even though it's not actually his day. This weather has turned everything on its head.'

'Dick?' The Warden swivelled to his right, 'Any sightings of Martin?'

'No, Warden,' Congleton said. 'But Roger is right, it's still raining cats and dogs out there. He's probably sheltering in some nook.'

The rain was driving hard, bouncing off the slates and gargoyles of Merton. The drone from the student body was always less in wet weather, perhaps because half of them were sitting soaked, dripping onto the flagstones.

Chaucer, still a little battered and confused, smiled as the scullion poured his wine, but the lack of progress in his enquiries was beginning to depress him. He had hoped to discuss things with Zouche but of course, that had come to nothing. And although Hattie was not a silent bedfellow, there was not much of import in her conversation, consisting of, as it did in the main, exhortations of delight or requests for him to put his back into it, which Chaucer didn't think possible, but with Hattie one never really knew.

He had two dead clerks and every stone wall in Oxford rose up sheer before him. One would soon, if God was willing, be safely stowed in the ground with the proper offices, and hopefully before too long the other would be likewise, so there was that at least for comfort. But as to who put them in the way of needing a Christian burial, he was no further forward.

He leaned to one side to allow his portion of conger to be placed in front of him. He noticed he did not have the crayfish egg dressing and his despondency grew. He did love a nice crayfish egg dressing now and then, and it was in short supply in London. Something about the wrong sort of river, Alice always said. He felt a crack and he was reminded anew of his clash with the quarter-staff as his back froze for a moment. Then his head gave a twinge and then his stomach gave a slight heave ... he sighed. Just lately, no day had been his day.

He was crumbling his bread and eying the butter with suspicion when a college servant scuttled in, wringing wet and grim of face. The man bowed before Warden Bloxham, then whispered in his ear. Chaucer could not remember seeing a man turn white before, although it was less of a change than it might be for other men and Bloxham grabbed convulsively for the man's cloak. Allard and Selham didn't appear to notice; neither did the other guests at the high table. Congleton was studying the wine list with the air of a man who knows his vines; anything north of the Loire left him decidedly unmoved.

Warden Bloxham struggled to his feet and beckoned over the College chaplain, a man as ghostly and cadaverous as the Warden himself, albeit several years younger. He whispered in the man's ear and the chaplain crossed himself. Bloxham tapped on the table-bell with his knife and the hall, eventually, fell silent.

'Gentlemen and scholars.' His voice wavered and he suddenly looked all of his three score years and ten. 'I ... I have just been given the news that Dr Martin Frisby is ... dead.'

There was a moment of stunned silence, apart from the rustle of cloth as the entire company crossed themselves. Then there was an audible gasp, a cry or two of 'No!' From the furthest corner, a subdued group of scholars muttered 'Arrmen,' out of respect, perhaps the last time they would do so.

'What's happened?' Chaucer heard Allard hiss in Bloxham's ear.

'He's been found dead,' the Warden told him, 'at the far end of the High.'

'The town?' Congleton touched Bloxham's arm. 'Was it one of Treddler's thugs?'

'I don't know, Dick.' The Warden spread his arms. 'Nobody does.'

'Where's the body now?' Chaucer asked, suddenly painfully aware that this was none of his business.

'Um ...' Bloxham turned to the college servant, who whispered once more in his ear. 'The crypt of St Frideswide.'

'Coming, Dick?' Chaucer asked. 'Warden, if we may?'

'Er ... of course. Of course.' He waved them away.

'Roger?' Chaucer looked at the man.

'Absolutely. We must do all we can for poor Martin.'

'By all means, by all means.' The old man cleared his throat.

'Chaplain, a prayer for the departed, if you please. A *Te Deum* before we continue the meal.'

And the chant began before Chaucer and friends reached the door.

Spring showers didn't do justice to what was happening over Oxford that night. The trio scurried along the cobbles, their cloaks wrapped around them and their hoods pulled down over their eyes.

'First the scholars, now the staff,' Allard was muttering. 'What the Hell's going on?'

'It's a college thing,' Congleton grunted. 'Balliol, I shouldn't wonder.'

'Geoffrey,' Allard said, 'you're an outsider – and I mean that in the most positive way. Do you have a view?'

Chaucer's only view at the moment was the rain running around the rim of his hood and soaking into the front of his houppe-lande. 'Insider, outsider,' he mumbled, 'I'm not sure it makes any difference.'

The appalling weather made no difference to the town watch. They were nowhere to be seen; any more than they would have been when the night was fine. 'I don't know what we pay our taxes for,' Allard moaned. 'We're not kept safe in our beds.'

'You don't pay any taxes, Roger,' Congleton reminded him. 'Any more than I do.' He caught Chaucer's look. 'University exemption, Geoffrey,' he explained.

'That's not the point,' Allard insisted. 'Ah, here we are.' He hammered on the well-worn oak of the door of St Frideswide's crypt as they waited. A suspicious face appeared through the grille in the wicket.

'Yes?'

'Dr Roger Allard,' he announced. 'Master of Medicine at Merton. I understand you have a body recently brought in.'

'Who says?' the face said, eyeing up the wet trio.

'I do,' Congleton said in his best court voice. 'We have it on good authority that Dr Martin Frisby of Merton was brought in not half an hour ago.'

'Wait there,' the face said and before anyone could protest, it had gone.

'Bugger this,' Allard grunted and pushed the wicket. It swung wide into the darkness and all three went inside. There was an immediate commotion and the face had returned, along with the prior himself. Chaucer felt a little guilty; he and Zouche had crept along these passageways after dark before, breaking God alone knew how many laws, to check on the body of Hal Golightly. Now he was about to do it again, but this time with the full weight of authority at his elbow.

'Gentlemen.' The prior stopped the trio in their tracks. 'May I remind you that this is a house of God?'

'May I remind you,' Congleton squared up to him, 'that the Thirteenth of King Henry III gives the faculty of Oxford University the right of entry to any building within the precincts of said university.' It was not a question this time, but a statement.

'I see,' the prior bridled. 'And you are?'

'Livid and distraught,' Allard snapped, 'all in one. Where is the body of Dr Frisby?'

The prior turned to the face.

'The stiff,' the face mumbled. 'Just brought in. Well, he's not stiff yet, of course. More a figure of speech, really.'

'Dr Frisby?' the prior repeated. 'Martin Frisby?'

'The same,' Congleton told him. 'Late Master of Mathematics of Merton College. A tragic loss.'

The prior fumed quietly. He looked at Chaucer – he'd seen that nosy bugger off already, but college faculties were a different proposition. He half-bowed. 'Follow me, gentlemen,' he said, and led the way.

It was all coming back to Chaucer now, the twists of the crypt, the spiral of the steps. It was cold at this level, far underground and the catacombs around the walls didn't help. Dusty clerics, long dead, lay in their niches on all four walls, their seals laden with Latin prayers and exhortations. The face had scuttled behind the prior and hastily lit two candles, which he passed to Allard and Congleton. On the dais in the centre of the room, where Chaucer had examined Hal Golightly, a body lay, wrapped up in a cloak stitched with the arms of Merton and various mathematical symbols, only a few of which the comptroller recognised.

Everybody crossed themselves. 'Roger?' Congleton jerked his head towards the corpse and the doctor of physic pulled back his hood and flexed his fingers. 'Gentlemen,' he said, 'what you are about to see may shock you. I shall be handling the body in a way that is not strictly approved by the Vatican.'

The prior tutted.

'Perhaps you'd like to leave, Father?' Congleton snapped.

'Thank you,' the prior said. 'I will. Humphrey,' he turned to the face, 'you will stay and watch. I expect a full report.'

Humphrey was not best pleased; laying out was one thing. Mucking about with one of God's creatures was altogether more blasphemous.

Gingerly, Allard placed his candle near to the body's head. Then he peeled back the hood, soaked as it was in rain and barely congealed blood. He crossed himself. 'Mother of God.'

'Nasty?' Chaucer asked. He couldn't see much from his position.

'You might say that,' Allard murmured. 'And not at all what I expected.'

No one remembered when dinner at Merton had been eaten in such silence. Other meals, yes – that was the custom. But dinner was a time of joviality, tall stories and boyish banter. The Quadrivium told dirty jokes to the Trivium, who did their best to respond as men of the world might. It didn't impress, but it was the Oxford way and had been for generations.

The Warden was about to push his marchpane around the plate for the final time, the third course he hadn't touched, when there was a commotion at the door and a figure, dripping wet, burst in.

'Sorry I'm late, dears,' he apologised to the serving wenches lined up against the wall. The he stopped, suddenly aware of the silence. 'Good God, has somebody died?'

Several of the company rose to their feet as if in the presence of a ghost.

'I know,' said the new arrival, in his well-known West Country burr, holding out his thin, clerical cloak ruefully. 'I picked a Hell of a night to end up with the cloak of a librarian. They just don't have the heft that masters' cloaks have, somehow.'

'Mother of God!' Warden Bloxham managed, his eyes wide, his hands trembling. 'Dr Frisby!' and he dropped, poleaxed, to the floor.

'Are you sufficiently recovered, Warden?' Allard released the tourniquet from John Bloxham's arm. 'You chose a hell of a night to faint. I am completely out of leeches.'

'I will survive, Doctor, thank you,' the old man croaked. He had never had so many people in his bedchamber before – at least, not since he had first seen the light of day and that was a *long* time ago.

'Well, your humours are unbalanced, that's for sure.' Allard warned.

'Yes, yes.' Bloxham fluttered his hands. 'Don't fuss. I shall be considerably more balanced when I know exactly what is going on. Dr Frisby, they told me you were dead.'

'That *was* rather exaggerated, Warden,' Frisby smiled. He was still in his soaking wet robes, dripping onto Bloxham's straw.

'Clearly,' Bloxham was becoming more irritated by the moment and Allard's fiddling with a phial and tutting didn't help. 'Master Chaucer, as possibly the only sane person in the room, will you explain what is happening?'

The comptroller looked at the others. They all had seniority over him in terms of academic qualifications and their links with the Warden, but he had been asked a civil question and felt it his duty to oblige. 'As I see it, Warden, Brother Anselm, late of your college, has been murdered.'

'Lackaday,' Bloxham sighed. Everybody else looked at him because they had no idea what that meant.

'The question we must ask,' Chaucer went on, 'is why.'

'Somebody had it in for him,' Congleton muttered. 'Saving your presence, Warden, as the man who appointed him, but Anselm was a pompous little shit.'

'Oh, come, now, Dick,' Bloxham frowned. 'A little harsh, surely?'

'I don't know,' Allard said. 'I had heard various things ...'

'Such as?' the Warden pressed him.

'Well, I don't like to speak ill of the dead, but he had his favourites, if you catch my drift; most of them the little boys of the Trivium.'

Bloxham's mouth hung open.

'That's just an ugly rumour,' Frisby said.

'It's ugly, Martin,' Quentin Selham butted in, 'but it's rather more than a rumour, I'm afraid. Brother Anselm's favourite passage in the Good Book concerned the cities of the plain.'

'He was also a Grecophile,' Congleton remarked. 'Used to read Aristophanes to the boys.'

Eyebrows were raised. Bloxham shuddered.

'Nothing proved, though, surely?' Frisby found himself increasingly alone in the court of character assassination.

'No smoke, Martin,' Congleton murmured. 'No smoke.'

'You, of all people, Dick,' the Master of Mathematics turned on the man. 'In your profession, don't you deal in truth, proof, hard evidence?'

'When I can,' Congleton bridled. 'It isn't always possible.'

'Gentlemen, gentlemen,' Chaucer all but clapped his hands. 'I can't help thinking we're all missing the point here. Dick, Roger, when we went to the crypt, we expected to find Dr Frisby's body, didn't we? Why was that?'

'McDermid, the servant,' Allard answered. 'He got it wrong.'

'But *why* did he get it wrong?'

They looked at each other, all those high-flown academics. The Warden looked at all of them. Then Dick Congleton clicked his fingers. 'The cloak,' he said. 'Anselm was wearing Frisby's cloak. It was wet. It was dark. Obviously, our murderer was in a hurry. Er … perhaps he was unfamiliar with Anselm's appearance, close to. He'd have been an outsider, not of the college.'

'Oriel,' Selham said.

'Balliol,' Allard offered.

'Martin,' Chaucer said quietly, 'Can you think of anybody who'd want to see you dead?'

There was a stunned silence, then Frisby lightened the mood. 'Well, half the Quadrivium, for a start.'

'Half the Quadrivium?' Ralph Strode freshened Chaucer's wine. 'He was joking, I assume?'

The pair were sitting in Strode's rooms at Tackley's and it was well past midnight. 'You tell me, Ralph,' the comptroller sipped the Romonye. 'You're more familiar with all this than I am. Do scholars kill their masters? Do clerks run amok?'

'Oh, they run amok all right.' Strode sat down again. 'You saw that the other day at the St Frideswide shenanigans. Riots. Pranks. Thumping the locals – they can't get enough of it. But *murder*? That's in a different league.'

'Wasn't there that business in Bologna not so long ago?'

'God, yes,' Strode said. 'I'd forgotten that. One of the Trivium took exception to one of the faculty's interpretation of Boethius and challenged him. You'd think that would lead to a scholarly debate, wouldn't you?'

'But it didn't.'

'No. This was Bologna, where the clerks themselves decide not only what they are taught, but what sort of salary their masters get.'

'Outrageous,' Chaucer muttered.

'Italian!' Strode countered. 'No, the magister in question clouted the lad and cast some doubt on his parentage. The lad took even more exception this time and called him a ... well, I can't remember the precise Italian, but it's not a phrase I'd use in front of a mother superior. The magister hit the boy again. This time, when the session was over, said boy and half a dozen of his cronies waylaid the magister and beat him to death. Was

Martin Frisby of such a disposition? When he said that "half the Quadrivium" want him dead?'

'I don't know, Ralph,' Chaucer ran his finger around the rim of his cup. 'But I intend to make it my business to find out.'

Chapter 13

'I had the most appalling dream,' the Warden muttered, clawing at his bedsheets. 'I dreamt that Frisby was dead and his ghost came unbidden to the feast.'

'You'll have to take more water with your Romonye, Warden.' Allard was peering into a phial of yellow liquid. 'There are twenty-four varieties of urine, but I'll confess I've never seen one with *quite* this colour. Have you been eating oysters?'

'No.'

'Lampreys?'

'No.'

'Larks' tongues?'

'Never to excess.'

'Well, then, it must be shock. Can the college funds run to pomegranates?'

'Pomegranates, Allard? Pomegranates? Don't be ludicrous. We aren't made of money. But tell me,' he grabbed the doctor's sleeve. 'This Frisby business ...'

'Martin Frisby is as alive as you and me, Warden.' Allard sniffed the urine bottle and tried not to turn away in disgust. 'It wasn't a dream. The librarian, now – that's a different matter entirely.'

The different matter lay on Merton's largest kitchen table, his body naked, his swollen head a mass of blood. Chaucer and Congleton had lost their sense of time, but they were vaguely aware that this work must be done soon or the scholars would be in for their breakfast.

'What did Roger say?' the Master of Logic asked. With help from the proctors, Chaucer, Congleton and Allard had got Anselm's body from the crypt of St Frideswide, but Congleton had had to take his leave; officers from the King's Bench had arrived with urgent news of John Wyclif's trial and he had had to attend to that. It was Chaucer's idea to move the dead man here, under Merton's roof. He didn't altogether trust the prior of St Frideswide and the malevolent wandering eye of Humphrey gave him no confidence at all. Watchers of the dead routinely desecrated corpses, helping themselves to teeth and hair. Chaucer himself had once owned a psaltery bound in the skin of a double murderer. But then he had married his Pippa and when she noticed an ear on the rear leaf, he had sold it. He still regretted that, sometimes. Chaucer was determined that nothing like that was going to happen to Anselm, whatever the rumours were about him.

'It's what he didn't say that bothered me,' Chaucer said, peering at the dead man by the candle's flickering flame.

'Oh?' Congleton was all ears.

'He didn't say he'd seen these wounds before.'

'And he had?'

'If, as he assured me, he examined the corpse of Hal Golightly,' yes. See these parallel cuts.'

'Hmm,' Congleton nodded. 'A sort of ridge and furrow pattern.'

Neither man was much versed in the ways of the countryside, they had people for that. It was not an analogy that Chaucer would have chosen. 'Same goes for Alfred Herbert,' he said.

'So,' Congleton eased himself back against the wall, resting a buttock on the roasting spit, 'What are your thoughts?'

Chaucer chuckled. 'Dick, I'm out on a limb here. This is not my town and these are not my people. You tell me.'

'All right. Let's assume – for now – that all three have been killed by the same habitual homicide. Why? What have they in common?'

'Merton,' Chaucer said. 'Two of them were clerks of the Quadrivium, the third the librarian. Except the third was a mistake.'

'It was?'

'Undoubtedly. I've just come from Dr Frisby's. He's in shock, poor fellow, and having to be consoled by … someone.'

Congleton rolled his eyes. 'If you mean my sister, Geoffrey, say so. I am fully aware that Harriet is the university tester; she's been like it since girlhood. Never met a cock she didn't like, although she has the refinement to call it a *membrum virile*. Each to his own in that respect. What of Frisby?'

'He was in the library this evening – last evening, that is, poring over old mathematical treatises with Anselm. He'd lost track of the time, realised that he'd be late for dinner and grabbed the nearest cloak on his way out. It was bucketing down by this time and by the time he had realised the cloak was not his, he was soaking wet and forced to shelter in the Golden Cross. One thing led to another and several cups later, he thought the rain had lessened enough for him to continue his journey. His arrival in hall caused the Warden to collapse and the rest you know.'

'And Frisby left Anselm in the library?'

'He says so, yes,' Chaucer nodded. 'Which brings me to the next question; where was Anselm and what was he doing for the next hour?'

'And how did he get to the far end of the High?'

'We can assume he walked.' Chaucer was ever a practical man. 'But what for? If he realised that he'd got Frisby's cloak, why was he travelling in the opposite direction, rather than coming to Merton to return it to him?'

'Let's backtrack,' Congleton suggested. 'You knew there was bad blood between Anselm and Waldemar, didn't you?'

'Waldemar?' That wasn't a name that Chaucer knew.

'Librarian at Balliol; Anselm's opposite number, so to speak. Decrying my own kind though I am, Geoffrey,' the lawyer said, 'we academics are a spiteful, petty bunch. Any veiled nuance, any slight, any badly judged *bon mot* and it's daggers drawn.'

'Literally?'

'Well, until now I'd say "no". It's usually name-calling, childish pranks.'

'Ah, like kissing St Frideswide,' Chaucer nodded, a rueful look on his face.

'Something like that,' Congleton laughed. Then he was serious again. 'No, Waldemar is ... No, I mustn't.'

'Damn it, Dick,' Chaucer fumed. 'You can't leave me dangling like that. What is Waldemar?'

'Malevolent,' Congleton said flatly. 'I believe him to be a practitioner of the Black Arts.'

'The ...?'

Congleton closed to his man. '*Malefecia*,' he murmured. '*Diabolis*.'

'Seriously?'

Congleton nodded. 'I haven't seen it myself, of course, but there's no smoke without fire. This defence work I've undertaken for John Wyclif – it's unearthed all kinds of darkness. Of course, I can't elaborate.'

'No, no, of course, but in the case of Waldemar?'

'He and Anselm used to be boon companions, preternaturally close, if you get my drift. Think Patroclus and Achilles, David and Jonathan, Roland and Oliver. Oh, a lot of that sort of thing goes on at Oxford and everybody turns a blind eye. That's one reason why Hattie gets away with her … what did you call it? Consolation? She provides a healthy outlet for young loins.'

'Whereas Anselm and Waldemar …' Chaucer raised an eyebrow.

'Quite,' Congleton said. 'We're men of the world, Geoffrey. We've seen things going on in the Southwark stews that'd turn your hair white … er … whiter.'

Chaucer nodded. 'I blame the crusades, myself.'

'Me too,' the Master of Logic said. 'Me too. Well, while Anselm and Waldemar were on good terms, no one batted an eyelid. What they got up to in their rooms was entirely up to them. But when they fell out … well, things got ugly and personal very quickly. Both men, as I understand it, took their favourite clerks under their wings, so to speak, telling tales of outrage and encouraging said clerks to wreak havoc on the other lot.'

'Which is why you mentioned Balliol as being behind all this with the murder of Herbert.'

'Exactly. I didn't want to bring up Anselm and Waldemar directly but now, well …'

'Nothing more dangerous,' Chaucer mused, 'than a librarian scorned.'

'You've never said a truer word, Geoffrey,' Congleton nodded. 'What will you do?'

Chaucer looked at him. 'Beard the black magician in his den,' he said.

The inns of Oxford were thronged with clerks later that day, despite the fact that Warden Bloxham had decreed a day of mourning for Brother Anselm. The clerks of Balliol were delighted because the arch-enemy of *their* librarian was dead. And the clerks of Merton were equally delighted because their *bête noire* had had his head stoved in. While sixteen men and true of Oxenford were deciding, in the hastily-convened crowner's court, that murder had been done by 'person or persons unknown', the more enterprising of their brethren were selling Anselm buns from their stalls, Anselm ales from their flagons and even phials of the dear man's blood scooped from the Very Spot at which he died.

And at the Very Spot, within an arrow shot of Carfax, a solemn ghoul wearing a scrounged Cistercian habit was telling passers-by, for a fee, exactly how the poor man came to die.

'How did he come to die?' Chaucer asked the 'Cistercian'.

'Bless you, sir,' the man growled from under his hood. 'Let those women and children move aside. It's not fit for their ears. And that's a groat, by the way.'

Cheap at half the price, Chaucer thought, if this rogue could give him any pointers. He passed the coins over. The 'Cistercian' bit each one and pocketed them. Then he raised his scrawny arms to the Heavens. 'A bolt,' he screeched, 'a bolt from the Heavens struck him down.'

'Get away,' somebody in the crowd grunted.

'As I live and breathe,' the ghoul said. 'And I saw it with my own eyes. Oh, he was a wicked man, was Lanfranc.'

'Anselm,' Chaucer corrected him.

'Anselm,' the ghoul went on without a pause. 'Debauched, he was, deflowering virgins even here in dear old Oxford. Why, he even ravished the novices up at the nunnery.'

'He preferred men,' Chaucer murmured in the man's ear.

'That, too,' the 'Cistercian' went on. 'No creature was safe from his roving eye, his wandering hands, his huge… I'm not saying Anselm was well hung. I'm saying God struck him down as he was, as He will strike us all at the Day of Judgement.'

'Did he have any help?' Chaucer asked.

'Who?' The ghoul had lost track of this conversation.

'The Almighty.'

'Er … how do you mean?' Tackling hecklers was not the mock Cistercian's forte.

'Well, did any human direct the Lord's thunderbolt?'

The ghoul screeched at him, 'Look, mate, the ways of the Lord are strange, y'know.' He leaned in to Chaucer. 'Best not ask too many questions, eh?'

Chaucer chuckled. 'No, indeed,' he said. 'That would never do.' And as he walked away, he heard the 'Cistercian' catching a new audience.

'Roll up, lordings, ladies, knarres, hear all about it.'

'So, there he was,' the big clerk was holding forth at the Golden Cross moments later as Chaucer arrived. 'Dead as a nit.'

There were cheers all round and the thud of tankards hitting oak.

'You saw him, did you?' Chaucer asked when the hubbub had died down. 'I assume the nit in question is Brother Anselm? Er ... Fingle, isn't it? Merton College?'

'What of it?' The clerk's piggy eyes looked even more sullen when he was challenged.

'Just answer the question.' Chaucer sat down on an empty stool, the criminous clerks all around him. 'Did you see the body?'

'Well, I ... no, not actually.'

'And can you tell me why a man's death is the cause of so much frivolity?'

Fingle slammed down his cup, spilling froth over the polished oak. 'Look, Master ... Chaucer, or whatever your name is, why don't you bugger off? You're not Oxford.'

Chaucer smiled. 'No, I'm not,' he said. 'And I'm very glad of it. I understand your warden has decreed a day of mourning for Anselm. So,' he looked around them all, 'why don't you little boys finish your drinks and go to the chapel? Spare a thought – and perhaps a prayer – for a dead soul.'

There was a silence. Then it ended. 'You didn't know Anselm, not like we did.'

It was Neville Cross, sitting across the table from Chaucer with a look of chilling hatred on his face.

'Meaning?' Chaucer asked.

'In polite circles,' Cross said, 'he was not as other men. In reality, he was a Bulgar, guilty of the crime of Sodom.'

'You know this for a fact?' Chaucer asked.

'We all do.' It was Harry Latimer, sitting to Cross's right. There were *hear hears* all round and some muttered oaths.

Chaucer looked from one face to the other. 'Who here was accosted by Anselm?' he asked. 'You, Latimer?'

The clerk blinked. 'Well, no, but ...'

'You, Fingle?'

The big lad licked his lips. This wasn't going too well. He had seen Chaucer defeated in the Great Debate, but now ... surely, *somebody* had an answer.

'Temple, isn't it?' Chaucer's gaze fell on the runt of the party. 'You?'

'He offered me some marchpane once.' It was defiant but somehow lacking in peril.

'Did he offer you anything else?' Chaucer's voice was level.

'Er ... as it happens, no.'

Chaucer's eyes flicked to the far side of the room, where the blond-haired Van der Gelder was licking the neck of a town girl. 'I assume that friend der Gelder was immune to any advances Anselm might make. Which leaves me with you, Master Cross, debater extraordinary, quarter-staff handler without peer, how many hours did you spend in Anselm's bed?'

Cross was on his feet in an instant, his face scarlet with rage, his fists clenched.

'Temper, temper,' Chaucer smiled. 'I should tell you, gentlemen, that under the table is a poignard point approximately three inches from Master Fingle's unmentionables.'

A squeak from Fingle confirmed that this was so.

'Now, once again, you will down your ale and leave. I believe that Merton chapel is that way.' He jerked his thumb towards the door.

One by one, the scholars rose to join the still-standing Cross and shuffled towards the street and the light. At the door, Cross turned back. 'There'll come a day, Chaucer,' he said.

'Depend on it,' the comptroller nodded.

Fingle hadn't moved, aware as he was what damage a poignard

could do at close quarters. Given his situation, it was brave of him to say what he said next. 'Not us, maybe,' he whispered, 'but Golightly and Herbert, *they* were Anselm's targets.'

'That's as may be,' Chaucer said, 'but they're dead, Fingle, and we can't ask them, can we?'

The comptroller stood up, a piece of wood in his hand. His poignard hung, still in its sheath, at his hip.

'What's that?' Fingle asked, suddenly realising that it had been sticking in his unmentionables for the last three minutes.

'This?' Chaucer threw it into the air and caught it expertly. 'Oh, it's my comptroller's tally-stick. Never go anywhere without it.'

And he made for the door. On his way out, he murmured to the large man propping up the bar, 'Thanks, Will. Didn't need you after all, but I'm grateful for your presence.'

The shipman smiled. 'Pity,' he said. 'Long time since I broke up a tavern. And that little shit Cross needs taking down a peg or two.'

It had been no simple matter to get past the proctors of Balliol, but Chaucer, with a mixture of royal name-dropping and old-fashioned English silver, had managed it. For a while, he wandered the quadrangles that stood beside Broad Street, admiring the mellow stone with all the ardour of a tourist. He wanted to find the library and, above all, the librarian.

'Can you tell me where the library is?' he asked a pair of clerks scuttling towards a lecture as the bell tolled.

'Yes,' one of them said and they vanished into a passageway, leaving the comptroller no further forward.

'*Tcha*!' a voice behind him made him turn. 'The youth of today. That's the Trivium for you. Can I help you, Master ...?' The man's face was more or less the colour of the college stone, but his robes marked him as a Benedictine.

'Chaucer,' the comptroller said.

'Good God,' the Benedictine paused, his hand still extended. 'The king's poet, here at Balliol!' And he seized the comptroller's hand in both of his. 'Welcome, Master Chaucer, welcome. This is an honour indeed.'

'Well, that's very nice of you, Brother …?'

'Waldemar. Waldemar of Lucerne. All rather a long time ago now.'

'You're the college librarian.' Chaucer couldn't believe his luck.

'For my sins.' Waldemar raised his eyes Heavenward. 'Can I offer you a little repast? Gascony? Romonye?'

'Well, I …'

'Excellent. Come this way.'

Chaucer followed the man across the quad and up a winding staircase. He saw the library, its dusty leather kissed now and then by the midday sun.

'I'll show you all that later,' Waldemar said, 'the books aren't going anywhere, believe me. Ah, here we are.'

The librarian's room above the collection was small and sparse. There was a crucifix on the wall and a large cabinet with bars and bolts. Waldemar ushered his guest to a chair and, turning his back momentarily, rattled keys in locks and let the cupboard door swing wide. Outside an inn and perhaps John of Gaunt's former palace at the Savoy, Chaucer had never seen so many bottles in his life.

Waldemar beamed with pride. 'My little indulgence,' he said. 'Shall we broach this one?'

He slid a dark bottle out of its niche and uncorked it. He put it to his nose and breathed in. 'Savour the moment, Master Chaucer,' he said and passed it to his guest.

Geoffrey Chaucer was no stranger to wine. Part of his stipend from the king came in the form of the stuff. He had sipped with His Grace, more than one Archbishop of Canterbury, nobles and burgesses without number. Even so, he had never smelt anything like this. The look on his face said it all.

Waldemar laughed. 'Yes,' he said, 'it takes a lot of people that way. I get it from a little man I know in the Pyrenees passes near Roncesvalles. And of course, I only share it with *very* special people.' He poured for them both.

'I am honoured, Brother.'

'Oh, Waldy, Master Chaucer, please,' and he raised his cup. 'To the blessed Dervorguila,' and he sipped appreciatively.

'Dervorguila?' Chaucer had drunk many a toast in his time, but he liked to know what he was drinking to.

'Dervorguila of Galloway,' the librarian explained. 'Wife of Sir John Balliol, founder of this college. Actually,' he leaned forward confidentially, 'she was the real founder in that Sir John, apparently, was only a little more blessed in the brains department than some of his sheep.'

'Devorguila.' Chaucer toasted and drank. There was a rushing in his ears and his tongue recoiled. He felt his eyeballs rolling and a tightening in his chest. Then, after a moment, a warm glow and a feeling that all was right with the world after all. 'I wanted to say,' he said when his tongue would let him, 'how sorry I was to hear of the death of Brother Anselm. I understand he was a friend.'

Waldemar's face fell. The bonhomie had vanished and there was a sudden chill in the room. 'He was,' he said. 'Very much past tense.'

'Dreadful thing, though.' Chaucer wasn't prepared to leave it there. 'Murder.'

'It is,' Waldemar nodded. 'But some men are the instruments of their own ends. Anselm wouldn't heed the warnings.'

'Warnings?'

The librarian leaned closer to Chaucer. 'Are you familiar with the works of Albertus Magnus, Master Chaucer?'

'Bishop of Ratisbon, wasn't he? Not specifically, no.'

'Alexander the Paphlagonian?'

'Er … no, I don't think so.'

'How about Roger Bacon?'

'Ah, the gunpowder man. Yes, vaguely.'

'Peter of Abano?'

'No.'

'Aristarchus of Samos?'

Chaucer shook his head.

'The late Anselm was familiar with all these people. They were practitioners of the Black Arts, Master Chaucer. Not to put too fine a point on it, they worshipped the devil, kissed his arse as you and I kiss the face of Christ. Anselm had a damnable library containing all the Devil's works, as practised by the Egyptians and the Mohammedans. I could have nothing to do with that. As soon as I learned of his revolting habits, I wanted nothing more to do with him.'

'I see,' Chaucer said. 'But wasn't there a certain … rivalry between the two of you? Both librarians of Oxford's oldest colleges.'

'That accolade belongs to me alone, Master Chaucer, as librarian of Oxford's *very* oldest college.'

'But Merton's books – Ptolemy's *Cosmographia*, for example.'

'That pamphlet,' Waldemar all but spat. 'It doesn't hold a candle to our possessions.'

'Be that as it may, Waldy,' Chaucer was determined to stay friendly. 'Someone killed Brother Anselm; I wanted to find out who.'

'Good for you,' Waldemar beamed, his bonhomie back. 'Now, let me show you the books that Balliol has. But first,' he reached across for the bottle, 'let me refresh your tincture. One for the road, eh?'

The rain came back that night with a vengeance, large drops bouncing off the *Madeleine*'s canopy. William Zouche had watched for Chaucer for hours. He had not been happy to see the comptroller, middle-aged, more or less unarmed and rather out of condition, in the middle of a gang of entitled thugs who had nothing but contempt for him. The shipman would go further; he had agreed to bring the man to Oxford to take back the body of a friend's ward to London for burial. But that was then. And since then, two more men had died, their skulls smashed, their brains exposed. Chaucer himself had been knocked from pillar to post with a quarter-staff. He had climbed a church spire for no good reason. And to cap it all, he had had the mother of all food poisoning. What else could go wrong?

William Zouche didn't know, but he felt it incumbent upon him to find out. When he captained a ship, he made it a matter of honour never to abandon a mate. The original *Madelaine*'s crew had been like family to William Zouche; so it was with Chaucer. Inevitably, Merton was his first stop.

'Geoffrey?' Ralph Strode was knee deep in vellum in a corner of the college library, a pair of spectacles on the end of his nose. 'No, I haven't seen him. Not since … No, sorry. No idea.'

So much for old friends, thought Zouche. His next port of call was the Senior Common Room where three of the unlikeliest birds were nesting together, ready for the shipman's stone.

'Last night,' Richard Congleton remembered. 'We were talking about poor Anselm. Roger, you were there.'

'Earlier, yes. You were called away, though. King's Bench or something.'

'Yes, but that didn't take long. I came back.'

'I haven't seen him since dinner last night,' Quentin Selham told Zouche.

'Where might I find Dr Frisby, Masters?' the shipman asked.

'Frideswide Grange would be my guess,' Allard said, sipping his wine and not making eye contact with Congleton.

'But it's hellish late, Zouche,' the lawyer said. 'I doubt they'll let you in.'

None of the Merton men appreciated the arcane skills of William Zouche. He trudged along the High in the pouring rain and saw the two heavies on either side of the door to the Grange, the livery of Merton sodden on their shoulders. It was highly likely that Martin Frisby hadn't seen Chaucer either, but the woman Dalton now – that was a different matter. Zouche kept his head down and didn't look directly at the proctors. High above him, in the black of the wall, candlelight peeped out between the slats of the shutters. He turned the corner and, checking that the coast was clear, shinned up the tracery and onto the roof.

From here, with the leads glossy with rain, Oxford lay dreaming. Smoke from the day's fires still drifted across the silent streets and the low hills to the south were lost in mist. No one at Merton had taken much notice of the rope slung around the shipman's waist, assuming that that was how people from Dartford probably dressed. Zouche unslipped the knots and looped the cord around the nearest gargoyle. He kept the rope taut and swung out to land silently on the nearest windowsill. The room beyond the panes was in darkness, so he tried another. A clerk sat upright in bed, poring over a book. Zouche kicked out and landed on a third sill. He could clearly see the heads of two men in the bed here. To each his own, he thought, and tried again. The fourth room was full of pure gold in the form of an open door and a light burning in the passageway beyond. The bed was empty. This was the one. From nowhere, Zouche's fish-gutter was in his hand, clicking open the casement latch. Then he was inside, prowling like a cat on the boards. The passageway stretched from left to right, candles glowing in their sconces. He counted eight doors, but three he already knew, so he turned left, padding silently past the others.

He had not been in Oxford all that long, but he already knew plenty about Hattie Dalton and her habits. Those habits were best employed a little way away from the common herd, and that meant the room at the far end.

In the room at the far end, Martin Frisby was indulging Hattie Dalton's habits to the full. What with his grunts, her squeals and the creaking of the tester, no one heard the door hiss open or the arrival of a man from Porlock.

'Evening,' Zouche murmured.

Had anyone asked Martin Frisby before that night, he wouldn't have said he could have moved that fast, but there he was, on his feet, on the floor, his nightshirt covering his embarrassment as best it could. Hattie hauled the coverlet over her and then saw the muscles on the shipman and wished she hadn't.

'What the devil …?' The Master of Mathematics was not known for his repartee, especially at moments like this.

'Sorry to bother you, master … mistress. I was looking for a friend.'

'Well, you won't get any sneaking around like that,' Frisby bellowed.

'*Hisht*, Marty,' Hattie quietened him. 'You'll wake the boys.'

'Boys be buggered,' Frisby snarled, although he had lessened the volume.

'Probably,' Zouche said, 'three doors along, unless I miss my guess. Have you seen Master Chaucer?'

'Chaucer?' Frisby was still trying to take all this in. 'No, not for … oh, I don't know; day before yesterday. Explain yourself, knarre.'

Zouche looked at the man levelly. 'No one seems to have seen him for the past day,' he said. He looked at Hattie. 'I wondered if you had.'

'Certainly not,' Frisby snapped.

'Now, now.' Hattie's approach was altogether softer. 'This gentleman is clearly concerned. Master …?'

'Zouche, Mistress,' the shipman said. 'William Zouche.'

'William,' she smiled. 'Sit down.' She patted the bed. 'Let's see what we can do. Thank you, Marty; we'll say goodnight, now.'

'What?' Frisby looked as if he had been poleaxed.

'Tomorrow night, my dear,' she said. 'Oh, no …' she did some private calculation in her head. 'No, that's no good, let's make it … oh, dear, this is awkward. I'll send a note.' She smiled to take the sting out of the words.

A strangled squeak was all that Frisby could manage but he took in the bulk of the shipman and the ugly knife stuffed into his waist

216

belt. He grabbed his houppelande and liripipe and stormed off into the night, slamming the door behind him.

Harriet patted the coverlet again. 'Now … William. How can I help?'

'Geoffrey Chaucer,' the shipman said. He hadn't moved yet.

'His room is two along from here,' she said.

'It's empty,' Zouche told her. 'Cold and unslept in. Is there anywhere else he might spend the night?'

Hattie raised an eyebrow. 'He's a deep one, is your Geoffrey Chaucer,' she said. 'I wouldn't be at all surprised.'

'He was investigating the murder of Brother Anselm of this college,' he told her.

'Ah, yes, what a wretched business. You've talked to the others? Dick and the rest?'

'All except the warden,' Zouche said.

'Don't waste your time. Johnny Bloxham doesn't know what day it is. What about …? No, that's ridiculous.'

'What is?'

'Well, Anselm was a funny old cove. Used to be bosom buddies, if you catch my drift, with his fellow librarian at Balliol, Waldemar of Lucerne.'

'Thank you,' Zouche said, secretly impressed that she could insert a seafaring term on such short notice. Hattie Dalton was indeed a woman of many talents.

'I don't know how you got in here tonight,' she laughed, 'but I'll guarantee you won't find Balliol so easy. Nothing to be gained by rushing off into the night. Leave it until the morning. And take those clothes off; you're soaked through.' She pulled the covers aside and lay there, naked as the day she was born. 'Besides, I was just coming to the boil. Poor old Marty, he tries his best but, well … I suspect his best is nowhere near as good as you on a real off day.'

Zouche smiled, unbuckling his belt. 'Well,' he said, 'never let it be said that I didn't oblige a lady.'

Chapter 14

Geoffrey Chaucer had been told throughout his life, by people from his mother to his wife and many in between, that he had no sense of time. It was certainly very true that he had been known, when mulling a stanza or two, to go a couple of days without noticing their passing. Often, when comptrolling could not be staved off any longer, he would spend what seemed like days brandishing his tally stick– only to discover that only thirty minutes had passed. So he wasn't amazed to find himself, in an apparent blink of an eye, to have gone from having a pleasant cup of something glorious with a librarian to lying on his back in the almost pitch dark, surrounded by the sounds of what could well have been souls in torment.

Chaucer knew that he was not in the best of shape. There were parts of his body he had not seen first-hand in years– although he sometimes caught a glimpse in a darkened windowpane or other shiny surface and quickly looked away. When he went to bed at night, either in his little room above the Aldgate or, more recently, in the opulent goose feather of Hattie Dalton's establishment, with or without human embellishment, he often lay quietly, letting his limbs relax. He was used to the twinge in his left knee and let that joint go slowly, taking it past the point of pain with care and precision. His right elbow gave him gyp in wet weather, so he usually tucked that into his side and let it settle slowly until it was happy.

But tonight – he assumed, from the dark, that it *was* night – none of this seemed to be happening. For a start, if this was a goose feather bed, the maker needed a sharp talking to. It was as hard as iron and dug into his shoulders something awful. His legs were crossed, something he had not willingly done for many years, and he wanted that to not be the case and yet he didn't seem able to do it. His knees were feeling the twist of the unfamiliar position and he became aware of a dull throb at the back of his head where it seemed to be resting on a sharp edge.

Chaucer had been brought up strictly as a child and an old nagging worry began to surface, alongside all his unfamiliar aches and pains. Had he – perish the thought – overdone the wine and perhaps disgraced himself in some way? Fainted, perhaps. Become raucous. Over familiar. He could remember none of these things, but they haunted him all the same and he blushed to himself in the darkness. Whatever it had been, it must have been quite serious for him to end up in this pickle. He was becoming increasingly convinced that he was tied up, at least at the ankles, possibly also at the wrists, which he had worked out were crossed on his chest.

The noises were getting louder and he set his teeth to make sure the sounds were not coming from his own throat. He had sometimes done that, remonstrated with Alice about the noise from downstairs, when in fact it had been him, snoring, keeping the district awake as far as the Tower. But no, this time, it really was someone else. But who? He listened carefully, to see if he could detect a pattern, words. But no – it was just a shapeless ululation, but clearly from many throats and not old throats, either. Chaucer tried to determine whether the voices were getting nearer or simply louder. He couldn't hear any footsteps, but that told him nothing. The owners of the voices could be barefoot, slipper-shod or just very, very careful in their approach. He clenched his fists. Or, at least, he tried to clench his fists but although he couldn't see them in the velvet dark, he knew that his hands hadn't moved. Testing carefully, it seemed the only muscles he could move with any certainty were the ones controlling his eyelids and his lungs. Other than that, he was helpless as a new-born kitten.

He looked down his nose and along the bulge of his torso, cursing the many dinners which impeded his view. There was no doubt, the voices were definitely getting louder because they were nearer. He could almost hear words now, although they stayed on the very cusp of understanding. His mind took on the rhythm, one *two*, three *four*, five *six*. One *two*, three *four*, five … He fought against it, but it brought its own kind of comfort, so he lay back in it, as he would in a warm bath.

The sound stopped suddenly, with the crash of a drum and Chaucer could hear the hiss of his own blood in his ears, taking the same tempo as the chant. One *two*, three *four*, five *six*. One *two*, three *four*, five *six*. That really couldn't be good. Even after one of Hattie Dalton's workouts, it sounded quite normal, if a little fast. This was not right.

'IT'S NOT RIGHT!' Chaucer shouted, but no sound came. A tear ran down the side of his face and into his ear. This was death, he knew it. If death had not already come, leaving him in purgatory.

William Zouche, freed from Hattie Dalton's clutches, decided to take the bold way out and strolled past the two proctors on the door with no preamble. One of them, with a bad squint and an unkempt beard had never been in Hattie's sights and so was rather startled to see the big shipman leaving the house where no one had gone in. The other, not so ill-favoured, expressed no surprise.

'Evening, sir,' he murmured. 'Help you?'

Zouche stopped and turned. He knew it was just something the man had learned to say by rote and hardly heard himself say it half the time, but it was worth a try. 'Yes, you can, as a matter of fact.'

The proctor gave himself a metaphorical slap across the chops; when would he learn not to volunteer before volunteering was required? But he was polite and helpful by nature – another thing which had endeared him to Hattie more than once – and he relaxed his stance a little and prepared to listen.

'Master Chaucer – you know him?'

The proctor nodded. 'Lives here, just temp'ry, like.'

'That's correct. Well, I don't seem to be able to find him.'

The proctor looked askance. He would have put money on this knarre knowing how many beans made five.

'No, he's not there. I've checked.' Zouche didn't meet the man's eye – he didn't need to. 'I have also checked at Merton and he isn't there. In fact, no one has seen him since this morning.'

The proctor balanced first on his toes and then his heels and looked up to the sky, sucking his teeth. 'Well, sir,' he said at last. 'Master Chaucer is of sound mind, I take it?' He asked the question and knew the answer would be yes, but from what he had heard it was by no means a foregone conclusion. The man fought professionals with a quarter-staff and climbed church spires.

'Of course he is,' Zouche snapped. 'He's Comptroller of the King's Woollens and Hides, man!'

'And that means … what, exactly?' the proctor wanted to know.

His almost silent companion, taking no part in the conversation but perceiving that the usual watching stance was being relaxed somewhat, began to pick his nose with single-minded concentration.

'Does that matter?' hissed Zouche. 'He's important and I can't find him. Surely, that's enough, isn't it?'

'*He* might be himportant, ho yes,' the proctor said, falling into his habit of over aspirating when he was getting annoyed. 'But *you* hain't himportant, har you?'

Zouche took two calming breaths through his nose and then decided to punch the man anyway. He drew his fist back and was about to let fly with something from which few men had recovered when the door was flung open and Hattie Dalton stood there, looking like a warship in full sail.

'Is there any reason for fisticuffs on my doorstep?' she asked, looking from one to the other as though she had never clapped eyes on them before.

Zouche swept off his cap and looked contrite. 'This man is being flippant about Master Chaucer being missing,' he muttered.

'Sorry, Mistress Dalton,' the other said. 'I didn't quite understand what this gentleman was after.'

'It's not difficult, Hopestruck,' she said, smartly. 'Go with Master Zouche here and find Master Chaucer. I don't need a guard at my door and I'm sure my boys don't. They are safer here than in any building in the town. And as for you,' she fetched the other proctor a slap upside the head which made him ricochet off the door post, 'if you must indulge in that revolting habit, do it elsewhere. This is a respectable house.'

And with that, she slammed the door.

'Well,' said Hopestruck, 'that's us told.'

'Yes, indeed,' Zouche agreed, tugging his cap back down over his brow.

The second proctor was seeing stars and said nothing.

'I tell you what,' Hopestruck said. 'I know most of the places in Oxford where men go when they don't want to be found. Been hunting down clerks all my adult life. What do you say to me taking you round? Some need special knocks, handshakes and that.'

'That would be very civil, umm …'

'Nathaniel. Nathaniel Hopestruck, You can call me Nat.'

'Thank you, Nat. You may call me Master Zouche. Is your friend all right?'

Hopestruck looked at his colleague and shrugged. 'He usually looks like that,' he said. 'He'll be all right here for the rest of the night, I'm sure.' He tugged on Zouche's sleeve. 'This way,' he said. 'We'll start nearby and work outwards.'

Chaucer held his breath. Something familiar was creeping into his senses, something that made him feel somehow comforted. The cadence of the chant had left him now and he was aware of tiny things, of rustling of mice in close proximity to where he lay, of the settling of the building around him, the wood groaning as it swelled in the teeming rain. Somewhere behind him and to the left, he could hear a drip as water sneaked its way in and fell to the floor, drop by insistent drop. He snuffed in the air, held it in the back of his throat, swallowed it. That smell. What *was* that smell? The knowledge was curled there, in his hindbrain, waiting to tell him its news when it was good and ready. And meanwhile, outside the ill-fitting door, a mass of tormented souls gathered, silently now, waiting to come in and tear him apart with talons of iron before throwing him into the flames of Hell.

* * *

Zouche, had he been asked in the cold light of day, would never have guessed that there were so many dubious hidey-holes in a town the size of Oxford. He was also somewhat surprised to find that a numbskull like Hopestruck could possibly remember the dozens of secret knocks and passwords which he had come up with in the past hour or so. But, amazing feats of memory notwithstanding, Chaucer had not been in any of the places they had visited, be they garrets, basements or rooms hidden in the walls. Zouche was becoming desperate, as well as soaked to the skin.

'Well, Nat,' he said, as the two men sheltered in the lee of a cottage near to the river, more to stop the drumming of rain on their heads than any attempt to keep dry. 'What now? That must be all, surely.'

The proctor sucked his teeth and did his rocking manoeuvre. He didn't look up this time, because no one likes rain in their eyes. 'Well, Master Zouche,' he said finally, 'I think it may be. There used to be one more but … well, the sheriff put paid to it a while ago. It was …' he plumped down on the soles of his feet and spread his hands in embarrassment at the depravity of his town '… depraved, no other word for it.'

'Depraved?' Zouche was surprised at the word and the clear discomfort of the man for just mentioning it. 'In what way?'

'Well, a *depraved* way.' Hopestruck was disappointed. He had taken Zouche for an intelligent sort of knarre.

Zouche had travelled the seven seas and knew depravity came in many shapes and sizes – he had tried quite a few himself and didn't judge. But he could see that perhaps Hopestruck didn't have his experiences, so asked the question again, in a different way. 'Drinking?'

'Nah. Drinking's not depraved.'

'Umm … *congress* of some sort? Animals, perhaps?'

'Eeurgh! No!'

Zouche was beginning to run out of options. Sex and drink covered most of the definitions of depravity, as far as he could tell. There were a lot of scholars in the town, so he tried his last shot. 'If not animals, then … boys?'

'No. But there were scholars there. It was some sort of ritual, we never got to see the details. The sheriff kept it to himself – he's got … he *had* a lad himself and it was all best kept under the carpet.'

'I see.' Zouche could tell that Hopestruck had no more to impart, so he changed tack. 'Where was this, before it was closed down?'

'You're moored on the river, are you?'

'Yes. The *Madeleine*.'

'Then you'll know it. It's the old wool shed, on the other bank from the town. Near derelict now, with the wool trade dead as mutton in Oxford, near as dammit. But you can't miss it.'

Zouche knew the one. He broke into a run, with the proctor keeping up with him with surprising ease. Perhaps it was all that rocking from toe to heel – it kept his knees supple.

Chaucer's hindbrain gave up its secret. *Wool*, that's what he could smell. Years and years of the fats from the fleeces soaking into the walls and floor. They'd had at least one dead bale in here as well, he could tell, that smell of rotting flesh creeping over the fresh smell of meadow and sheep shit. Before he could congratulate himself on his returning memory, the door was flung open and an extraordinary figure was outlined against the light of what seemed like a thousand candles, gathered in the room beyond.

It was tall. That was the first thing Chaucer noticed, it was head and shoulders above the crowded people behind it. And that wasn't counting the horns, which curled above its brow, which was covered in coarse, springing hair which stood in a nimbus against the light. The head was held high, proudly, and slightly at an angle, first one way, then another. Chaucer was reminded of a blackbird eyeing a worm on wet grass on a fine summer's morning. The analogy was strangely comforting, a little bit of normality in a world gone unaccountably mad. But there was an evil about this thing that made him cringe, or try to, because he could still not move a single limb, not even to twitch a finger.

Another smell now overwhelmed the comfort of the wool– acrid, acid, like the ashes of an old bonfire left out in the rain. As the creature moved its head, the smell came in waves, making the bile rise in the comptroller's throat. The murmuring crowd was becoming restive, waving their candles above their heads, adding another nauseous layer to the smells which now were filling Chaucer's world. As far as he could tell, the candles were black and dripping, the smoke thick and heavy. He closed his eyes, but not knowing what was happening was worse and he let them spring open again.

In those few seconds, the goat-headed creature had moved nearer, slyly, slimily, and stood over him, his arms outstretched so that all Chaucer could now see was a black shape like an enormous preying bird, with rays of light thrown from the monstrous mockery of a crown of thorns slung between the horns. The thing leaned closer and from deep inside its throat, it began to laugh, a laugh that had its beginnings at the mouth of Hell.

Behind the creature, the invisible crowd were beginning to chant again, starting at a whisper, getting louder and louder by infinitesimal degrees. Soon, though, the maniac laughter and the chant filled the comptroller's ears and he closed his eyes against the terror.

'Ne-*ca*,' the crowd cried. 'Ne-*ca*. Ne-*ca*.'

And the poet translated the Latin in the only way he could. 'Kill *him*. Kill *him*. Kill *him*.'

Zouche and the proctor ran through the streets running with rain, keeping their feet with difficulty. When they reached the river, they could tell at once that they had found the right place. The old wool shed loomed blacker against the black sky, with faint beams of light showing through the broken wattle and daub and the sliding tiles. For a derelict building, it was showing rather overt signs of life. Zouche extended an arm and both men slithered to a halt.

'The lights,' Zouche said. 'Did they show lights before, before they were closed down?'

'I dunno,' Hopestruck said. 'I was off that night.'

'So, let me get this right, you don't know anything about the goings-on in the wool shed? Because you were off that night.'

'Nah. Yeah.' Hopestruck was having difficulty choosing which question to answer.

'So apart from the depravity, you have no idea what we're going to find in there?'

Hopestruck grabbed at the opportunity. 'Well, Master Chaucer, hopefully,' he said. 'But apart from that, no. No idea.'

'Are you armed?' Zouche asked the question more in hope than anything else.

'A 'course.' The proctor whipped out a club from somewhere and Zouche gave him full marks for his concealment skills. This was followed by a couple of wicked-looking blades and a small axe.

'Well, I need to just stop at the *Madeleine* to stock up,' Zouche said, impressed by the mini-armoury with which Hopestruck now positively bristled. He decided on just one club and one blade – used properly, they would be enough. 'Do you know the ways into the wool shed?'

'Now, that I do,' Hopestruck said proudly. 'On a fall evening when it's starting to cool, there was warm lying in the old wool shed, back in the day. With a nice soft armful and an unrolled fleece, you could …'

'I'm sure you could,' Zouche stopped him before he could give details it would be hard to forget later. 'Where is it?'

'Round the back from the river, there's a little wicket, saves opening the big doors. It lets you straight into the big room, where they rolled and graded the wool. There's a wool press in there as well, like a table with rails at either end. I think that got left when the merchants stopped using it. Too big to move and not much use to anybody. Stinks of wool, for a start, and oily as anything. You couldn't get a purchase …'

But Zouche wasn't listening. With his club in his hand and his blade up his sleeve, he was off at a loping run. Hopestruck ran down Memory Lane and caught him up and soon, the two big men were listening intently at the wicket gate of the old wool shed.

'What's that they're saying?' Hopestruck whispered in the shipman's ear.

'I don't know,' he breathed back. 'It's Latin, but not from the church. *Sshh*.'

From the shed, the words came above the hiss of the rain. 'Ho*la*, No*a*, Mas*sa*,' over and over, and then, suddenly and much louder, 'Ne*CA*!'

'It sounds like gibberish to me,' Zouche said, louder now he realised that nothing from outside would be heard above that cacophony. 'I've heard a lot of rituals in a lot of countries and to me, that just sounds like something to get a crowd riled up. What do you reckon as to numbers?'

Hopestruck cocked his head. 'Hard to say. A dozen? Twenty? Can't be more.'

'I agree. Are you ready to take on ten, perhaps more?'

Hopestruck smiled and nodded, rain streaming down his face, and hefted his club.

Zouche nodded. The man was an idiot, but he was a big idiot and could obviously handle weapons. It was going to be all right. He could feel it in his bones.

Chaucer had decided that he wasn't actually in Hell, or even Purgatory, Hell's waiting room. He was somewhere all too earthly, that smelled of wool and old clothes, mouse urine and cat shit. He was faced with a man, albeit one in the last stages of insanity and dressed as a goat. He was proud of himself for being able to think logically against the insistent chanting of gibberish laced with threats. He could feel the hard wood at his back, with rails under his head and feet. He was lying on a wool press, in a wool shed. Where there was wool, there was sanity. With all his might, he lifted his legs, bound at the ankles as they were, and kicked the goat-headed madman right where it hurt the most. He felt the squelch and heard the groan and rolled sideways as the great horned head plummeted down towards his face.

'On three,' Zouche said, bracing himself for the impact with the wicket. 'Three!'

The two big men hurtled through the gate which buckled under their weight like parchment and found themselves at the back of a crowd of candle-waving … children? They looked at each other. Could this be right? There wasn't a soul in the place even up to their shoulders, and the faces turned to them in panic had never seen a razor. Some were still round with puppy-fat and spots were well-represented.

Hopestruck recognised a few. 'These are Trivium scholars,' he said. 'From …' he cast his eye across the crowd, 'Balliol, unless I miss my guess.'

One round-eyed child, a little more collected than the rest, stepped forward. 'It's just in jest, Master Hopestruck,' he said, blowing out his candle. 'We wouldn't hurt anyone.'

'*Jest*?' Zouche was astounded. How on Earth could this be a jest? 'Where is the jest in this? A wild, wet night, candles made of …' he sniffed. 'God alone knows what. Have you got women in here?' His knowledge of adolescent boys was scant, but he had an idea that that was usually the case.

'Women?' The lad was aghast. 'No, no women here. Just us and Brother Waldemar.'

'The librarian?' Hopestruck was becoming more confused by the minute. 'Where is he?'

'Over there.' The lad pointed. 'Oh … well, he *was* over there. I don't seem to see him now. Oh, no, look, there he is. He seems to have fallen into the wool press, somehow.'

Sepulchral groans reached the men now and the goat-headed monster lurched half-upright, clutching himself in the time-honoured fashion of all men who have been kicked soundly in the balls.

The other boys were backing away from the apparition which now emerged from the main room. It hopped ungainly on bound feet, its arms tied across its breast. Its houppelande was soiled and wet, hooked up somehow and half tucked into its hose, which were holed and filthy. It only had one shoe. It was also in a temper.

'Is that you, Will?' it said, closing one eye in an attempt to focus. 'Don't let these little bastards go, and certainly not this idiot in the goat costume. They were trying to kill me.' And with that, he keeled over and lay prone at the feet of the groaning goat.

The boys clamoured around Zouche and Hopestruck. Their spokesman clutched the shipman's arm. 'No, sir, no. It was a jest. Brother Waldemar asked us to come here one last time, to invoke the Devil and to frighten Master Chaucer. He said it was …' He turned his head and looked at the comptroller, in a dead faint on the floor. He sobbed and looked at Zouche and Hopestruck with tears in his eyes. 'He said it was a jest.' His voice broke and he was just a child again. 'I am in trouble, am I not, Master Hopestruck?'

The proctor was not an unkind man, but he was always truthful. 'You are indeed, my lad. You are indeed. But at least you're in good company.' He lifted his head and raised his voice. 'You, you all know me, so don't try and weasel out of this. I want you to form a line and follow me; we are going to knock up your warden at this ungodly hour and report this to him. Master Zouche here is going to take …' he shook his head, it was still almost unbelievable 'Brother Waldemar here to …' He turned to the shipman. 'Where *are* you taking him, Master Zouche?'

'I need to deal with Master Chaucer here first,' Zouche said. 'He needs the help of a doctor of physic and quickly. This one,' he tossed a laconic head at Waldemar of Lucerne, who was leaning on the wool press, breathing hard, 'won't suffer over much if I tie him up in here for a while. I might remember to tell someone before he dies of hunger and thirst, I might not.'

The librarian hauled off the goat's head and threw it aside. 'It was just …' he said, still gasping for breath, 'a jest.'

'Hmm,' Zouche said, untying Chaucer with hands adept at knots and using the rope to retie the librarian. 'So is this.'

Chaucer was no lightweight, but even so the shipman lifted him with ease, pulling an arm around his shoulders. The comptroller was starting to make small whimpering noises in the back of his throat, which Zouche chose to take as a good sign. They left the wool shed at the rear of a phalanx of sobbing boys, shepherded by Hopestruck, who turned to say a last word to Zouche.

'A good night's work, Master Zouche,' he said, looking anxiously at Chaucer's face, which was slack and rather grey.

'A good night's work indeed, Nat,' Zouche said. 'And you can call me Will.'

Chapter 15

Chaucer spent the next day recovering. To him, time was still a little uncertain, but everyone told him it was the next day and who was he to argue? His experiences with powder forte were as nothing to this and he jumped at shadows. Some of his extremities still took a while to work out what he wanted them to do and he spent minutes at a time staring at his thumb, just waiting for it to twitch slightly; although things were improving, that improvement was slow. He had declined Roger Allard's offer of some slithery, ghastly poultice and certainly wasn't up to anything served in Merton's buttery. In the end, it was only Hattie Dalton's dumplings that did the trick, washed down with nothing more threatening than water from the Cherwell.

And another uneventful Oxford day had gone by before Ralph Strode visited the victim in his room at Frideswide Grange. William Zouche had proved to be a treasure and intended to sleep, like a Mohammedan guard, across the entrance to the comptroller's room all night. The shipman and his trusty club would deter anybody.

'We were very worried about you, Geoffrey,' Strode sat himself down in the chair beside the bed. 'How are you feeling now?'

Chaucer narrowed his eyes. 'That depends on how many of you there are,' he said. When he had woken up after his midnight rescue, he had found that his eyes worked as and when they fancied it, but Allard had breezily told him that was entirely normal.

'Spoken like a true sacrifice,' Strode smiled.

'What the hell was in that drink?' Chaucer assumed it had been the drink, which was a shame, because it had been truly delicious.

'Allard isn't sure. He is trying to decide between the nut of a tree only found growing on the eastern slopes of Mount Olympus and a root found in the foundations of a temple in the foothills above Constantinople.'

'In other words…?'

'He has absolutely no idea. Who would have thought that a harmless little librarian would have been a magus in league with the horned one?'

'Was he?'

Strode spread his arms wide. 'That depends on your view of the Netherworld,' he said. 'I am a logician, Geoffrey, trained to trust my senses to pursue the rational. Men like Waldemar, well, there are three possibilities. He is either a servant of the devil, up to his tonsure in diabolus, in which case we'll probably burn him. Or he's just a failed miracle play actor who likes to dress up.'

'Or?'

'Or?'

'You said there were three possibilities.'

Strode laughed. 'Just checking you were back with us,' he said. 'Or, he's a Lollard and I've got my man, the heart of the conspiracy. I, personally, bend to that.'

'On what grounds?'

'Red hot pincers,' Strode said, a slightly mad gleam in his eye, 'a great – and much underrated – persuader of men, in my opinion.

That's why I'm late. I intended to be here an hour ago, but once he saw the pincers, old Waldy sang like a troubadour. They've got a whole range of persuaders up at the castle.'

'He only *saw* the pincers?'

'Oh, Lord, yes. I'm a civilised man, Geoffrey and this *is* Oxford, not some appalling German hell-hole. I even went to the lengths,' he held up the singed edge of his houppelande, 'of proving how hot the iron was without going to the trouble of pressing against his cheek. I doubt that the Inquisition will be so obliging.'

'He'll have to face them, too?' Chaucer asked. 'He didn't seem … I don't know how to put it. He didn't seem to really have his heart in it, somehow. Will tells me that all he had around him for acolytes were some boys.'

'Doesn't that make it worse?' Strode asked, reasonably.

'Of course. I have the Archbishop's writ in my rooms at Tackley's. And you don't mess with William Courtney. They'll take him to Rome, I shouldn't wonder; make an example of him. Oh, there might come a day when all men will think like Waldemar. But for now, well, the rule of law must be upheld.'

'Speaking of which,' Chaucer sat upright, with some effort and to his own surprise, 'does all this mumbo-jumbo have any bearing on John Wyclif's case; Dick Congleton's job?'

'If they can prove a link between Waldemar and Wyclif, yes. It's in the bag from the prosecution's point of view; Dick might as well not turn up.'

'I don't envy him,' the comptroller nodded carefully. 'When Waldemar was singing, what did he actually confess to?'

Strode frowned. 'I assume you mean "to what did he actually confess", Geoffrey?'

'Sorry,' the comptroller said. 'I haven't been well.'

'I'll let it go this once,' Strode said, smiling. 'Waldemar had to admit that he regularly presided over Esbats with various clerks, Sabbats on certain appointed nights – never on college property, of course; it would draw too much attention. He didn't always involve the same boys, either. He weeded out the ones who were just there hoping for drink and loose women; which was most of them, I imagine. But he was growing quite a band of proper adherents and they are being rooted out. The boys who were there last night hadn't been before; I think he was thinking on his feet when you fell into his clutches and so he had to put up with what he had to hand.'

'How many boys were involved?'

'On any one night, thirteen, traditionally, in mockery of the Lord and his disciples. There had been a raid a while ago, so the proctors tell me, and some of the boys were sent home, so he was building his coven almost from the beginning.'

'And Waldemar was the Lord?' Chaucer checked.

'Complete with goat's head and fiery brands. Well, candles – as I say, he had to work with what he had. But I'm not interested in all that tomfoolery. The man scorns the actual Mass, kissing the devil's arse and so on, which of course is linked with his other pastime.'

'Sodomy?'

'The same,' Strode nodded. 'He also challenges the celibacy of priests, and the saying of prayers for the dead. He believes – and this really is too laughable for words – that all men are created equal.'

He and Chaucer guffawed.

'I have every reason to believe,' Strode was suddenly serious, 'that this thinking will spread unless it is stopped. Most Lollards seem to be of the peasant persuasion, like those unwashed idiots last year, but if it takes hold in the universities, God help us.' The logician stood up and looked down at Chaucer, taking his hand in his. 'Are you going to be all right, Geoffrey?' he asked.

'I will be all right,' Chaucer said. 'I've been through worse and lived to tell the tale.'

Strode looked at him for a moment, then nodded and let go of his hand. 'Then I'll take my leave. I have to report to Canterbury. My work here is done.'

Chaucer smiled. 'I'm happy for you, Ralph,' he said. 'I wish mine was. I still have a murderer to catch.'

The next day, the comptroller was well enough to walk along the High, albeit slowly. Marriot, Mayor Treddler's man from the Safety Commission, smiled at him, which reminded Chaucer of the silver plate on a coffin. The rain of the past days had well and truly gone and Oxford basked in a mellow sunshine, gilding the awnings of the market stalls and dappling in the sheltering arms of the birches.

Grandpont was busy as usual, with boats of all sizes, skiffs and wherries flitting about with the rattle of rowlocks and the stiffening of canvas. The *Madeleine* rocked gently under her trailing willows and William Zouche was sitting amidships quaffing ale. He had left the comptroller to his breakfast, during which Warden Bloxham had whispered in Chaucer's ear (the meal supposedly to be taken in silence) that he had a vacancy for a librarian and was he interested? The comptroller's reply had not been recorded.

Zouche handed a cup to the comptroller. 'There's something in the wind, Geoffrey,' he said.

Chaucer wobbled onto the boat and took the cup. The sky hadn't a cloud in it. 'Really?' he asked. 'More rain, do you think?' These seafaring men knew all there was to know about the weather, not like landlubbers like him.

Zouche was shaking his head. 'It's not the weather,' he said. 'It's the people. There's a mood – I can't put my finger on it, but I've seen it at sea; twice now.'

'What is it?' Chaucer eased himself down. He still ached all over. 'What does it signify?'

'A mutiny,' Zouche said. 'The twice I've seen it at sea, mutinies followed. And on board ship, Geoffrey, that's a serious thing. Men are confined, cramped in their quarters. Their world is forty feet long and fifteen feet wide. And all around it is the ocean. When even the seabirds are silent and there's no wind, you can hear men's hearts beat, hear their thoughts even. I'm getting that feeling now.'

'Hmm.' Chaucer looked across to the busy town, unaware in its everyday bustle. 'You may very well be right, Will,' he said.

Impending mutiny or not, life on board the *Madeleine* had to go on. Zouche rummaged in his secret hidey-hole while Chaucer politely averted his eyes, and pulled out the astrolabe. He carefully unwrapped the sacking and started to polish the ornate brass.

It was then that a thought occurred to Geoffrey Chaucer. 'How much would you say, Will,' he asked, 'that thing is worth?'

'All the riches of Arabia,' the shipman said, 'if you're becalmed in a watery world with no horizon.'

'But here,' Chaucer said, 'on the Thames just south of Oxford. What price?'

Zouche laughed. 'Do you want to buy it, Geoff?' he asked.

'Not exactly,' Chaucer said. 'More of a borrow. But if it should be damaged?'

'Five nobles,' Zouche announced and Chaucer nearly swallowed his tongue.

'Shall we say three?'

'I won't haggle with a friend,' the shipman said. 'Call it four and it's a deal.' And they shook hands.

Chaucer took the astrolabe and traced the arcane symbols with his fingers.

'I always say …' Zouche began, but he never finished his sentence. The comptroller brought the astrolabe crashing down on the *Madeleine's* deck, the rim biting into the oak, sending the splinters flying. Then he did it again. And again.

'Mother of God!' Zouche restrained him. Clearly, all that the man had been through had unhinged his mind.

'There,' Chaucer smiled. 'No harm done, I don't think. The astrolabe's in fine fettle and a few minutes' work with a chisel will neaten up the *Madeleine.*'

'What …?' Zouche was still lost for words.

'That's just oak, will,' Chaucer said, quietly. 'It can be fixed. But somebody's head? Think back. Where have you seen these parallel cuts before? Hal Golightly. Alfred Herbert. Brother Anselm. This,' he held the astrolabe up, 'or one just like it, is what killed them all.'

He looked into the shipman's face and smiled, 'and if I didn't know you better, I'd have to ask you where you were on the nights in question.'

'There's something brewing, Jack; I'd stake my life on it.'

Jack Treddler sat in his solar in the Guild Hall. It was that time of year again – the spring tax returns – guaranteed to give him the mother of all headaches. He had never really wanted to be mayor, least of all of Oxford. Why not a nice non-university town, like Wisbech or Coventry? The colleges had their own systems, of course, but he had to collect ground rent for them all and they were always difficult about it.

'Brewing, Marriot?' the mayor repeated. 'What are you talking about?'

'The colleges, specifically Merton and Balliol. They're squaring up to each other.'

'Again? What's that got to do with us?'

'Nothing, if they kept their shenanigans confined to their property, but it'll spill out into the streets and then it *is* our problem. And I saw that knarre Chaucer this morning. He smiled at me. *Smiled*. Like I don't know he thinks of us as the shit on his cordovans. He's up to something as well, that's for sure.'

'I hope he's up to finding whoever killed the sheriff's little boy,' Treddler sighed. 'That's what I told his lordship he was doing and he's going to come back expecting results any day now; you'll see.'

''Ere,' Marriot slumped into a chair alongside a pile of documents. 'Did you hear about the latest one? That librarian knarre at Balliol?'

'The devil worshipper?' Treddler nodded, grateful for the chance to put down his quill. 'Yes, yes I did. Course, it didn't surprise me at all.'

'It didn't?' Marriot didn't know his boss was so perceptive.

'Stands to reason, doesn't it? Can you read, Marriot?'

'Yes.' The man stood on his dignity. 'Well, no, not the long words.'

'I only read law reports and tax material because I have to – and, as you know, the prior of St Frideswide translates the Latin for me. But *those* people,' he jabbed the air with a malevolent finger, 'those university knarres read *for pleasure*. Can you imagine that?'

'It's not healthy,' Marriot knew.

'So, it leads them into dark ways. They say that when they caught that Waldemar knarre, he had three sheep in bed with him. Not one, mark you – *three*!'

'Disgusting.' Marriot shook his head. ''Ere, you don't think this is what those murders are all about, do you? The Black Arts?'

'How d'you mean?'

'Well,' Marriot dropped his voice lest the Guild Hall walls had ears, 'he needs victims, don't he? The horned one? Needs sacrifices.'

'True.' Treddler pondered the quandary. 'But that's virgins, isn't it? Young nubile things on the threshold of womanhood.'

'S'pose so. Mind you,' a sudden thought occurred to Marriot and he burst out laughing, 'you won't find many of *them* in Oxford!'

Treddler laughed so hard he spilled his ink. That Marriot, he had a way with words. Even if they were only the short ones.

The Black Arts. Was that what all this was about? Geoffrey Chaucer needed a little reflection that night, but the man he would have bounced his ideas off, Ralph Strode, the companion of a mile, had left Oxford by the last town carriage. So Chaucer's thoughts merely bounced off the walls in his room at Frideswide Grange. He knew that Zouche lay outside his door and he was glad of that. Who would have thought that a shipman picked up by chance could become a saviour and a guardian angel all in one? Even so, it was not fair to inflict still further worries on the man; Chaucer had already dented the rim of his astrolabe and cut grooves in his boat.

Time and time again, their faces swam into Chaucer's vision. Hal Golightly, youngest member of the Brembre clan, a light-fingered ingenue who stole books. That hadn't surprised Chaucer much – Nicholas Brembre had been routinely stealing other people's property all his adult life. On the other hand, the only one to accuse Golightly was Anselm the librarian, a man who had friends of a certain disposition. Had young Golightly been a target of Anselm and had he rebuffed him? Did the librarian kill the boy as an act of revenge or perhaps to shut him up? Then there was the hapless Alfred Herbert, a drunk and a penitent, an odd weak offspring for the High Sheriff of the county. The lad seemed to have been genuinely affected by Golightly's death. And he was afraid of somebody – or rather, somebodies – the calculators. Was the boy just rambling nonsense in his cups, on the night when Chaucer had put him to bed? Then there was the most perplexing of all – Anselm, the waspish librarian who despised the Quadrivium. Had they all turned down his advances? Why had he and Waldemar quarrelled, gone from lovers to sworn enemies in the blink of an eye? Had Waldemar, the black magus, killed Anselm? And, like the others, done it with an astrolabe? And why an astrolabe? What was wrong with a knife, a sword, an axe? Who kills with a scientific navigational instrument? Above all, there was the business with the cloaks. Chaucer had made his enquiries as if Anselm was the intended target; but what if it was Martin Frisby, whose cloak he had been wearing that night? One thing was certain. There would be no more opportunities to question Waldemar of Lucerne; he was under lock and key in Oxford castle, bound for the Vatican and the fire; Frisby, on the other hand, at least for the moment, was still very much alive. When this forever night had passed, the comptroller would go and see him.

'I don't think I care for your tone, Master Cross.' Martin Frisby had been ambushed, if that wasn't too strong a word, by a sizeable rabble of the Quadrivium of Merton and he was not best pleased.

'Dr Frisby,' the clerk said, standing four-square at the head of a little army, 'we are concerned that whatever is going on at Balliol is having an effect on us.'

'How so?' The Master of Mathematics wanted to know.

'Now it has been proven beyond all doubt that certain scholars of Balliol and their librarian have been indulging in devil worship …'

'That's just hearsay,' Frisby insisted.

'Indeed,' Cross came back at him, 'but the man we all heard say it is Geoffrey Chaucer, court poet and Comptroller of the King's Woollens.'

'And Hides,' Fingle felt it only right to add.

'I got the distinct impression that you weren't too impressed by Master Chaucer, Cross.'

'My personal feelings don't come into this,' the clerk said. 'That wretched business with the hanged effigy, for which *our* lads were beaten, was clearly the work of Waldemar and his minions. They're Lollards, Doctor, and Balliol is crawling with them.'

'I don't see what we can do,' Frisby said.

'We can go to the warden and demand an official apology from Balliol, from their warden to the lowest kitchen scullion. If we don't get that, then Merton men cannot be held responsible for what may follow.'

'Was that a threat, Frisby?' John Bloxham was being helped into his gown for the morning's lecture.

'I asked Cross that, Warden,' Frisby said, 'and he replied it was a promise. Bit of a cliché, I thought, but he meant it.'

Bloxham burbled to himself, 'I don't like the sound of this. It'll be St Scholastica's Day all over again. Blood. Teeth. All manner of unpleasantness. Get over to Warden Muncaster; arrange a meeting between us. If two erudite wardens of our respective colleges can't iron this out, I'm a witch's tit.'

It had to be said that Martin Frisby was feeling a little apprehensive that night. He had been hurt that his light o' love was so keen to kick him out of her bed *in flagrante* and possibly to replace him with a mere boatman. Surely, Hattie knew that he was a scholar *par excellence*, holding the chair of Mathematics at the oldest college in Oxford. Generations of young bloods, many of them now senior churchmen, lawyers, knights of the shire, had passed through his steady hands on their way to greatness. All right, he was a mathematician, but he appreciated the finer things in life. He played the lute for Hattie and read her poems in Greek. His *agape mou*, spoken with his soft West Country burr was guaranteed to buckle the knees and melt the heart of the most ardent nun in Christendom.

Then there was that wretched business with the Quadrivium and that arrogant shit Cross. All that posturing and pretence. Didn't they know that they were just children alongside him? Nobody understood Boethius and Pythagoras like Martin Frisby; no one could interpret Euclid with such clarity.

But what worried Frisby most, like a louse in a hair shirt irritating his skin, was the fact that Anselm might have died because of that stupid mistake over the cloak; that *he*, not the librarian, was the target of a madman.

He had taken to looking at everybody, far longer than usual. Was that a murderous cast in Quentin Selham's one good eye? The cup that John Bloxham had passed him at breakfast – was it dripping with poison? And what about that oaf from the kitchen who had dropped that pitcher? It could have broken his foot. Gangrene could have set in and he could have died horribly and slowly, the most cunning murder attempt of them all. Then, there were the outsiders. The riffraff of the town he'd known for years— not by name, of course, but by appearance and reputation. They all hated him; not the university, not Merton College, *him*, Martin Monachorum Frisby.

And so, he was watching his back as he made his way to Frideswide Grange that night. So much so that he wasn't looking where he was going. He half turned in time to see a figure, black and silent, focussed before he felt the most shuddering shock to his head and saw flashing lights. He didn't see the cobbles come up to meet him, didn't feel the pain as his knees hit the stone. Something warm and sticky was trickling down from his head. It stung his eyes and blocked his nose. He could taste its salt on his lips.

'Hoo!' a voice called, but Frisby didn't hear it. 'Who goes there?'

He knew he was on his hands and knees, looking bemusedly at two pairs of feet. One had cordovans, velvet, well-stitched; the other had wooden clogs with iron studs.

'Who are you?' Frisby heard a familiar voice ask.

'Tom. Nightwatch.' That was the man with the clogs. 'You?'

'Congleton. Merton College. Martin? Martin, can you hear me?'

Frisby felt himself being turned over to lie on his back. 'Dick,' he thought he said.

'It's all right,' Congleton was cradling the man's head. 'You'll be all right. You've taken a blow to the head.' He turned on the nightwatchman. 'One of *your* lot, I presume.'

'Presume what you like, mate,' Tom scowled. 'I didn't see nobody.'

'Neither did I,' Congleton said. 'Here, help me get him up. This man needs a doctor. His home's not far.' Together, they hauled the staggering man upright, supporting him between them. 'How many fingers am I holding up, Martin?'

'Fingers?' The Master of Mathematics couldn't see any. That worried him on a very distant level – surely, he was usually quite good with numbers.

'All right, I'll take it from here, Watchman,' Congleton said, taking most of Frisby's weight.

'I can't do that, sir,' Tom said. 'The mayor'll have my guts for garters. I've got to see him to his quarters.'

'Very well, but handle him carefully, man. Merton College can't afford to lose a man like him.'

The three of them huddled around the candles in Allard's rooms as the first glimmer of dawn lent its glow to ogee arches and crenelations across the still-sleeping town.

'I'd say you saved Martin's life, Dick.' Allard was pounding something evil-smelling in a mortar on the table. He caught Chaucer's eye. 'I know you don't care for this stuff, Geoffrey, but, trust me, it's a life-saver, rather like Dick here.' The doctor laughed, pleased at his bon mot.

'Come on, Roger,' Congleton said. 'I just happened to be in the right place at the right time.' He looked at Chaucer. 'My weekly visit to Harriet. Oh, I know, she hardly needs my protection, but I promised our father on his deathbed.'

'And you didn't see anybody?'

'Not a soul. Not until the watchman turned up. We got to Martin together.'

'Did he see anything?' Allard asked.

'No,' Chaucer told him. 'I asked him earlier. He was having trouble with his lanthorn, so he wasn't looking up. He may have heard the padding of feet, but he wasn't sure.'

'Couldn't be robbery, could it?' Allard asked. 'I mean, university men are not the best paid in the world – hence my private practice and Dick's – but, by comparison with the hoi polloi of the town …'

'I've said it before and I'll say it again,' Congleton leaned back in his chair, 'this is a college thing. Roger, what did you make of Martin's head wounds?'

'Metal object,' the doctor said. 'Not particularly sharp.'

'Just like Hal Golightly, Alfred Herbert and Brother Anselm,' Chaucer said.

'Oh, I couldn't be as positive as that,' Allard said.

'Come on, Roger,' Congleton was exasperated. 'If you gave me that sitting on the fence tripe in court, I'd crucify you. *Of course* the wounds are the same. And they were all delivered by a Balliol man; I'll stake my reputation on it.'

It was, of course, William Zouche who saw it first, a single boat winding its way along the Cherwell, carried by the run of the river. One oar trailed in the water, the other only God knew where.

'Geoffrey,' Zouche was standing at the prow of the *Madeleine*, checking the banks on either side. 'Trouble.'

Chaucer was fiddling with the astrolabe, trying to make sense of it all. He saw what Zouche had seen, a hand half-raised in the hull, a foot sticking out at a rakish angle. 'What in God's name …?'

As the boat swept past, Zouche leaned out with his boathook, grappled the edge of the boat and pulled it alongside the *Madeleine*. Someone was lying inside, groaning, his face a mass of blood, his knuckles bruised.

'Help me get him aboard, Geoff.' Zouche was hauling the oarsman across and the two of them struggled with the almost dead weight.

'Good God, I know this boy!' Chaucer was cleaning the face of blood.

Zouche slapped the lad across the face, which the comptroller thought was overdoing things, and the boy came to, his eyes rolling, his mouth gasping for air. For a moment, he struggled, fists clenched and teeth bared.

'It's all right, Antonio,' Chaucer said softly. 'You're among friends, you're safe now.'

The Italian calmed down once he recognised a familiar face. 'Signor Chaucer,' he gasped. 'Thank God. Thank God.'

'What happened to you, man?' the comptroller asked. The lad's shirt was all but shredded and his Balliol device had been ripped from his sleeve.

'I met a little trouble,' the clerk said. 'The Quadrivium from Merton.'

'Neville Cross!' Zouche spat in the river.

'They've been planning for days, trading insults with Balliol men. I was just unlucky to be alone. All I wanted to do was to row my boat gently down the stream.'

A deep groaning bell shattered the moment. Da Silva was struggling upright. 'That's Great Tom,' he said, 'from the Abbey at Osney. There's a riot in the town.'

'Great Tom,' Jack Treddler muttered. 'Oh, shit. Marriot, get your Safety Commission boys out on the street. I don't care about personal injury to bystanders, but property, that's paramount. Don't let those university bastards touch a stone.' The mayor was muttering to himself now, buckling on his sword. 'Now, of all times,' he said. 'It would be election year, wouldn't it?'

'Great Tom?' Warden Bloxham was in the middle of his afternoon nap. 'It's not the French, is it? Couldn't be the French, surely? We'd have heard something.'

'What you can hear, Warden,' Quentin Selham snapped, striding through the old man's apartments, 'is all Hell breaking loose. Our boys and Balliol's. The only question is where the battle will break out – Broad Street or the High.'

'I've been here before.' Bloxham was peering out of the casement into Mob Quad. He thought it had all gone rather quiet. That was because the builders had gone, snatching up their tools and scattering to their homes. A kind of peace had come to Oxford; the lull before the storm.

'Sorry, Hattie.' Van der Gelder was dragging himself out of bed in Frideswide Grange, pushing the woman aside as best he could and fumbling for his hose. 'That's Great Tom. The boys'll need me,'

On the *Madeleine*, Antonio da Silva was trying to pretend that all was well, that his arm wasn't broken, and he didn't have a lip the size of the castle keep. 'I must get to them,' he was mumbling through the swelling. 'Balliol cannot survive without the Italian School.'

'That's as may be, son.' Zouche held him down. 'But you're going nowhere with an arm like that. Now, just hold still while I …'

Nobody was ready for what happened next. There was a sound that none of them had heard before, a boom from the south that was not a boom, a wind that came from nowhere. Zouche turned to see the trees along the Thames flutter their leaves and he saw the bore hurtling towards him, a solid wave of water, furious and foaming, making straight for the *Madeleine*.

'Hold on, Geoff!' he shouted, but the warning came too late and the wave hit the boat squarely in the stern, lifting it, dropping the bow and slamming her sideways. It ploughed on under the keep, to crash into Grandpont and overturn a skiff on the far bank. A fisherman on the jetty got his line tangled with it all and was yanked from his seat, hurtling with a shout and a splash into the water. When Chaucer's head cleared, he was lying alongside da Silva, who was groaning and holding his arm.

'Will,' the comptroller said in the unearthly silence which followed. 'What in the name of all that's holy was that?'

The shipman shook himself. 'Could be the mouth of Hell opening,' he grunted. He could see from Chaucer's face that the comptroller wasn't going along with that. 'Or – and this is less likely in the scheme of things, there's an earthquake somewhere down river.' He shook himself again. 'No, that's nonsense. Forget I spoke. I'm going with the mouth of Hell.'

'I think we all are,' Chaucer said. 'Look after the lad, will you, Will? I've got a fight to break up.'

'You, Geoff?' Zouche blinked at him.

'I know at least one of the leaders,' the comptroller said, 'and he beat me once in debate and then again with a quarter-staff. He owes me a rematch.'

Zouche laughed. 'All right,' he said, rummaging for his club beneath his seat, 'I'll leave the debating to you. *If* you leave the quarter-staffing to me.'

The pair shook hands. 'It's a deal,' Chaucer said.

'You,' Zouche pointed his club at the Italian, still groaning on the deck, 'stay there. If you don't, I'll break your other arm.' And, at that moment, that sounded like good advice to Antonio da Silva.

For the briefest of moments, Chaucer felt himself lost in time. A year ago, almost to the day, he had sat his grey alongside his king facing the expanse of Smithfield. Ahead of them had stood the peasant army of Wat Tyler, armed with their stolen weapons and flying their false flags. Now, he was here again, on foot this time and in place of the Lord's anointed, a rough shipman with a club, standing like Hercules.

On the flat stretch of meadow, shin-high with spring grass, two armies faced each other. To Chaucer's left, in front of the town walls, the men of Merton, the college device fluttering from makeshift banners. To his right, above the Cherwell, the equally motley rabble of Balliol. What struck Zouche most about this sight was the eerie silence. He had never seen anything like it.

'What do we do now, Geoff?' he hissed in Chaucer's ear. There were a few townsmen dotted on the meadow's fringes, some against the town walls, others along the riverbank. Some of these, Chaucer realised, wore the livery of Oxford. He even saw Jack Treddler briefly, hedged round as he was by heavily armed men. He noticed that the mayor had a convenient avenue of escape at his back, should the need arise.

'We wait for our moment,' the comptroller said.

'You've seen this before?' Zouche was incredulous. Neither army was really an army. No one was over twenty-two and the weapons cradled in folded arms or dangling from belts were home-made, chair legs and cooking utensils lifted from the butteries of their respective colleges.

'Sort of,' Chaucer nodded.

The front ranks of both sides were beginning to creep forward, the wings curving in. There were shouts, insults, scholars spitting into the grass. Here and there, a clerk would turn his back, lower his breeches and waggle his arse at the opposition.

'Not just now, thank you,' Chaucer shouted. This was his moment. 'But thanks for the offer.' He sauntered out into the ground between the armies as though he were shopping in Eastcheap. The armies looked at him in amazement and the sound which had begun to build died away to a few mutters.

'Master Cross.' The comptroller beckoned to the man. 'Do you speak for Merton?'

'I do,' Cross said, and with Fingle, Latimer and Temple at his elbow, marched forward.

'Who speaks for Balliol?' Chaucer asked.

'I do,' a voice called and a large clerk came forward, his henchmen with him.

For a moment, William Zouche watched all this as though in a trance. Then he realised he could no longer see Chaucer in the knot of miscreants at the centre of the field and he hurried forward to join the man.

'Why do you knarres not know how this is done?' Chaucer asked. 'If you're going to pick a fight, there are rules, you know.'

'What rules?' Cross snarled. All his life, Neville Cross had known that rules were for other people.

Chaucer closed to him. 'The rules of chivalry,' he said, 'as laid down by Edward of Woodstock, the Black Prince.' Instantly, everybody crossed themselves. That was gratifying; no Lollards here, at least. He waited for just long enough, 'My old friend.'

Glances were exchanged. This plump little man who was not from Oxford had known the Black Prince?

'Master … um …?' Chaucer was looking at the leader of the Balliol crew.

'Michael Langdon,' he said, as though as a challenge.

'Master Langdon,' Chaucer took his hand. Then he reached out for Cross's. 'Well, give me your hand, man. Priorities must serve.'

He held both men's hands together between his own. 'Why have you come here,' he asked them in a voice that re-echoed off the town walls, 'at this hour and to this place?'

Both scholars looked at Chaucer, open-mouthed.

'Do what?' Cross said.

Chaucer let out an exasperated sigh. 'The protocols of Najera,' he said, 'and for that matter of Poitiers and Crecy. Since time immemorial – that's 1189, by the way – contending parties on a field of battle have met to parley, to discuss conditions.'

'What conditions?' Langdon asked.

'Apart from the fact that Master Cross here is an arrogant, nay, insufferable shit, what have you got against Merton College?'

There were hoots of laughter from the Balliol ranks, jeers and boos from Merton.

'And you, Master Cross, apart from his woeful dress sense and that rather feeble attempt to grow a beard, what do you have against Master Langdon and his people?'

Cross pulled himself up to his full height. 'Langdon is a liar and a pederast. His college is an abomination.'

Jeers this time from Balliol, cat calls and the rattling of pans. Chaucer turned to Langdon. 'Would you say pretty much the same about Cross and Merton?'

254

'Pretty much,' Langdon said.

Chaucer still held their hands closed, looking from one to the other. 'In that case,' he said, 'the matter must be decided by the ordinances of Madeleine.'

'The …?' Neville Cross queried it first.

'Master Zouche, if you please,' Chaucer said.

To his dying day, William Zouche didn't know whether he read Geoffrey Chaucer's mind in that moment. Or perhaps it was just instinct. He strolled between the warring clerks, facing Chaucer. He placed one hand on top of Chaucer's, the other underneath. Then, as the clerks frowned, looking at each other, Chaucer and the shipman, Zouche broke the circle, grabbing the backs of both their heads and slamming their foreheads together with a crack that reverberated to Osney Abbey, making Great Tom hum in his tower. Both of them fell, poleaxed, and Chaucer and Zouche bowed to each other.

For a moment, the field below the walls fell silent, both armies staring in disbelief at the sudden collapse of their leaders without so much as a knife being drawn. The Merton henchmen pulled back, leaving Cross in the grass. The Balliol men did too and each cohort retreated to their own lines.

'What now?' Zouche muttered out of the corner of his mouth. 'Do you take on the rest of the Merton bunch and I'll have the Balliol crowd?'

But before Chaucer could answer, a trumpet shattered the afternoon. All eyes looked to the town. Swarms of armed men were pouring out of the gates, trampling the grass and herding the Merton cohort into a corner. A second group steered the Balliol army out of the way.

'Well, well,' Chaucer smiled. 'The cavalry.'

A knot of horsemen came cantering across Grandpont, their hoofs clattering on the woodwork and they reined in on the high ground near the walls. The Safety Commission, suddenly brave as lions with Jack Treddler at their head, were now everywhere, prodding the clerks with spears and halberds.

'Stop that!' the leading horseman yelled at them and they froze.

'I am the High Sheriff of Oxfordshire,' he said as his horse snorted and pawed the ground. 'Sorry to interrupt your little game, gentlemen, but I am looking for Geoffrey Chaucer.'

'Here I am.' Chaucer stepped forward.

'So you are,' the sheriff said. 'You're easy to lose in a crowd. What news of the murder of my son?'

'I intend to unmask him tonight, my lord, at Merton, should you care to be present.'

'Wild horses,' said Herbert, 'wouldn't keep me away. Treddler!'

The mayor scurried forward. 'Sire?' he bowed.

'Don't grovel, man. *Sire* is reserved for the king, as you well know. Plain *my lord* will do. Vallender!' The ever-officious secretary urged his horse forward, his lectern swung into position over the animal's neck. 'What time, Chaucer?'

'Shall we say eight of the clock, sir?'

'Vallender.'

The secretary scratched with his quill. The sheriff looked down at Jack Treddler like the shit on his solleret. 'I want the wardens supposedly in charge of this riffraff at the Guild Hall within the hour. I've already stopped my donation to Merton and with the links I've got, it's a dead certainty that Balliol will close too. Vallender here will accompany you around the town, making a careful note of damage done to property by these overgrown schoolboys. Good day to you, Master Chaucer.'

And he wheeled his horse away as his men broke up the crowd and the clerks slunk back to their lectures, sheepish and shamefaced. Nobody picked up Cross and Langdon and soon all that was left of the great battle was their spreadeagled forms in the middle of some trampled grass.

'Geoff,' William Zouche shook Chaucer's hand, 'that was pure genius. Thank God you knew the protocols of Najera, eh?'

'Protocols of Najera?' Chaucer echoed. 'Nah. I just made them up.'

Chapter 16

Warden Bloxham was in an unforgiving mood. He had just been told, along with his opposite number, Andrew Muncaster of Balliol, that one more occurrence of random street violence among the student body and both colleges would be closed. Both wardens knew that the High Sheriff did not have that legal right, but it was a moot point and the wrangling would go on for years, denting the colleges' reputations forever. More, Bloxham had just learned that Sir Herbert Herbert, irrespective of his high office, had withdrawn his annual donation to Merton College. When the Warden had remonstrated with him, the sheriff's advice was simple – 'Sell a book or two, Bloxham. They won't be missed.'

He was now sitting looking at a sheet of Vallender's immaculate script, listing the damage done by the Merton scholars. The red mist in front of Bloxham's eyes made it hard to see detail, but he could see that the townsfolk were taking full advantage of a temporary cash cow – he was almost certain that the scholars of Merton had not broken the pump in the cellar of the Widow Poumphrey's house, no matter how insistent she was about it. Similarly, he couldn't see how a rampaging horde of mad oxen, let alone some clerks out for a bit of rough and tumble, could have completely destroyed the stables of the Sun in Splendour, which wasn't even on the right side of town. With a sigh, he added the sheet to the piles already on his desk and lay back in his chair, with a hand over his eyes.

So, it may have been vengeful of the Warden to deny the Quadrivium dinner that night. The Trivium could eat, as they had not been involved in that nonsense in the meadows. But the Quadrivium must make what arrangements they could elsewhere in the town. He was a man with economies to make, after all. One thing was definitely certain – there would be no comradely invitations to Balliol that evening.

'Warden, what's going on?' It was Roger Allard asking, sweeping into the Merton library as minions lit the candles and departed and the chained books rattled a little as they left.

'*Going on*, Roger?'

'Well, I was just in the middle of my applemoy when I received a note from Watkin summoning me here.'

'I had one of those, too.' Richard Congleton was padding across the floorboards of the upper landing before gliding down the stairs with their vicious twist.

'So did we.' It was Martin Frisby and Quentin Selham, speaking as one.

'*I* didn't get a note.' Hattie Dalton swept off her broad-brimmed hat, having entered from the street, 'just Watkin grunting with his usual finesse. If you have a problem, Johnny, with the way I run the Grange, a more personal approach would be appreciated.'

Bloxham was beside himself. 'Johnny, Harriet?' he all but screeched. 'Remember where you are, woman! I don't think this is about you.'

Hattie looked around her. She hadn't set foot in this inner sanctum for years and she suddenly realised that all the faculty were dressed in their academic finery, as though a founder's day or graduation ceremony was about to take place. 'Sorry, Warden,' she simpered. 'I apologise.'

'I don't know,' Bloxham said to them all, 'in answer to your questions. I didn't call this meeting. I too received a note. I was to attend here in the library at eight of the clock, in full fig. The note was unsigned.'

'I couldn't be bothered to use my seal of office.' A voice boomed from the darkness at the far end and Herbert Herbert strode into their midst. He was wearing his robes, too, full plate armour and armed to the teeth. 'I'll thank you to vacate that chair, Warden. I am here in my official capacity.'

There was a silence. Richard Congleton broke it. 'If this is some kind of court, Sheriff ...' he began.

'You could call it that.' Another voice echoed high in the fan-vaulting and Geoffrey Chaucer stood on the landing, looking down at the mass of brain power below him. 'But it's not one that you'd recognise, Dick. Neither would I, from the memory of my days at Lincoln's Inn. But needs must, when the Devil drives.'

'The Devil?' Selham raised an eyebrow.

'Warden,' the sheriff barked. 'Your chair.'

Bloxham raised himself up and took his place alongside the others, forming a semi-circle around the dais that was now occupied by Herbert Herbert.

'I called the meeting,' Chaucer was still standing at the top of the stairs, 'and I must thank Master Vallender here for copying out the letters.'

The sheriff's man half bowed, lectern across his chest as usual, quill dipped in ink and ready to go.

'You all know,' Chaucer began, 'that I came to Oxford to take home the body of Hal Golightly. What I found was a hot bed of conspiracy and murder. Doctor Frisby, you are very lucky to be alive and your would-be killer is in this room tonight.'

Eyes swivelled from side to side. Here and there, knuckles whitened, backs straightened and jaws flexed.

'Some of you will remember the recent Great Debate,' Chaucer went on.

There were murmurs and not a few chuckles. The comptroller held up his hand.

'Not my finest hour,' he said. 'Then, I held up a book with which we are all familiar.' He produced it now. 'The Vulgate, the word of God translated from the Hebrew to the Greek to the Latin. It takes six months, give or take, to transcribe it, which is why this book is so precious. Master Wyclif, however, has taken an estimated ten months to translate the Latin into English.'

There were shouts and growls, especially from the warden and the sheriff.

'Please, gentlemen,' Chaucer quietened them. 'No false outrage. Wyclif was a Merton man; Dick, you're about to defend him at the London Synod. Let me show you another book.' This one took both hands to lift. 'Ptolemy's *Geographica Cosmographica*, from this very library, where Brother Anselm was, until recently, *Defensor Libri*, defender of the books.'

'Er … be careful with that, Chaucer,' Bloxham entreated. 'It's unique, you know.'

'Yes, Warden,' the comptroller said, 'I do. And yet I've heard it described by Waldemar of Lucerne, no less, as *a mere pamphlet*.'

'That madman?' Allard snapped. 'What does he know?'

'A great deal,' Chaucer told them. 'Perhaps as much as some of you. Somebody else who knew something although he didn't know he knew it, was young Antonio da Silva.'

'Who?' Selham asked.

'He's a Balliol man,' Chaucer said. 'A keen oarsman, or at least he was until somebody broke his arm. He had some insightful comments about your college, gentlemen. It is a laughingstock because of its silly clubs. Who can translate Italian for me? Dr Selham? Dr Frisby?'

'We all speak Latin, Chaucer,' Congleton said. 'That's close enough.'

'Very well, then. *Colcolati*. What does that mean?'

There was a silence.

'Oh, come now, gentlemen. You wouldn't pass the Trivium with a response like that. *Colcolati* is Italian for calculators. And I'll come back to that. That great scholar, Waldemar, told me, shortly before he drugged me, that Anselm had a library of blasphemous books. He didn't. I've checked. But Waldemar did. I checked that too. And among them …' he held up another tome, smaller than the *Geographica*, 'this. The works of Aristarchus of Samos, who lived in the third century before Christ. You let it slip, didn't you, Martin, with your toast to the king – "Here's to his Grace and Aristarchus".'

'Frisby, you bloody idiot!' Allard hissed.

'This book is why Hal Golightly believed that Merton's whole collection should be torn up and thrown away. Because he believed, no, he *knew* that all of it, from Ptolemy onwards, was fiction; the nonsense that we in our oh, so smug European universities have invented over the centuries.'

'The boy was ill, Chaucer,' Allard said. 'Martin, you saw it. I said to you, didn't I, his urine …'

'His urine is neither here nor there, as well you know,' Chaucer cut in. 'No, what Martin Frisby saw was a 'flaky, unreliable' young man. Flaky because he was afraid; unreliable because he might break whatever oath he may have taken, reveal the secrets he knew.'

'What secrets?' Congleton asked. 'This is all preposterous, Chaucer.'

'The secrets that you all keep, even you, Hattie, although you are not part of it in the literal sense. When I asked you about the calculators, you changed the subject, left the room.'

'This is men's work, Geoffrey. I ...'

'Sins of omission, Hattie,' Chaucer said softly, 'are sins, nevertheless. How many died because you didn't speak out? Martin, you hid Lollard tracts in your garderobe – Ralph Strode found them.'

'*Lollardy*?' Bloxham was aghast. 'Mother of God, no. Not in Merton!'

'And the pentagram in which I found you sitting, the arcane scribblings on your desk.' Chaucer held up the Aristarchus again. 'It's all in here, isn't it? "Most of my colleagues" you told me once "are blaspheming hypocrites. And so they are – you included.'

'That's rubbish!' Frisby was on his feet, roaring defiance.

'Alfred Herbert was afraid of the calculators. He was afraid of the Sand Reckoner. Well, now I know why. With the exception of Hattie and I believe you, Warden, *you* are the calculators, the conspiracy that forced acolytes to keep your secrets. You taught your unprovable claptrap and you told your hapless charges to keep your mouths shut. Or else.'

'Or else what?' Allard wanted to know.

'Or else there would be a series of random accidents like those at a dangerous building site, right here in Mob Quad. A clerk called Firth explained it to me. "We were warned," he said.'

'Chaucer!' It was the sheriff's turn to be on his feet. 'What the hell are you talking about?'

The comptroller smiled, then chuckled. 'They won't tell you, my lord, so I'll have to. Your son died because of the terrible "truth" these men have uncovered. Whether Waldemar of Lucerne was part of it, I don't know. Young Firth was a friend of your boy. On the same day he told me he and others had been warned, he cowered in the shadows of his room and told me something else. He said "I don't like the sun". Now, why should he say that?'

'Because he's barking,' Allard said, 'college madness. I've seen several cases ...'

Chaucer grabbed Ptolemy's tome and thudded down the stairs. He hauled open the leather covers and slammed it onto the dais at Herbert's feet. 'What do you see there, my Lord?' he asked.

'Er ... the universe,' the sheriff bent and picked the book up, turning it right way up. 'God's universe.'

'Precisely. And where is the earth?'

'At the centre of the universe. Where it should be.'

Chaucer had brought the other book with him, tucked under the sleeve of his houppelande. 'And what about this one?' he asked. 'Where is the Earth now?'

'Um ...' Herbert peered closer at the Aristarchus. 'It seems to be to one side, with the other planets.'

'And what is in the centre?' Chaucer asked.

Herbert blinked in disbelief. 'The sun,' he said. He looked up, scanning the room. 'But, surely, that's ridiculous. It can't be the sun.'

'The sun,' Chaucer repeated, 'the sun that young Firth is afraid of. The sun that led to the deaths of all of them – Golightly, Herbert, Anselm and, very nearly, Frisby.'

'Oh, but this is nonsense, Chaucer,' the sheriff said. 'Some ancient Greek twaddle.'

'Is it, my lord?' The comptroller looked the man in the face. 'Is it, Martin? Roger? Quentin? Dick? Is it twaddle? It's ancient and Greek, I will grant you that, but what else is it?'

'It's the truth,' Allard growled.

'We've proved it,' Frisby chimed in, 'with calculations, measurements, radians.'

'And what did you use for your calculations?' Chaucer asked.

There was a silence. And it was Chaucer's turn to break it. 'You used an astrolabe, gentlemen; just as one of you used it to kill three men.'

'But ...' Herbert was trying to take it all in 'This is blasphemy, Chaucer. To say that the sun, not the earth, is at the centre of the universe is to ...'

'Invite Hell fire,' Chaucer said. 'The Church will burn these men. And who are we to say that the Church would be wrong?'

Everyone who had been on their feet now slumped into their chairs. Warden Bloxham couldn't believe it; his entire faculty were followers of the horned one; there was no other way to look at it.

'Vallender,' the sheriff said after the dust of damnation had settled. 'Summon the guard. I want this nest of hornets in irons in the castle.'

'One moment, my lord.' Chaucer was still on his feet. 'Would you take a moment to reconsider?'

'Reconsider, Chaucer?' Herbert snapped. 'Reconsider? I can conceive of no crime more heinous than that which these men have committed.'

'I can, my lord,' the comptroller said. 'Murder.'

'Ah, yes, well, possibly.'

'There is a world of difference between having an idea, an idea, can I remind you, that isn't new but comes to us from the ancients and killing to keep that idea secret.'

'But it's a dangerous idea,' Herbert agreed. 'The ancients were pagans; they had no concept of the one true God. The world has changed.'

'No,' Chaucer agreed. 'They followed scientia, the laws of nature and the way of things. Who knows that one day, we will regard scientia as our God?'

'That's blasphemy, Chaucer!' the sheriff shouted. 'Do you want to join these misfits in the dungeon?'

'Do you want to know who killed your son?'

'Of course.' Herbert was calmer now.

'If I give you the murderer's head on a plate,' Chaucer looked at the man, 'will you let the others go? Warden Bloxham, I am sure, had no knowledge of their dabblings. Hattie,' he looked at her fondly as she sat sobbing quietly in the corner of Anselm's library, 'may have known of the calculators, but she didn't know where their studies had taken them. It isn't a common subject for pillow talk, after all.'

'So, what do you propose?' the sheriff asked.

'Let them go. Oh, they'll never teach at any university again, of course, never poison more young minds. All except one.'

'Which one?' Herbert was sitting in the Warden's seat again but was on the alert now, leaning forward, ready to pounce.

'At first,' Chaucer prowled the room, 'I suspected you, Roger.'

'Me?' The doctor was outraged.

'You were vague about Hal Golightly's wounds. When I challenged you, you flounced out, refused to discuss it. I realise now that you are simply a bad practitioner whose grasp of his job is, to say the least, insecure.'

'How dare you?' Allard was on his feet again.

'Sit down!' Herbert barked. 'Better humiliated, I would have thought, than dangling at the end of a rope or smouldering at the whim of the Inquisition.' Allard duly subsided.

'Then, I considered the late Brother Anselm,' Chaucer went on, 'who hated his clerks of the Quadrivium while at the same time perhaps harbouring less than pure thoughts about them. A man who puts books before people is not a man to trust. His own death, however much it was a case of mistaken identity, put paid to that.'

'Ha!' Quentin Selham guffawed. 'Common sense at last!'

The others crowed and Chaucer smiled. 'Don't feel left out, Quentin,' he said. 'You're a musician by inclination, never the brightest apple in the barrel. Without wishing to be unkind, you haven't the intellect to plan these murders. I suspect you only went along with the heliocentric universe because the others told you to. What did they say? That it all boiled down to the music of the spheres, something like that.'

The look on Selham's face told him he was right. The Master of Music bridled. 'Well, really!' He was lost for words, as Chaucer knew he would be.

'Then, Martin, there was you. Loose of mouth, calling your colleagues blaspheming hypocrites; toying with magic before my very eyes in your rooms. You read, if not disseminate, Lollard tracts. You leave damning evidence on your table. When I saw the scribbles, I couldn't decipher them. Now, I understand them – the positions of the planets as you believe they are. You were key to it all, weren't you? Aristarchus, whom you toasted in my presence, because you forgot yourself, he needed someone with a firm hand on figures to prove the theories right. A pity, because with all your West Country

tarradiddle and schoolboy lovesick nonsense for Hattie, you are the
true genius of the calculators.'

Frisby didn't deny any of it. He just slumped in his chair.

'But you weren't the leader, were you? You weren't the Sand
Reckoner. That was you, Dick.'

All eyes turned to the Master of Logic. 'I've said it before and I'll say
it again, Geoffrey,' Congleton murmured. 'Despite the Great Debate,
the Law lost a great mind when you opted for Woollens and Hides.'

'As leader of the pack,' Chaucer said, 'you had to control the others.
Selham would do as he was told. Allard was nearly as bent as you are,
a man of the establishment (in this case the calculators) whose only
god was money. He knew without you he would soon be driven to
wandering the roads as some kind of hedge wizard – if we searched
the town of Oxford, we wouldn't be able to find a single body he
had healed and Logic is a dying art, I would say. So he went along
with anything you wanted him to. But the lads who you'd inveigled
into all this ...'

'Those dark arts,' Herbert cut in.

'Those dark arts,' Chaucer repeated. 'Most of them were depend-
able and loyal – Neville Cross, I'm thinking, foremost among them.
But Hal Golightly, he was flaky, unhappy at what he saw, unable to
square that with his upbringing. So too, Alfred Herbert. His father
over there taught him one way; you were teaching something else
altogether and in the end, his father's way won.' Chaucer looked at the
sheriff. 'You can be proud of your boy, my lord,' he said. 'One more
day and he would have brought this whole farrago crashing down.'

'You bastard!' the sheriff growled, his hand on his sword hilt, his
eyes burning into Congleton's.

'But the biggest problem was Frisby, wasn't it? As my enquiries continued, you couldn't trust him. Your first thought was to silence me – ridiculing me in the debate, getting Cross to beat me with his quarter-staff. Getting Hattie, your obliging sister, to arrange that nonsense with the cat up the church spire. Persuading the street hawker to give me lethal amounts of powder forte …'

Congleton shrugged. 'None of that is true but while we debate the first three, I must say here and now that I have never colluded with a street hawker in my life.'

Chaucer looked aghast and turned to Vallender, waiting patiently at his master's elbow as usual. 'In that case,' he said, 'you should perhaps try to find the man and make sure he sells no more pork or anything else, for that matter. The man is lethal. Where was I? Oh, yes, well, anyway, any of those could have killed me, but they didn't. So, if Frisby could have his mouth shut, you reasoned, everything would still be all right. Unfortunately, it was a bad night, wasn't it? You couldn't see your hand in front of your face because of the rain and Anselm was wearing Frisby's cloak.'

Chaucer was standing in front of the man now, looking him squarely in the face. 'A nice touch of symbolism, by the way, to use the astrolabe, the calculators' gadget. It's just a pity you used it on the wrong man. So, you had to try again. And this time, the nightwatchman nearly caught you in the act. It must have been infuriating that the knarre insisted on getting Frisby to safety.'

'He was a peasant,' Congleton said, his head held high. 'Just like you, Chaucer. You really have no clue, have you? I tried to put you off. I told you it was the town, it was the Lollards, it was Balliol. I even led you a merry dance with that murder-map nonsense.' Congleton laughed. 'Ha, the look on your face! You believed it, didn't you? Every single word. I am not the Sand Reckoner, you ignorant knarre.

Aristarchus was. Whatever you do with me, with us, you can't shut us down. Not you, Chaucer, nor you, sheriff. We are the future. We are scientia. We are the truth.'

'You may be,' Chaucer said. 'You just didn't want to burn, did you? That's why others had to die, to keep you safe. Men have been dying for their beliefs since language was born but you – oh, no, not you, Master Congleton. You are immortal, after all. And you have the principles of a louse.'

Congleton looked Chaucer in the face and got up, slowly, making the comptroller step back to give him room. All eyes were turned in their direction – their lives as they had known them may be over, but what happened to Congleton would tell them how bad their futures might be.

Congleton carried on walking, forcing Chaucer back, until his heels were against the edge of the dais and Vallender leaned forward with a kindly hand to help him up the step without falling. Congleton looked at them both with contempt.

'Look at you,' he said to Chaucer. 'Heaven only knows how you have got to where you are today. You can't even walk straight without help. Without that shipman at your back, I could have murdered you a dozen times since you arrived here and none any the wiser who had done it.' He flicked a glance at Vallender, who stood, imperturbable behind his lectern. 'Men like you,' he spat, 'lackeys, lickspittles. You would not survive in the world I have planned. Science. Not kindliness. That's what matters. The truth. The *sun* is king!'

Only three men could see the strings of spit beginning to bedeck Congleton's chin as he got nearer and nearer to the edge of madness. He walked forward still, pace by slow pace until he was toe to toe with the sheriff, who sat in his chair, showing no emotion as the man who had killed his son spat his venom.

'I could kill you now,' Congleton hissed. 'There are more of us than there are of you. We would be out of Oxford and never to be seen again before they even found your bodies.'

A quiet voice behind him made him turn.

'What about me, Dickie?' Hattie said. 'Am I to be killed or to run with you, I wonder?'

Congleton looked at her as if she were a stranger. 'Do what you like, Hat,' he said. 'You were never really part of this. You were just ...' he waved a hand over the calculators 'entertainment. Something to keep them happy, keep them from wandering off and talking in their sleep to less trustworthy ears.'

'Entertainment?' Her voice was sad. 'I didn't know I was entertainment.'

Chaucer, who had spent most of his time in Oxford being mildly afraid of Hattie Dalton, wanted to take her in his arms and comfort her. He looked at Frisby. Surely, if the man still had a soul, he would feel the same. But no; the Master of Mathematics looked firmly at his feet, nervously pleating his houppelande between trembling fingers.

'Well, you were,' Congleton said, turning his back on her. 'So, sheriff, what's to be done?' He reached round to the small of his back to where he kept his dagger, purely for personal protection, he always said. 'Because we have a conundrum here. You're the sheriff, and of course, there is a special penalty for killing you.'

Herbert, his head high, nodded. 'Indeed there is,' he said, a small smile on his lips.

'Whereas I am a lawyer, and as everyone knows, you can't kill a lawyer.'

'No,' the same gentle voice came from behind him. As he heard it, his groping fingers closed on nothing. His dagger was not in the small of his back any longer. It was between his ribs and deep in his heart. 'But brothers... everyone knows you can kill those.'

Chapter 17

Chaucer was in a quandary. In some ways, he just wanted to get out of Oxford, to be on the river, floating downstream towards the Port of London and don't spare the horses, or whatever the phrase might be when speaking of a boat. But he knew that, as a man with a soul and a kind one at that, that there were things to do, people to see, wounds to heal, albeit invisible ones this time. William Zouche understood, as he understood most things, and he was busy on the *Madeleine*, making things shipshape and ready for the off. He had some goodbyes to say as well, but they were best said in private.

Chaucer had not returned to Frideswide Grange. Somehow, it was just too difficult. One of the serving maids from the college had been sent to pack his trunk and get it to a carrier; it would probably arrive in London before him and Alice would see to it, do the darning, get the stains out, all the things she was so good at. Chaucer found that he really missed Alice and his little bed under the eaves of the Aldgate, and that made him fleeter of foot than usual.

He had seen Hattie for the last time that night, the night of the long knife. The sheriff was in a cleft stick. He had witnessed a murder being done before his very eyes, but the murder of a murderer who he, given time, would have despatched himself either at the end of a rope or more painfully and slowly in a dark cell with the warder's eyes averted. But … a murder was a murder, and it had been witnessed by too many people to pretend otherwise.

Vallender, he knew, would say nothing. Warden Bloxham was so deep in shock he didn't count. Chaucer, of course, would say nothing. But the remaining calculators – by doing nothing to bring Hattie Dalton to justice, he was playing into their hands. Martin Frisby would probably be on her side, though that was by no means definite. Allard and Selham on the other hand would shout loud and long if they thought it would do them any good. So, Hattie Dalton had to be arrested and taken, with much ceremony, to the castle, to be thrown into a dungeon.

Chaucer had visited her there and one thing struck him straight away. He had been shown into a room with woven hangings and a great tester bed. A fire to drive away the recent damp was burning merrily in the hearth and in front of it sat Hattie, dressed in a plain gown, her hair loose and tied back by a plain kerchief.

Chaucer smiled at her. 'I can't help noticing, Hattie,' he said, 'that this doesn't look much like a prison cell.'

She made a face at him. 'I can't go out, Master Chaucer,' she said. 'So that makes it a prison, I think.'

'It's not terribly *dank*, though, is it, Hattie? Not really dreary, in the accepted sense of the word. No stone. No dripping water. No rats to speak of.'

'That's very true, Geoffrey,' she said. She patted the low seat beside her and he shook his head. 'I'm safe to sit next to,' she said. 'I only kill brothers who have killed some very nice boys because he believed things which fly in the face of God and nature. I won't kill you.'

He laughed. 'No, I know you won't,' he said. 'But one thing and another since I have been in Oxford have conspired to give me a bad back. Beatings. Climbing church towers. Kidnapping.'

'Me?' she said and looked up, the firelight glittering in her eyes.

'I've had backache for worse reasons than you,' he reassured her. 'But I'll just sit on this high settle, if I may.'

'Please yourself,' she said. 'I had to agree to quite a lot of rules tonight. 'I can't go out of this room, is one. I can't ... Well, you know what. I can't bring myself to use the word *entertain*, not anymore.' Suddenly, her eyes filled with tears. 'I shouldn't have killed him, Geoffrey, should I? I shouldn't have stabbed him like that. Our father always said not to do anything in anger and I was just so, *so* angry with him. He was my *brother*. And he used me, used me to keep his friends quiet. That's all I was.'

'Not to Frisby,' Chaucer said. 'You were the world to him.'

'Yes,' she agreed. 'But a world that orbits the sun. So that won't do, will it? That's no great thing.'

'Of them all,' Chaucer reassured her, 'Martin was the most misled, I think. He just needed something to believe in. And sadly, he found Aristarchus of Samos before he found you. It would have been different otherwise.'

He was by no means sure that this was true, but she looked so sad, and he hated people to be sad.

'So, he loved me, d'you think?'

'I know he did. Does, probably.'

'What's going to happen to them, Martin, Allard and what's his name, the music teacher?'

'You didn't … entertain Quentin Selham, then?'

'If I did, I don't remember it. And with an eye like that, I probably would have.'

'The Warden, though …'

Hattie's face was soft in the firelight. 'Dear old Johnny, yes, we do see each other once in a while. I go and see him. Sit and chat … and things. Not always *things*, he's not as young as he was, after all. But yes … what a lovely, lovely man. He doesn't deserve all this.'

'Never mind,' Chaucer said, kindly. 'When all this is over, you can go and chat and things with him again.'

'Really?' Her eyes were wide. 'When all this is over, things will be back to normal?' She paused. 'I mean things, not *things*. Umm …'

Chaucer looked at her, sitting there, her life in tatters but still able to joke. 'Yes, Hattie. I have had a word with the sheriff. He will have to keep you here for a while, until the calculators have been dealt with. Run out of town is probably as bad as it will get – tar, feathers, a bit of whipping at the cart's tail – and if the townspeople get wind of it, it may be with a few brickbats to see them on their way. But then, well, you are free to go.'

'To go where?' She spread her arms.

'Are your parents still living?'

'No. The dear things are dead and just as well. This would kill them. That's why I stayed close to Dick. We were all …' Her face filled with horror as the events of the evening came back to her. She swallowed hard and carried on. 'We *were* all we had.'

'I don't know the law of this, but Vallender will help. Vallender knows everything.'

'Vallender?' A lot had happened and some facts had passed her by.

Chaucer sketched a lectern in front of him.

'Oh, him. He did seem nice. He helped you when ... when Dick tried to knock you down. I wonder if he ...'

'I have no idea. Perhaps you can find out when you discuss your inheritance. Dick had a good practice in London. There is bound to be some money.'

Hattie stood up, like a tidal surge in her white shift and went over to Chaucer and snuggled onto his knee. 'You are a good man, Geoffrey Chaucer. A good, kind man. As well as being unusually athletic for a man of your build. I don't suppose you would like to ...'

Chaucer wagged a finger. 'Rule number two, Hattie,' he admonished her. 'Don't forget rule number two.'

'Really?'

'I'm afraid so.'

'I can kiss you, though?'

He cradled her cheek in his palm. 'Yes, Hattie. You can kiss me. You can kiss me goodbye.'

The next morning, having spent the night as a guest of the sheriff in his permanent apartments in the Guild Hall, Chaucer had gone to Merton, to see how Warden Bloxham was managing with the news which had broken over his head like a tidal wave the night before.

He had gone first to his rooms, only to be told that the Warden was at breakfast. Chaucer was a little surprised; had he been asked for his best guess, he would have said that the man would probably stay as reclusive as possible until the dust had started to settle. So he was intrigued as to what he would find when he got to the Great Hall.

Warden Bloxham sat in his appointed seat, at the head of high table. The student tables at right angles to it were but sparsely populated. The Trivium numbers were almost as normal, but of the Quadrivium only a fraction was present. Cross and his acolytes were conspicuous by their absences and not just because they had always made the most noise, even when meals were supposed to be taken in silence. They were also bigger and more arrogant in their bearing and somehow had always seemed to take up more room per head than was quite natural. At the high table, the gaps were fewer but were more obvious for being at Bloxham's right and left hand. Towards the bottom of the table a few Masters still sat. Chaucer thought he had been introduced to a few; the Master of Theology was there, trying to catch no one's eye. A pasty-faced man with a long strand of hair wound round the back of his head in lieu of a decent tonsure led, as he remembered, a new subject which had but one scholar, the economics of prehistoric cultures. Chaucer had always suspected that it was made up and the man just needed a roof over his head.

Bloxham was spooning up oatmeal with evident enjoyment and waved his spoon at Chaucer when he took a place usually filled by the spare buttocks of Roger Allard.

'Chaucer, Chaucer, my good man. How wonderful to see you. Not too tired after last night's excitement, I hope.'

'Umm … no. No, I slept well at the sheriff's lodgings.'

'Good, good. Poor Hattie, she won't be keeping house any longer, I don't suppose.'

'That must be up to the sheriff … and to you, of course.'

'All in due time, I understand.' The man went back to his oatmeal. Chaucer pulled a piece of bread from a fresh loaf which had no one else to eat it. 'Do you …' he cleared his throat. 'Do you have any plans? For Merton?'

Bloxham's blue eyes were guileless as a child's. 'Well, I shall need some new Masters, of course,' he said, looking solemn, difficult to do with oatmeal on his chin. 'And a new Quadrivium, though one is tempted, very tempted, to just kick the whole boiling out and let nature take its course, wait for the years below to … mature, so to speak. Yes,' he pushed a lump of oats to the side of his plate. 'Yes, I do believe that is what I shall do.'

'Not *all* of them, surely?' Chaucer felt sorry for the rare members of the Quadrivium who were apparently simply there to learn.

Bloxham peered short-sightedly down the Quadrivium table, to the clerks who tried to avoid his eye and look terribly studious, all at once.

'Well, perhaps not all. I will ask for anyone who thinks they deserve to stay to apply to me in the library. And that's another thing, I suppose. A new librarian. Have you given any more thought …?'

'I'm afraid I would be too busy, Warden. The king, you know. Calls on my time.' The man was clearly in shock and Chaucer let him down gently.

'Quite so, quite so.' He looked down the Quadrivium table again and then at his decimated Masters. 'There will be changes, of course.' And he bent his attention back to his oats. Chaucer, waiting for some kind of formal farewell, realised after a moment that there would not be one, and left, still clutching his hunk of bread, which he ate on his way back down to the *Madeleine*.

Zouche had turned his craft and was waiting to cast off when Chaucer arrived, brushing crumbs from his ample front. He knew from bitter experience what eating was like on the *Madeleine* and wished now that he had taken more from the Merton table. But Zouche had a surprise for him. He nodded towards a basket in the stern, covered in hessian. Chaucer clambered aboard and made his way crabwise to it. He would need to work on regaining his river-legs, he could tell. Under the hessian was a world of wonders. Cheese encased in wax, bread, salty butter packed into a jar. A ham, black with treacle and, surrounding the food, a fence of wine bottles of every size and hue.

'There's a bag of apples there as well,' Zouche said. 'We'll eat well on our way home, one way and another.'

'Who is it from?' Chaucer couldn't take his eyes off the ham, which wasn't green at all.

'Sir Herbert Herbert sent most of it,' the shipman told him. 'The mayor sent the apples. I didn't think you'd want anything from the wine cellar of Waldemar of Lucerne.'

That sounded about right and Chaucer took an apple, a little floury and musty as all apples must be in May, but still welcome. He settled down on a bench in the prow and watched Zouche do his magic. He could see the little bed that he had made his own still there and waiting for him and he found himself looking forward to a quiet river journey back to London. The *Madeleine* had taken quite a knock in the tidal surge she had ridden so well, and Zouche had mended it as best he could – it was river worthy but not very beautiful, and he had promised the boat that he would take her to the best shipwright in London when they got home. After all, when he added on all the extras, he was going to be a rich man. For a while.

Zouche poked Chaucer with his toe. 'Home, Geoff,' he said. 'I suppose it will be Master Chaucer from now on, will it?'

Chaucer looked at the dock, fast approaching on the starboard side and sighed. 'I suppose it is, Will, yes. But I hope you'll visit me when you're in port and it will be Geoff and Will then, for certain. Have you got your bill? I told you to keep a tally.'

'I have indeed, Master Chaucer,' Zouche said. 'But it is lore of the sea not to open any documents of that nature on board. Bad luck, see. I'll send for the money in a day or so, if that's all right with you?'

'What an odd superstition,' Chaucer said. 'But I don't want to bring bad luck to you or the *Madeleine*. Oh, look!' His eyes were landward now and his river days almost forgotten. 'There's Alice! How did she know?'

'I sent word,' Zouche said. 'It's marked down as extra number twenty-seven B.'

The *Madeleine* came to a graceful stop and quick hands grabbed the rope Zouche threw. Some hefty lightermen hauled Chaucer ashore and he was soon engulfed in a wave of humanity; when he looked back, the *Madeleine* was in mid-stream, making for the Pool.

'Oh, Master Chaucer,' Alice babbled. 'It's been ever so exciting while you've been away. We had an earthquake and everything. All my pots and pans fell down and the cat nearly had kittens.' This last was not news. Alice's cat had kittens regularly under much less exciting circumstances. Chaucer had his thumb under the flap of the folded paper Zouche had slipped to him so discreetly but paused.

'An earthquake, you say? When was this?'

'Ooh, let me think. It was the twenty-first, I remember that because I said to Doggett, I said, twenty-one is an unlucky number, I said, so no wonder …'

'Do you know what time?' Chaucer was enthralled.

'It was two o'clock, or as near as makes no nevermind. 'Cos all the bells were chiming the hour and they just kept on and on, jangling and jangling. Ooh, Master Chaucer, it was that frightening. I says to Doggett, *Master Chaucer would be enjoying this*, I says.' She finally seemed to have the earthquake out of her system and gave him a beaming smile. 'I have missed you, Master Chaucer. You're room's all ready for you. And a nice pie for your dinner.' She glanced down at the paper in his hand. 'I'll get along back now. I've hired a man to help you back. I'll leave you to your business.' She was still just in earshot when she heard an eldritch cry.

'*How much?*'

Chaucer turned to where the Madeleine was still just visible and raised an arm, ready to shake his fist at the shipman. If he wasn't passing on these expenses to Nicholas Brembre, who was richer than God, he would be in penury for the rest of his life. Then he thought of the dark alleys, of the man always at his back, of the loyalty and devotion this randomly chosen shipman had unfailingly shown and he changed his mind and made it into a wave.

And across the water, he swore that he could hear the shipman laughing, just for the sheer joy of being alive.

Printed in the USA
CPSIA information can be obtained
at www.ICGtesting.com
LVHW030254061224
798486LV00025B/252

* 9 7 8 1 8 3 9 0 1 5 1 1 3 *